THE RIGHT ONE

WENDY SMITH

ARIADNE WAYNE

Edited by
LAUREN CLARKE

Illustrated by
MOSS BOOK COVERS

ISBN: 978-1-991303-17-2

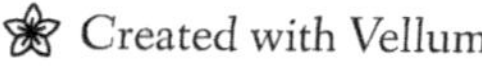 Created with Vellum

Dedicated to anyone who has a Frozen obsessed child.

1

ALEXANDER WAS WORKING LATE *AGAIN*.

As the girlfriend of a busy lawyer, I was used to the long hours, but this case he was on had taken up so much time lately, it was driving me nuts. Besides, springing a surprise dinner on him gave me the excuse to buy takeaway, rather than the swanky restaurant food we normally ate.

McDonald's was the choice tonight, complete with Fanta, that guilty little sugary pleasure. I'd never been allowed soft drinks when I was growing up, and it was my absolute favourite.

I climbed out of the car, dragging the bag of food with me, the drinks in their little cardboard cup holder. I'd driven carefully with them balanced on my lap—not the safest, but the drive from the restaurant to my destination wasn't far, and I had a bet with myself that I wouldn't spill a drop.

Smug that I'd achieved my goal, I walked up to the front entrance of Clarke and Thompson, the law firm Alexander worked for. I smiled at the security guard as I walked past, and he opened the door, letting me in so I could make my way to Alexander's office. His assistant wasn't at her desk, and I listened at the door, just in case he had a client with him despite the late hour. It was quiet so I pushed the door, beaming as I entered.

"I went hunting and found this for dinner," I announced loudly.

"Shit."

Alexander looked up at me. I dropped the bag of food, along with my jaw, at the sight of my boyfriend, pants down, lying on top of his assistant on the beautiful white leather couch that I'd helped him pick out.

I felt faint, my head swimming as every part of me tried to comprehend what I was seeing. Tears formed even though my mind was blank of thought. "No." My voice sounded tiny.

"Rebecca. It's not what it looks like," Alexander said.

He made the mistake of pushing off the couch, exposing the fact that his penis was not only out of his pants, but had seconds ago very much been inside her. I clamped my lips together, plucking a cup from the holder and threw the contents of it over him, swiftly following it with the other cup.

Bright orange liquid was everywhere. His assistant, whose name I couldn't remember in the first place, screeched as the ice cubes inside hit her.

Alexander had a pretty impressive penis at the best of times. Now it had kind of shrivelled away, no doubt at the combination of being caught and the very cold drink that had just hit it.

Does Fanta stain leather? The random thought ran through my head as I turned on my heel and bolted.

"I hope you get your dick stuck in your zip," I yelled as I passed through the door. The guard raised an eyebrow at me as I left the building. "Excuse me, I'm afraid Mr Davis has had an accident. He seems to have fallen and dropped his penis inside ..." *Shit, what was her name?* "Sierra."

The guard's mouth fell open and I pushed my way out of the building, running to my car, fumbling with the keys as I tried to see through the tears.

Alexander was seconds behind me, his shirt and pants covered in

Fanta, and he hammered on the car window. "Rebecca. Stop. We need to talk."

"No, you need to leave me the hell alone. Don't bother coming home. I'm changing the locks."

I turned the key in the ignition, slamming the car into reverse and backing up, hitting the accelerator to get the hell out of there and get home. Would I change the locks that quickly? It was seven pm after all. It just felt so good to say it.

Home wasn't far and I ran to the bathroom as soon as I got there, retching into the toilet, my stomach not settling despite there being nothing in it.

I collapsed on the floor beside the vanity, leaning my head against the wood and crying harder than I ever had before. Three years of my life down the toilet. Loving him, being only with him, wanting to spend the rest of my life with him ...

How long had he been screwing around on me? Was she the only one? How many times? So many questions, but I didn't want the answers. They were no use to me. All it took was one time to betray me, to betray us.

Screw him. I didn't need him anyway.

CHAPTER TWO

EIGHTEEN MONTHS LATER …

LONELINESS STRIKES at the weirdest of times. It doesn't matter if you have the never-ending love and support of friends and family, all the adoration in the world can't stop your heart from being broken. And then the loneliness takes over and you end up crying into your corn flakes, unable to cope with the day ahead and singing power ballads as you drink an entire bottle of wine while watching *X Factor*.

A year and a half ago, I walked in on my boyfriend of three years having sex with his assistant on his office couch. Afterwards, I went through all five stages of grief.

Denial. That lasted all of five seconds. About enough time to yell 'no' at the top of my voice and sounding like a mouse. Anger came next as I exploded, dumping the cold drinks I was carrying all over that couch. I bargained with myself all the way home about whether to turn back and give him another piece of my mind or not.

Instead, I locked myself away and spent three days crying and eating every piece of chocolate I could find. And even though I hated him, never wanted to see him again, some tiny little part of me waited for the phone to ring, for him to say sorry, beg me for forgiveness.

The call never came.

My father had thought the sun shone out of Alexander's arse. I mean, who wouldn't? He was this gorgeous man—he looked like he'd been carved from marble—but he was also so down to earth. Perfect for me, or so my father had thought. I think in the end, Dad was more traumatised by our break-up than I was.

Acceptance was the most beautiful stage of the whole deal. Apart from the chocolate eating—that bit was pretty damn good.

It was the nights alone, the cold bed, the wanting so badly to be held that if he'd walked in the door, I might have taken him back. That was never, ever going to happen. It couldn't.

The most adult relationship of my life had become the worst as I battled the sadness that weighed heavily, the misery that was my existence.

Snap out of it, Rebecca.

Eighteen months later, and there was only one thing for it. Well, lots of it.

Tequila.

BACON.

My head swam as I opened my eyes. The jackhammer wouldn't shut up, drilling through my brain. And all I could smell was bacon.

I lifted my hand to wipe the drool that had run down from the corner of my mouth, probably from a combination of falling asleep while drunk and the delicious aroma that filled my house.

Looking around the room, the wallpaper came to life, littered with dancing flowers. *No bacon here.*

And yet, I could still smell it.

I wobbled as I stood, pushing myself to my feet and holding the wall for support as I made my way to the kitchen. Maybe coffee could help me focus, remove the errant smell from my nose.

The aroma only grew as I approached the kitchen, my mind springing awake, and I realised someone really was cooking bacon.

He had scruffy hair, and was clad only in a T-shirt and boxer shorts. No pants.

He's in my house with no pants. What on earth did I do last night?

Scanning my memory for something to ignite and remind me, I struck nothing. I might have been drunk, but I didn't usually forget things. Especially bringing home men.

He turned, grinning at me, spatula in hand.

Whoever he is, he's freaking hot.

Blond stubble covered his chin, leading up to these gorgeous, cheeky blue eyes that twinkled, and I ...

WHAT THE HELL? HE'S IN *MY* HOUSE.

"What the hell are you doing in my house? I'll call the police." I grabbed the phone from the counter and squinted, trying to focus on the keys.

He laughed—*laughed* at me. "Relax. I didn't break in. You left the door open, I presume when you staggered in last night."

Staggered?

"So why are you in my kitchen, cooking *my* food?"

He shrugged, picking up a piece of bacon with the spatula and carrying it to the table where a couple of buttered bread slices waited. Drops of bacon fat dripped a trail in his wake.

"Can you not do that? You're making a mess on the floor."

"Relax, I'll clean it up."

"Can you please stop telling me to relax? You're in MY house."

Grinning, he slid the bacon onto the bread, slapping the other slice on top. He picked up the plate, holding it toward me.

"There you go, pretty lady, your breakfast awaits."

He thinks I'm pretty? Oh ...

No. No, no, no.

Maybe.

"Thanks," I grumbled, taking the plate and sitting on the other side of the table. "Who the hell are you?"

"I'm Elliot, and I live next door."

Last time I looked there was a blue-rinse granny living in the house next to mine. What?

"Serious? I thought my neighbours were much older."

"I just moved in with my nan."

Oh. Unexpected.

"Really? She okay?" I saw her sometimes in her garden, making her way between the rose bushes that littered her front lawn. My garden was empty in comparison.

"Just getting old. She needs a hand sometimes, but she's not ready to go into a home."

He went back to the cooktop, retrieving another slice of bacon, and returning to the table to make himself a sandwich.

"Elliot, it's really nice that you've come and made me breakfast, but I didn't invite you in here. And you've made a mess."

As he sat, he waggled his eyebrows. "Plenty of other ways to make a mess."

What the ...?

"Look, I could still call the police."

He leaned back in his seat with the biggest grin on his face, and I just wanted to smack it off.

"I wanted to make sure you were safe, seeing as the door was wide open. And then I thought you could do with some breakfast after that three am return home-time, so I hung around, watched some TV—"

"Were you watching me?"

"No. I heard you, though, cackling like a witch as you paid the taxi driver. I heard that snorty laugh and just knew I had to meet you."

I sat, dumbfounded at what he'd said. I think he propositioned me and insulted me, all in the same conversation. Damn it. What I really should do is to finish my sandwich and leave.

Leave? This was *my* house.

Clearly the alcohol had scrambled my brain.

"I appreciate that you were looking out for me, but you have to see how inappropriate this is."

He tilted his head to the side, boring holes in me with his eyes. "I'll admit, I don't usually walk into people's homes uninvited, but I'm sure you would have asked me over eventually."

He waved his hand across his T-shirt and I looked closer at the small holes scattered across the fabric. The man was an utter slob. "I mean, who can resist this, right?" And then he laughed, this deep throaty laugh that made every hair on my body stand on end.

"Take your sandwich and go."

His smile disappeared as he examined the expression on my face. As nice as it was to have solid food cooked for me, this was right up there on the Weird Crap That Happens To Me scale. At least I hadn't brought him home to have sex with, and then forgotten about him being there.

I had, however, woken up before not knowing where I was, and ...

Mind wandering again.

Elliot frowned. "I'm sorry. I just wanted to make sure you were okay."

I nodded, looking at the table as he made his way out. He turned, the sunshine streaming through the now open door, surrounding him with a big glowing halo of light. My heart skipped a beat. He was so beautiful.

"Before I do go, what's your name?"

"Rebecca," I said, and took a bite of my sandwich. I stifled a moan from the amazing combination of melted butter and salty bacon. This was really hitting the spot.

"Nice to meet you, Rebecca. Next time, make sure you close the door after you come in. Especially in the middle of the night. Never know who might just walk into your house."

With that, the door closed. The shining bright light faded, and I was left in my kitchen with a sandwich and bacon fat on the floor to clean.

I couldn't help but smile.

3

I WAS the girl who'd rebelled at school. The one who'd raised the hem on her skirt that extra half-inch, driving the teachers crazy, the one who would sneak out after dark to meet boys. How I'd escaped my teens without getting pregnant, I have no idea.

Anything to get my father's attention.

When trying hard to impress him didn't work, I resorted to all the bad things I could think of doing without actually putting myself at risk. Well, not too much.

Somehow, from those days I'd retained the friends I'd made. They didn't misbehave like I did, but they were always there to help me pick up the pieces when I got caught. They drove me insane at times, but I would be forever grateful for their friendship and support. Even if at times it didn't seem like it.

I pulled into the car park of the restaurant Le Grande. It was one of those pretentious places that pretends to be something it isn't, where all the cool and wealthy hang out. I had no idea how I came to be here.

The sound of giggling floated out the door as I approached,

wondering if I should suggest somewhere less fancy next time. It was tradition, but sometimes it was good to try something new. Right?

"Rebecca." Nicola's voice was rough as always, like she'd smoked forty cigarettes before lunchtime. I smiled sweetly as my friend waved to get my attention, nearly taking out a waiter in the process.

As if I didn't know where they were sitting. The same place they'd been sitting once a month for the past ten years.

This was the meeting of what I liked to call 'the lonely and shallow club', not that I would ever say that to their faces. And don't get me wrong—it wasn't just them I was targeting with that name. That included me.

It consisted of scratchy-voiced Nicola, whose exquisitely delicate features reeled the men in, but whose complete and utter focus on her looks usually put them off. Of all my friends, she was the one I worried about the most—her weight fluctuated so much that she often looked as if she could break. To her it was all about the way she looked, how attractive she was to men, and how much money they had. Yet, I adored her soft heart.

Gemma wasn't the smartest person I'd ever met, and was nearly as obsessed as Nicola with the way she looked, and perfecting how to hook a man. But she'd do anything for anyone, and I do mean *anything*.

And then there was Katya, recently engaged, and rubbing the noses of everyone she knew in it. I hadn't told her yet that while I was at uni, I'd blown her fiancé (before he was her fiancé) in a campus bathroom. From the way he looked at me whenever he saw me, he hadn't forgotten about it either.

"Rebecca, it's so good to see you." Gemma stood, and as I approached the table she came toward me and did that ridiculous air-kiss thing that I couldn't help but screw up by actually kissing her cheek. I smiled to myself as she wiped her face.

"You too, Gemma. You're looking well."

She smiled as she sat and Katya nearly backhanded me as I sat down, waving her hand with that diamond rock in front of my face.

As if I hadn't seen it last time we'd had lunch, when she was newly engaged. And at her engagement party two weeks ago.

"How are you?" Gemma's green eyes were full of empathy as she fixed her gaze on me, boring through me like some kind of emerald drill.

"I've been better. But onwards and upwards, or something like that," I said.

"So, no news on the Alexander front?" she asked.

I looked around the table. All three of them sat there with bated breath—waiting for what? They asked the same question every month, and the answer was always the same.

The problem though, was that when you split with someone who moved in the same social circles as you, you were bound to run into them sooner or later. And we had, two weeks before at Katya's engagement party.

"What Alexander front?" I frowned.

"We just wondered if you two were back together," Katya said.

"Why on earth would I ever let that happen?"

"He is gorgeous and rich," Nicola said. "And he showed a lot of interest in you at Katya's party."

My hands fisted, and I scraped my palms with my nails as I took deep breaths, trying to remain calm. "The only reason he showed any interest was because I went home with one of his old friends. What's his name?"

They all looked at me, horrified.

"Bryce. That's the one. That was a one-night wonder." I smiled. "Besides, Alexander is still a chauvinist pig who decided to screw some other girl while supposedly in a relationship with me. I spent three days at home eating chocolate and crying, and now I'm over it. It's been eighteen months. To be honest, I'm over men for a while. Serious ones, at least."

"Well, my Tim would never do that to me. He adores me." Katya ran her hand over the ring again.

I roll my eyes.

"Hey Katya, are diamonds supposed to be *that* sparkly?" I asked.

She pulled her hand to her chest, shielding the ring with her other hand. "What do you mean?"

"Are you sure that's not a cubic zirconia? I'd go and get that checked if I were you."

Her nose twitched, and she sucked her lower lip in, that little seed of uncertainty seeming to grow as she stared at me.

I laughed. "I'm just kidding. Of course it's a diamond. Tim wouldn't do anything less."

The waiter appeared with the same kind of wine we'd been buying from here for as long as I could remember, and I smiled at the glass as he poured it for me, catching glimpses of Katya out of the corner of my eye as she stared at the ring on her finger.

I shouldn't have been so bitchy, but it was hard not to. I hadn't fallen in love with Alexander's money. He was gorgeous, and for just a little while we'd been blissfully happy. Until he'd wrecked everything.

For them to think I would ever take him back was insulting. Why should I put up with that kind of behaviour? He'd broken my heart.

I barely paid attention as the waiter took the food order, Katya taking control as always. I stared at my wine glass, twirling it so the golden liquid swished around, taking care not to let it splash too much.

Taking a sip, I looked around the table. The other three were in animated conversation, not noticing that I wasn't taking part in it.

The food didn't take long to arrive. Apparently we'd all ordered salad, and I grimaced as I stared at it. What was I doing? The memory of the bacon sandwich three mornings ago brought a smile to my lips. It had been so messy, and possibly one of the best things I'd ever eaten. I had come here once a month for so long, and always had the same thing, the same boring thing. To my left was the same salad, to my right was the same salad. I was surrounded by the same damn salad.

I waved down the waiter and he approached me, one of his

eyebrows raised. Our usual afternoon was for the four of us to sit and talk, taking up valuable seats in this swanky place while the waiters hovered, ready to pounce and clear the table the second we were gone.

"Do you have something with bacon in it? Oh, and fries."

His eyes darted at the others and back to me. I hadn't looked, but I could only imagine the expressions of horror on their faces.

"The Caesar salad has bacon in it." He smiled, and I looked back down at my plate.

"No. I want something that doesn't have all this green stuff. I want something that's going to give me a big fatty rush. Do you have anything like that?"

He adjusted his tie, shaking his head, clearly uncomfortable.

"What do you have that I'll regret eating later? Maybe because I'm so bloated I can't move?"

"We do have a filet mignon steak with a very creamy sauce. It comes with crispy potatoes."

I grinned. "That, please. Sounds amazing. Medium rare, please. If it comes with salad, I don't want it. I think I've had enough."

Silence surrounded me as I tucked my napkin into my shirt. Knowing my luck, if there was creamy sauce it would end up all over me. I looked up to see my three friends gaping at me in utter disbelief.

"What?"

"Nothing," Katya said.

"I feel like something different."

She went back to picking at her salad, and the other two followed suit while I waited for my steak.

The aroma of onion and garlic made my stomach grumble. The food might be expensive here, but it was worth every penny. Thankfully it wasn't one of those fine-dining places that had tiny meals for a million dollars, so at least my steak would be decent.

In fact, I was pretty sure I drooled as my meal approached the table, dripping in creamy saucy goodness. The scent of red meat had my tastebuds watering.

I savoured each succulent slice, acutely aware that the others were watching me.

"Oh my God, you guys. You need to try this. It's amazing."

One by one they screwed up their faces, still watching as I lowered the fork and then raised it again with each bite.

"Live a little." Gemma looked horrified as I spoke with my mouth full.

When I was finished and the waiter came over to see if we needed the table cleared, I asked for the dessert menu.

***

BLOATED AND CONTENT, it was time to pay the bill and leave. As we walked out the door, Gemma grabbed my arm. "Look."

My stomach plunged as I spotted someone familiar climbing out of his car, and it wasn't from all the food I'd just eaten. Alexander walked around his SUV, opening the passenger door for a blonde woman, who flung her arms around his neck as soon as she stood. I'd cried as many tears as I could for him, but it still hurt.

"Is that the woman you caught him with?" Nicola asked.

I shook my head. "No, I'm sure he's been busy with several women since then."

She rubbed my back. It didn't help.

Alexander turned toward the restaurant and spotted me, the smile falling off his face as our gazes locked. I looked away, changing direction and heading to the right, where my car was parked.

"Turns out there are other benefits to this place," Nicola said, pulling on my arm to direct my attention across the street. I didn't notice what she was pointing out at first. *JP Motors.* It looked like just another car yard. *When did she get that excited about cars?*

And then I spotted him, sponge in hand, bubbles everywhere as he soaped up the car. A dirty blond Adonis if ever I saw one, the deep tan in his skin glistening in the sunlight from the water that covered his chest. When I raised my eyes above his abs, which took a *lot* of effort, I found myself looking into familiar blue eyes.

Elliot.

The moment recognition hit him, his face lit up and he grinned, my stomach lurching so much I thought I was going to hurl that big fatty lunch I'd just consumed.

"Rebecca," he called, waving at me, as I blushed and gave a little wave back.

"You know him?" Gemma asked, her eyebrows wiggling slightly as she stared at me.

"He's my neighbour."

"Just imagine hooking up with him. Gorgeous, and you'd get a new car every year." She giggled behind her hand, and I looked away as I rolled my eyes. How on earth would you ever draw the conclusion that the man cleaning the cars owned the lot?

"He's cleaning the cars, Gemma, he doesn't own them."

Her jaw dropped and if Katya's nose could tilt any higher, it would probably have leapt from her face.

"Oh." Gemma looked at the ground.

"I don't think that matters," Nicola said. "Turn around."

When I turned, Alexander was staring at me. He'd come to a stop outside the restaurant entrance and held the door for his date as he watched.

I smirked and turned my attention back to Elliot, this time raising my arm and waving it like a crazy person. His laugh echoed across the car park, and he shook his head as he went back to soaping up the car.

"See you next month, girls," I said brightly, blowing them kisses as I climbed into my car. In the rear-view mirror, I could see Alexander still standing there, the woman he was with frowning as he watched me back the car and drive out onto the road.

She was welcome to him, but getting that reaction was priceless.

Today had turned out pretty damn good.

4

IN THE EVENING AT HOME, the cupboards were empty, and I opened each one just to double check if any food had magically appeared. I'd clearly forgotten to go grocery shopping again.

Maybe I should employ someone to take care of me.

Actually, that wasn't the most stupid idea I've ever had.

I already had someone who mowed the lawn and tidied the garden. I was glad I never did as Alexander suggested and employed a housekeeper. He probably would have screwed her too. Maybe I needed a nanny for myself.

Giggling at the thought, I walked out to the back door. Someone was barbecuing out there, and the smell was amazing. I could go and get a burger. That'd fill the gap. There shouldn't be a gap after what I ate for lunch, but that smell was alluring, and I stood on the back deck sniffing the air, glad that no one was around to see me.

The yard felt so empty. There was a swimming pool just past the deck, fenced off and dry as a bone. I'd drained it so long ago when the upkeep got to be too much hassle. I hadn't been using it. Maybe I should get it pulled out, do something different with the space.

"Rebecca."

I froze, slowly turning my head to the left where the voice had come from, and spotted Elliot on the deck next door, barbecue hood open and flipping something as if the activity was a fine art.

"Hey again." I waved and turned to go back inside.

"Want some?"

I looked back over at him and he pointed at the hotplate. His offer was tempting, but I wasn't sure about encouraging him.

"I'm just going out for something to eat. Maybe I'll see you later," I said.

He turned toward me, stepping off the deck and walking to the fence line. " What a coincidence, I'm making something to eat. Want a burger?"

Damn it. He read my mind. It did smell good.

Maybe.

"Do you have enough for one extra?"

Elliot grinned. "Sure. I'm cooking burger patties for Nan. I'm the one having steak and there's plenty. She struggles a bit much eating it with her false teeth."

I grinned. "Only if you're sure. I'm happy to go for a drive."

He turned back toward the barbecue, and I took a deep breath watching him. That man had serious swagger. I was so busy watching him, I didn't see his grandmother come out of the house.

"Hello, dear," she called out.

"Hi." I waved at her. I'd been in this house a few years now, but kept to myself for the most part. I had seen her tending to her roses, fussing over the brightly coloured plants, and envied her quiet life. Mine wasn't hectic most of the time, but work could get busy, and I was good at not stopping to take a break from everything.

"Meet you at your front door in ten minutes," Elliot called, and I nodded, walking back toward the house.

Distracted by those warm fuzzy feelings from his kindness, I wasn't watching where I was going and tripped, stumbling back in the house. I looked over my shoulder. Elliot's grandmother was on her way back into the house, Elliot was watching the food cooking. Whew. No making an idiot of myself today, thank you.

I sat down on a recliner chair in the living room, twiddling my thumbs while I waited for a knock on the door. There was no reason for me to be nervous, but my heart was racing at the thought of spending time with Elliot. Especially after the view I'd gotten this afternoon.

Closing my eyes, I could see him in my mind, those big soapy bubbles running down the car, his chest dripping wet from the water splashing. I moved my hands to my thighs, gripping the fabric of my long skirt, tugging at the hem. Seeing him like that made me ache to be touched with those hands that squeezed the sponge and ...

Tap, tap, tap.

I sat up straight, the spell broken. *Get it together, Rebecca.* Taking a deep breath, I rose, smoothing my skirt down, wondering idly how quickly I could slip my clothing off. You know, if necessary.

Elliot stood on the other side of the door, large serving platter in hand, with four burgers, lavishly made with meat and lettuce and tomato, and holy cow they looked good. So did he with that big smile, glowing as if he'd won the lottery. My mouth watered, and it wasn't just from the food.

He was dressed far more tidily than he had been when I'd first met him, a white collared shirt buttoned to the throat and black jeans. Yummy enough to eat too.

"Come in," I said, standing back to let him in.

He walked toward the kitchen.

"Don't worry about that, just put the plate down on the coffee table. Want a drink? I think there's a bottle of Coke in the fridge. I'll grab it" I tried so hard not to babble, but the words all came tumbling out in one big long sentence. Elliot just grinned even more and turned, placing the platter on the coffee table.

"Sounds great."

"Take a seat. I'll be back in a minute. I'll grab a couple of plates too. Your grandmother not joining us?"

"Coronation Street is on. Nothing can drag her away from that."

As I entered the kitchen, I took a deep breath. This wasn't a date. It was my neighbour looking out for me, just as he'd made sure I was safe the other night. He wasn't interested, right? Even if he was, I wasn't ready for anything new. Not after having just today announced I'd sworn off men for a while.

I grabbed a couple of dinner plates and set them on the bench. Tucking two drinking glasses under my arm, I grabbed the Coke bottle from the fridge, picked up the plates in my other hand and set back to the living room.

Elliot sat on the couch, looking as if he were at home, leaning back and looking around.

"You've got a really nice place."

"Thanks," I said, placing the plates and glasses down.

"And hey." He waved at the food. "This is a peace offering. I must have scared the crap out of you the other morning and I'm sorry. This neighbourhood is so quiet I have trouble sleeping sometimes, and hearing you out there intrigued me. It scared me to see you leave the front door wide open."

I shrugged. "I was pretty drunk. I still don't think that you should have come in, let alone help yourself to food from my fridge."

He blushed, and I held my breath. Holy crap that was cute. "I know. I just felt like I should take care of you if no one else was going to."

Maybe I should have been more angry than I was, but I was grateful that he'd looked out for me, and thankful that no one else had wandered past, seen the door open and come in. I'd put myself in danger by being careless.

"I appreciate it."

"I couldn't let anything bad happen to you when I was right next door. I'd never have been able to live with myself."

We just looked at each other for a moment. I wasn't one to be lost for words, but right now he'd left me more touched than anyone had in a long time.

"How about we eat these burgers before they get cold." My voice wavered as I spoke, and I passed him a plate, wanting to shove the food in my mouth, as much to find something else to do other than talk as to abate my hunger. My stomach grumbled at the smell.

Out of the four burgers on the plate, we both went for the same one, and our fingers smacked together.

"Sorry." I laughed.

"This must be the best looking one. You take it." He grinned, the heat in my cheeks rising at the way he was looking at me. So earnest. And young. How much younger than me was he?

I almost felt bad for thinking such carnal thoughts about him.

"Thanks." I took the burger, sinking my teeth into it and sighing at the mixture of beef and cheese. None of the other stuff mattered; that was what made me happy today.

"Good, then?" Elliot waggled his eyebrows at me, and I laughed, still with a mouth full of food. He grinned that stellar smile. "I'm glad. I like a woman who enjoys her food."

I swallowed the first bite, laughing again. "It's a recent development. I also literally have nothing in the cupboards."

"Happy to help." He took a bite, closing his eyes as he chewed, a look of blissful surrender on his face. "Damn, that's good. I should have made fries to go with these."

"They would have been great, but I've been a bit of a pig today. It's probably just as well you didn't make them."

He laughed, waving his burger in the air. "I love this kinda thing. If we're going to hang out together, you'd better get used to them."

I cocked an eyebrow. "Hang out together?"

Elliot shrugged. "I guess I should have asked you if you have a boyfriend. I don't want to step on anyone's toes."

My stomach flipped, and I let out a large breath with a sigh. "No, no boyfriend." I leaned back in the chair. "I got burned badly by the last one."

He frowned. "What happened? Shit. I guess it's none of my business."

"It's fine. I don't mind talking about it now. It really sucked, but I caught him with his pants down. Literally."

The look on his face brought a smile to my lips. His jaw dropped and he gaped at me. "Wow. How could anyone do that to you? You're gorgeous."

That did it. I dropped the burger on my plate, and attempted to hide the blush on my cheeks with my hands.

"I mean, what a dick," he said.

I grinned, nodding like an idiot. "I poured drinks over him. Icy-cold Fanta shrivels things pretty quickly."

Elliot laughed. "I bet it does. And I bet that felt good."

"It did. He still broke my heart though."

He looked down at his plate. "I could never do that. Who cheats on someone they're supposed to love?"

His sincerity brought tears to my eyes. Finding a truly good man was hard, and I'd thought I had one once.

Now I knew I was looking at one.

There was only one thing to do after eating so much at lunch and then again at dinner. Sleep.

I don't even remember Elliot leaving. The last thing I recall was the heaviness of my eyes as they tried so desperately to close on me, the television so hard to watch.

I woke on the couch in the morning, a blanket over me, and it was as if no one had even been there. Yawning as I stood and stretched, I made my way to the kitchen where the dishes had been washed, dried and put back into the cupboard.

It appeared I'd found my nanny.

"Hrmm might keep you on," I murmured, smiling.

Elliot was not only charming, but apparently very sweet.

Maybe that was just what I needed.

5

OLIVIA.

Out of nowhere she'd come, and I adored the hell out of her.

Our friendship had started when she came to work for me, and grew when her dirt bag husband left her a week after she'd started. Something about her made me want to coddle her; she just needed someone to take care of her for a change.

We'd been through a lot together, and she was my best friend. Nothing like the girls I'd grown up with, the women I'd just had lunch with.

I couldn't have been more proud of her when she'd started writing, and I'd worked with her to self-publish her wonderful stories that made me hotter than hell to read. They'd sold like hotcakes. She'd also met and fallen in love with the sweetest, sexiest man I think I'd ever met.

She'd gone from being neglected to being treated like the queen she was. I'd always love Logan for taking such good care of her and her boys.

The best decision I'd ever made was hiring her.

Olivia had been the third person who had come in for an interview for this role. It had everything you could ever want in a job—finance, invoicing, general admin ...

The first person who'd come in was this mousey teenager. Her age hadn't been on her CV, but she'd said she had the relevant experience.

Relevant experience, my arse.

The second hadn't looked me in the eye, just kept her focus on the table the whole time. I didn't want someone who was scared of me; I wanted someone who would fit in and have coffee with the rest of the team, not hide in the corner.

The day she'd come in for the interview, my receptionist, Grace, had come into my office, one eyebrow raised with that holier-than-thou expression on her face that she was *so* good at.

"Your three o'clock appointment is here. She looks nervous. You could probably squeeze her on salary."

It had been my turn to raise an eyebrow. Dad owned the big finance company; the little lending company he'd bought for me was a subsidiary of his, but I got to run it by myself. As long as I didn't run it into the ground.

I'd been impressed by Grace's work history when we'd bought the company, but she could be a real pain in the butt. No one really liked her that much. She was straight up to the point of being rude, had an opinion on everything, and never approved of anything.

"Thank you for your advice. I think I'll stick to what I decided on."

Grace had shrugged. "Your loss."

She'd turned and walked away, and I'd shaken my head with a sigh. It was nice she cared, not so great she'd stuck her nose in where it didn't belong.

Olivia had been different. She was quiet, yet confident. Her dark hair had been tied up in a bun with wisps escaping at awkward angles, as if she'd been making an effort to look professional, and succeeding, but I'd seen what a busy woman she was. Especially when she'd told me she had two young children.

"Do you think you have any weaknesses?" I'd asked.

"I need to stop saying yes to everything," she'd said without hesitation.

I'd laughed, and her eyebrows had dipped, uncertainty written all over her face as if she'd been concerned about saying the wrong thing. This job must have been important for her to get.

"I have to be honest—there are times when this job will be demanding, other times when it'll be quiet. I'm not one of those people that dumps stuff on their staff without thinking about workload. I don't think you would be pushed to say yes to everything."

Her lips had curled into the tiniest of smiles.

"Tell you what—I have a couple of other people to see but I'll have a better idea of where I'm at tomorrow. I'll give you a call tomorrow afternoon and let you know."

Her smile had grown, probably in relief that the interview was over, and she'd nodded.

I'd watched as she'd left the building. Her car had seen better days, and part of me wanted to run after her, just give her the job. But I'd had to go through the process, or at least be seen to do it. She could do the job, that much was obvious, and she'd be good at it and work hard.

As she'd pulled out of the car park and onto the road, I'd turned back toward my office. Grace had smiled at me. "She's the one, right?"

I'd nodded. "I think so."

"She looks like she needs some help."

I'd nodded again, choking back tears that had stung my eyes. I'd gotten that impression too. "I think so."

"You're a big softy, Rebecca Wallace."

Grinning, I'd made my way back to my office. Maybe I was, but I still hadn't been about to screw myself over. I'd thought Olivia Grant and I could help one another.

Now I needed to see her.

She sat in her office, and I slipped in the door, sitting on the other side of the desk.

"Hey," I said.

Olivia looked up at me. Poor thing. She worked so hard and hated being interrupted.

"Hey." She smiled and I grinned back. Since she'd gotten together with Logan, every day was happy for Olivia. And I was so glad for her, even if I was a little envious at all the sex she was getting. That man was hot, and he worshipped her. I could only imagine he doted on her in bed as well. That was what I needed, but without all the crap that came with it.

"How's it going?"

She nodded. "I've reconciled those accounts you asked me about so they are all good. Just working on the payments for ..."

I rolled my eyes. "As if I'm talking about work. How are things at home? How are the boys? How is that gorgeous muscle-bound hunk you're entangled with?"

Olivia got this far-away look in her eyes, and an even bigger smile on her face at the mention of Logan and the boys. I loved seeing her so happy.

"They're all good. Thomas starting school has made things bit easier financially. Logan is taking them both to the workshop in the afternoons so we don't have to pay for childcare. Such a relief with the house renovations and everything else that's going on."

I nodded. "That's awesome. How much longer until you move?"

Since her breakup, Olivia and her boys had been living in this pokey little apartment, with barely enough room for the three of them. Logan had made four, but he had a house that he was doing up and they were due to move in sometime. Preferably sooner rather than later.

She rolled her eyes. "I don't know. Most of the structural work was done, but it had been pretty run down. It's taken forever to get council approvals and then get the work done. I can't wait for it though. I'm so over us all being squashed together."

I grinned. "I bet you are. Tell that man of yours to hurry up."

Olivia bit down on her bottom lip as if trying to decide whether to tell me something or not.

"You okay?" I asked.

"I'm pregnant."

Silence hung between us as we gazed at one another.

"Do you want to be?" I asked.

"It was planned, and I'm three months in—just been waiting for that safe time to tell anyone. Logan was so keen to have a baby and we're so happy that I said yes. I didn't want to say anything until I knew what was happening. But I'm scared."

I stood, walking around the desk and crouching beside her.

"Why? You guys are obviously crazy about each other. He's in it for life from what I can see. And I know your heart. So are you."

She nodded. "I love him, and I know he loves me and the boys. But we've been together just over a year, and I don't know if that's long enough. I want to spend the rest of my life with him. I didn't really hesitate before agreeing to a baby, but now it's really happening, I can't pretend it doesn't frighten me."

I smiled. "Sweetie, I think that's perfectly normal. After everything you went through, this whole thing must be terrifying, especially with your kids."

She sucked on her bottom lip and nodded. "Maybe I'll feel better a few more months in." She gritted her teeth. "Perhaps we'll be closer to moving into the house then."

I laughed and stood, leaning over to hug her and pushing Elliot from my mind. She had enough on her plate without worrying about me, and if I told her that I was desperately attracted to my unemployed neighbour, she'd worry. Although, she'd also worry if he was a lawyer, or a banker, or anything else.

"Thank you for listening. We haven't had a wine evening in forever." She looked up at me. "I mean, obviously that's out, but it would be nice to catch up for a real talk."

"That is a great idea."

"You know you're welcome any time, even when my mob is awake. You're family."

I grinned. "I know."

"I can't wait to get into the house. There's so much room. I'll have to take you over to show you sometime. I even have a little quiet spot where I can write."

I grabbed her hands, squeezing them. "Sounds amazing. I love how you've found the support you needed."

She nodded, a huge grin on her face. "I think sometimes the worst things that happen to you lead to the best things. I never thought I'd ever be this happy. My boys are doing well, I have Logan, and I have you."

My heart swelled with pride. Her joy made me warm all over.

Maybe it could rub off on me.

6

BY THE END of the week I was tired, bone tired. It had been a crazy busy seven days and we'd pushed through it all. Dad would be proud. *Crap.* I should really call him to catch up outside of business. We were both hopeless at that.

I stopped on the way home and grabbed fish and chips for dinner. There were a few things in the cupboards at home now, but nothing I felt like cooking.

The house was dark when I got there. Sometimes I wondered why I ever stayed here. When Alexander had been around, it had seemed lively enough. He'd moved in after six months, though looking back it never really felt like a home with him. He was so busy with his legal practice that he was often coming and going at all hours for work. I'd ended up with a replica of my father.

It's funny when I look back now how clear it is. Back then I'd been so star struck that I hadn't seen it at all. I guess that was why him cheating completely blindsided me.

I'd had sex a handful of times since that awful day, just the odd one-night stand. When you got dicked around on, it was kinda hard to want to trust again.

I flicked on the television, opening the parcel of food out on the coffee table and tearing the little sachets of tomato sauce to squeeze out onto the paper. My fingernails matched the colour of the sauce today, bright red and still immaculate despite the rough day I'd had. I'd gotten into the habit of applying nail varnish every evening. It was soothing after a stressful day and I must have had fifty colours scattered around the house.

Pondering what colour to change to tonight, I dipped a chip in the sauce and moaned as I took a bite. This fulfilled every food fantasy of the last week and then some. I'd behaved and kept up my daily lunch visits to the gym, apart from on the day I'd had lunch with the girls. I figured that made up for it.

I'd just eaten my third chip when there was a tap at the door.

No one ever visited me at home. The girls would all call first, and I didn't know anyone as spontaneous as me.

I grinned at Elliot on my doorstep, bottle of Coke in hand. "I thought it'd be polite to bring something over. Wondered what you were doing this evening?"

"I've just gotten this gargantuan pile of fish and chips. Wanna join me?"

Eyebrows raised, he nodded. "Sounds great. There's a movie on TV I want to watch tonight, but if you've got other ideas ..."

"I have no plans other than eating a lot of greasy food. Come in."

He entered, laughing as he saw the food pile on the coffee table. "You weren't kidding about how much there is."

"I thought it could keep me going all weekend."

Elliot flopped on the couch. "Do you always take such good care of yourself?"

Shrugging I moved toward the kitchen to get some glasses. "I'm just really bad at it lately."

"Are you usually alone on a Friday night?"

As I bent into the cupboard, I slowed, closing my eyes at the question. I'd enjoyed being able to swing around to Olivia's whenever I needed company, and she'd needed it, too. Now she'd formed a family with Logan, that seemed much less of an option now, no matter how welcome I was around there. She hadn't written much lately, so I didn't even have her dirty words for comfort. Boy, did she know how to stoke the old fire.

"Sometimes. I try not to go out drinking very often."

"Good." He was smiling at me as I re-entered the living room. "Don't want you leaving your door open. Anyone might walk in."

I laughed, sitting on the couch beside him, and taking the Coke bottle from his hands. I poured two glasses and nodded at the fish and chips. "Help yourself."

He looked around, lifting the paper and locating the remote, flicking though the channels, until he found the one he was after. "Hope you don't mind."

I shook my head. "It's fine. I didn't have any plans. It was just background noise."

We sat side by side on the couch while some reality show played first. I wasn't a big fan of reality TV and the food held more interest right now than the television did.

I don't know what it was about Elliot, but while he was easily one of the most gorgeous men I'd ever met, both inside and out, he was just so easy to be around. This didn't feel like a date or anything like that—it was just a casual visit from my neighbour, who just happened to be hot and sweet. My favourite combination.

It was, however, incredibly hard to concentrate with him beside me. Despite my just wanting to flake in front of whatever was on, I couldn't help glancing at him, all relaxed and engrossed in the show.

He just seemed to settle in, leaning back with his legs stretched out, burping when he finished his Coke. All I could do was laugh; this was clearly no date.

"Sorry." He laughed as I shook my head, one eyebrow raised.

"Not trying to impress me then."

The distinctive theme tune to *The Lion King* started and I roared with laughter. "This is the movie you want to watch?"

Elliot grinned. "It was one of my favourites as a kid."

Smiling, I nodded. "Mine too."

"Can I tell you a secret?" His blue eyes flashed with mischief and one of my eyebrows crept up involuntarily.

"What?"

"I cried like a baby when Mufasa died."

I patted his arm. "It is a sad part of the movie. Do you want to know a secret of mine?"

He nodded.

"I cried when Nemo and his dad got separated."

Elliot laughed. "Aren't we a couple of softies?"

I shoved his shoulder with the palm of my hand. "Speak for yourself."

"Let's see who gets through this without tears in their eyes then." He tilted his head as he gazed at me. When he grinned that widely, dimples formed at the corners of his mouth. It wasn't possible for him to be any more cute. And distracting.

"Fine." I stood.

"Where are you going?"

"To get a box of tissues. Just in case."

I thought I'd be self-conscious sitting with Elliot, but even as the movie got to the saddest part, I felt nothing but comfortable being beside him. We laughed and sang along with the songs, and when Mufasa passed I wasn't the only one reaching for a tissue.

"So, I guess that was a bit much for both of us," Elliot said gently as the film finished, and I dabbed at my eye for one last time.

"Maybe for you. I've just got something in my eye." I failed to keep a straight face and he laughed, rolling his eyes.

"Whatever."

There was a moment of silence as we looked at one another. He seemed to be trying to read my mind, the way his eyes bored into me.

"You know, I should warn you I have a habit of speaking my mind. And being bitchy. Though there's probably not too much to be bitchy about with you. Except if we start talking about my friends, who I absolutely adore, but sometimes it would be nice to have someone to moan at when they have these expectations of me and I'm just not who they think I am and—"

Elliot inched closer. "Are you nervous?"

"Why would I be nervous?" I swallowed hard as he grew closer.

"Because you're talking an awful lot about nothing, and you look tense, like you're about to explode."

I relaxed my shoulders, releasing the tension I hadn't even realised was there. "Sorry. I don't mean to be weird."

"You're not weird. I like you."

I smiled and he tilted his head. "You seem like a good person, Rebecca. I mean, we don't know one another very well, but I like spending time with you."

"I like spending time with you too."

Elliot grinned, those dimples setting me on fire. "Glad to hear it."

He reached for the remote, switching the television off and dropping the controller on the table.

"So, Rebecca. I don't even know your last name."

I grinned. "Wallace. It's Rebecca Wallace."

"I'm Elliot Franklin. Nice to meet you, Rebecca Wallace."

Laughing, I took his hand in mine as he extended it to shake. "Nice to meet you, Elliot Franklin."

"At least this time I knocked on the door before entering the house."

I nodded slowly, a smirk on my face.

His gaze was intense, but I couldn't look away. *You're still holding his hand.* I let go, laughing nervously.

"So, tell me about yourself," he said.

I shrugged. "I'm thirty, I own a small finance company."

Elliot had that dazzling smile across his face again. "I'm twenty-five. I play guitar in a band sometimes. I have no permanent job and no idea where I'm going with my life."

Instead of something witty, I nodded, not knowing what to say next. "Okay."

What was wrong with me? When it came to picking up men, I

was usually pretty good with it. Did I even want to pick him up? He was my neighbour. What if things went weird?

"So, uh. Why don't you know where you're going in life?" The words came out slowly; I must have sounded like an idiot.

He shrugged. "I was always in trouble at school," Elliot said. "I never took anything seriously, spent so much time goofing off. Even got suspended once for sneaking into the school pool at night. That just got extended into adulthood."

I laughed, pointing at myself and nodding. "Smoking in the bike sheds."

"Aren't we a couple of trouble makers?" His eyes twinkled with mischief, his face only inches from mine, and the gap was closing.

"It sounds like it." I swallowed hard, my heart beating like crazy as our faces drew closer together. He eliminated the distance, kissing me and after a moment his tongue found mine. I gripped his forearm as the kiss intensified while his hand landed on my hip. I didn't want it to stop, and the way he kept kissing me, I don't think he wanted that either.

When he finally pulled away, we kept our eyes locked on one another. This was new, exciting, something I hadn't anticipated. I'd just enjoyed having some company and him being a bit of eye candy wasn't hurting.

"So?" A grin spread across his face.

"So," I said.

"Where to from here?"

I could have said so many things. Instead I shrugged and giggled like a damn schoolgirl.

"You know I'm really crap at relationships," he said.

I rolled my eyes. "It was one kiss. Not a relationship."

Elliot licked his lips, tightening his grip, pulling me just that little bit closer to him again.

"What if I want more than one kiss?"

My body was on fire. This whole thing was insane, but I just wanted to see where the ride was going. And the way that kiss had gone, I was picturing some crazy journey.

"What if I want more too?" I asked,

There was no answer to that question as Elliot's mouth covered mine, his tongue performing a tango in my mouth as he ran his hand up and down my spine. He pushed me back on the couch, still kissing me, his body on top of mine.

I spread my legs, hooking them around his waist to pull him even closer, pressing myself against him, feeling him harden as we dry humped and kissed like it was going out of style.

My brain told me to slow down, get to know him a little better before jumping into bed with him.

Screw it, my body said. *We're on the couch, not the bed.* It was a small technicality, but I didn't care, I was ready to get that man inside me.

He laughed as I rolled us off the couch and onto the floor where I could grind my hips and rub against him, nearly getting off in the process. It seriously was not going to take much.

"Is this what you want?" he asked.

"I don't want a relationship; the last one nearly destroyed me. I've made it a rule not to get serious. But I could be open to being friends with benefits. You know, you clean my car the way you did in that car yard, with no shirt on and lots of bubbles, then you get to come in and do the same thing to me."

Elliot laughed, reaching up to pull out the clip that held up my hair. Dark curls spilled down around me, and he gripped them, pulling me down to his lips for another kiss.

"What do I get in return?"

"Sex. Lots of sex. With no strings." I reached for the hem of my shirt, pulling it over my head. He grinned, slipping his hands around me, unhooking my bra and cupping my breasts in his hands, rubbing his thumbs across my nipples.

"I think I can handle that."

I slid back, pushing his shirt up and letting him sit up just enough to get it over his head. That muscular chest I'd spied from across the road was even better up close, his skin the colour of bronze. Kissed by the sun, as my mother would say.

Leaning over, I kissed him again. He smelled so good, that soapy clean smell that told me he'd made an effort before coming to see me.

"So, uh, are we going to do it on the floor? Or is there somewhere more comfortable?" he asked. I was so into this, I hadn't even thought about it.

"Well, my bedroom isn't far. Plus, I have condoms in the drawer beside the bed."

"I always carry one in my wallet. Doesn't bother me where as long as we do."

I squealed as he flipped me over this time, pinning me to the floor, kissing my breasts and stroking them as if they were the most precious things he'd ever had his hands on. The mixture of tender and rough was really doing something for me.

"Let's go to your room. I'm picking your mattress won't be as hard on my knees as this floor. Or yours."

My eyes widened at his words. He wasn't just planning on one time and go. This was either going to be a marathon or lots of little bites. I could handle either right now.

"I don't care as long as we stop talking and start doing."

Elliot pushed himself off me, holding out his hand. "Come on."

By the time we got to the bedroom, his pants were on their way down and I was treated to the sight of this gorgeous, naked man who wasn't just big in stature. It was like every single damn Christmas had come at once.

My vagina was about to be very happy with me.

He'd grabbed his wallet out of his jeans and fished out the condom, which he now held in his hand. Standing awkwardly, a smile on his lips, I looked at him blankly before realising I hadn't taken off my pants and my gaze had been fixed firmly on his groin.

I grabbed his hand, sitting him down on the edge of the bed. I slipped off my jeans, and knelt before him.

Alexander was bigger than any man I had been with before. But Elliot took the cake. Hell, he had the whole damn bakery.

He looked down at me with wide eyes. That just excited me further.

As I lowered my mouth onto him, he groaned as I took him as far in as possible. The clean, soapy smell was really doing it for me; I couldn't get enough of the scent and I slid my mouth back and forward, taking deep breaths, enjoying this as much as he very clearly was.

As I ran my tongue up and down his length he moaned. I raised my eyes to meet his. "Want me to keep going?"

He nodded. "That feels amazing."

Pretty amazing for me too.

I had always been one to enjoy giving head. It was that fun, quick thing you could often get away with when sex was just too difficult to sneak in. Like that time in the bathroom at uni with Katya's now fiancé, or in Alexander's car in the restaurant car park before going to have dinner with Dad.

Tonight though, I could just take my time and savour this man who I hoped would savour me afterward. I could do with keeping my ankles around my ears for a while.

"Holy crap. I've never had a blow job like this before."

His words spurred me on, and I sped up my movements, gripping him tightly as he moaned.

"Get on the bed," he said, gasping.

"But I'm not finished."

"Rebecca," he growled, and a lightning bolt went up my spine

I did as I was asked and climbed up on the bed, rolling onto my back. Elliot pushed my legs apart, leaning over me to kiss me, running his fingers up my thigh and making me shiver in anticipation.

"Don't tease me," I whispered.

"That's all you've been doing to me since we met." His deep laugh vibrated in his chest as I stroked his skin.

He moved back, replacing his fingers with his lips, planting gentle kisses on my thighs before plunging his tongue into me. As he flicked it over my clit, I nearly took off, needing this so badly, wanting him so much.

"Elliot," I moaned, reaching down to run my fingers through his hair, torn between wanting this to go on all night and wanting him in me.

I shuddered, closing my eyes. It had been a long time since anyone had brought me to such heights and I wanted to revel in it.

When he moved away, I opened my eyes in time to see him tear open the condom packet and roll it on. I looked at him in awe, this magnificent man about to impale me. I'd really struck it lucky this time.

He slammed into me, and I moaned. Having him inside me felt as good as I'd imagined, and I closed my eyes, my arms above my head, my hips pushing back and meeting his every thrust.

"You'll be the death of me, Rebecca," he whispered.

"Why's that?"

"This feels better than anything in the history of everything."

When I laughed, he moaned loudly. "Do that again?"

I laughed again, and his biceps flexed, the tight expression on his face showing his effort to hold back and not finish this too early.

"I just want this to last as long as possible," he said, his words confirming my interpretation of that expression.

"Me too." I ran my finger up his arm. "Although, it doesn't really matter. After we've finished, we can always start again."

Elliot laughed. "I like the way you think."

He slowed, and my heart beat faster as we just gazed at one another. It would be so easy to fall for him, love him, want more than just sex.

But that was all I wanted right now. No strings, no commitments —just lots and lots of great sex. And this was amazing. Elliot knew just how to hit all my spots.

He called out my name, his body stiffening over mine as he came and leaned over, pressing his nose to my own. It was strangely the most intimate moment we'd shared.

His lips grazed mine. "That was amazing."

"For me too," I whispered.

"Strictly casual?"

I don't know if his half-whispered sentence was a statement or question, but I nodded.

Elliot rolled to my side, lying flat on his back and panting at the effort. "I can handle that." He grinned.

IT WAS a little after three in the morning, and we'd had sex three times. Good things come in threes. So had I.

"Have you ever thought about having kids?" Elliot asked.

We snuggled, Elliot with his arm around me, my hand resting on his chest, cuddled in for the warmth and comfort he brought in the afterglow of sex.

I frowned. What a weird question to ask when we'd just met one another. "Why?"

Elliot shrugged. "Just curious I guess. You seem to have everything else going for you; I'm just wondering what Ms Wallace thinks the future holds."

I stroked his chest with my fingers, closing my eyes for a moment. "I have thought about it, but I don't know if I'll ever do it. I'd be too scared they'd end up with the upbringing I had."

"Tell me about it."

I took a deep, loud breath. "Dad lost a lot of money in a deal. I was young, but I remember them fighting and then him moving out. After that I was bounced back and forward. Sometimes I'd wake up not remembering whose house I was in. Mum would drink half a bottle of gin and I'd come home from school and have to pick her up off the floor."

I nuzzled his shoulder. This wasn't something I'd spoken about often, and not with anyone so new to my life. Elliot was somehow different. "I couldn't keep a boyfriend. Either Dad wouldn't approve, or Mum would flirt with them to the point where I was ashamed to take anyone home."

His warm, gentle hand stroked my shoulder and he kissed my forehead softly. "Look, I don't know them to judge them, but I do know you're not your parents, Rebecca."

"I know. I don't know if I want to take the risk."

Elliot squeezed my shoulder, and I nuzzled his chest, so warm and safe. Something about him was comforting, reassuring. I didn't know what it was, but I knew I could trust him.

"I want kids," his soft voice said.

I looked up at him, wide-eyed. "Oh, not right this second," he said, his chest vibrating with his deep laugh. "I have this dream of all the pieces falling into place. Finding someone to love, someone to have kids with, sorting out my work situation. I can't keep doing odd jobs for a living."

"Don't look at me. I'm hopeless at relationships, and don't know what I want," I said.

His hand stroked my cheek as he raised my face to look at him. "Whatever this is, I like it. So, I'll be happy if you want to keep doing it."

"I want a friend, Elliot. A real friend. This is just icing on the cake. Lots and lots of icing."

He laughed again, dipping his head to kiss me. His kisses melted me, but I couldn't give in, wouldn't let myself be hurt so badly again.

"I can be your friend, and I'll give you lots of icing," he murmured.

I snuggled back onto his chest and closed my eyes.

He was gone in the morning, disappearing in the night I guess because I'd emphasised the no-commitment approach I was going to take to our relationship. I was used to waking in a cold bed.

But I kinda wished the house smelled of bacon.

7

IT'S hard to get over your ex when he still lives in the area. When we broke up, Alexander took his things and left, and not once had he called me to discuss us.

But there were days where I seemed to see him everywhere I went. That was why the ghost of our relationship had haunted me for so very long.

The time for buying constant take-out food had gone. I needed to pull myself together and look after number one. No one else was going to do it.

After work, I swung by the supermarket, determined to fill a trolley full of good, wholesome food. Like donuts. They had sugar, and sugar was natural, right?

Reluctantly, I scoured the fruit and vegetable section, picking out some beautiful fresh, vibrant looking things to eat. Maybe they'd help pull me out of the funk I was in. Maybe instead of burying myself in work and a good night out, looking after myself might just make me better.

That and Elliot's company.

Now that made me smile, and I grinned like a mad woman as I made my way through the rest of the store. Pretty soon the trolley was full, and instead of the junk I'd been sure I was about to buy, it looked like a pretty decent shopping expedition.

And then I saw him, just as I left the checkout and headed toward my car. Alexander, on his way in to buy food.

"Hey," he said.

I smiled and nodded. No point being too polite.

"Doing your shopping?"

What does it look like, numb nuts?

I gaped at him. "Is that what you do here?"

Alexander grinned. "Sorry, that must have sounded dumb. It's good to see you."

"Damn it," I said, looking at the trolley.

"What?"

"I forgot to get any Fanta." I smiled sweetly and walked away, picking up the pace as I crossed the car park, needing to get away as fast as I could.

Him being around still rattled me.

———

SOMEWHERE DOWN THE back of the cupboard was a wok, and I now fished through the cooking pots to find it. It had been forever since I'd made a stir-fry, and unpacking all the fresh vegetables had made my stomach grumble.

It didn't take long for the house to have that wonderful smell of cooking food, and it seemed a bit warmer somehow, homely, more so than it had done in forever. Who knew all I had to do was to cook a proper meal?

I couldn't get it onto the plate fast enough, wolfing it down as I made my way to the couch. My favourite spot.

Before I got as far as sitting down, there was a knock on the door.

Bowl still in hand, I scooped up another mouthful before making my way to open it, licking the fork clean and moaning at how good the food tasted as I pulled at the handle.

Elliot stood there with a grin a mile wide on his face. "I hope that sound was in anticipation of seeing me."

Chewing, I waved my hand to say hello and indicate I was eating. I swallowed and smiled. "Actually it was because I just cooked a mean stir-fry."

"Got any left?"

"I'm getting the feeling you only want to be with me for my food." I laughed.

"Hey. I did bring you over food once." He licked his lips, looking down at the bowl in my hand. "Actually, I raced around here as soon as I knew you were home. I wanted to see you."

My whole body was warm and not just from the hot food as I grinned at him. "I'm glad to see you too."

He took a step toward me, closing the space between us and making my heart beat faster. "Elliot," I murmured.

His blue eyes twinkling with mischief, he bent his head, kissing me. *Do I have anything in my teeth?*

"I haven't been able to stop thinking about you." He wrapped his arms around my waist, and leaned in to nuzzle my neck. I gripped the food bowl tight, resisting the urge to just drop it and hook my legs around him.

Torn between the overwhelming need to have this man inside me again and my grumbling stomach, I prodded him with my free hand.

"What?"

"Want some dinner?"

"I thought that was what I was having." He nipped at my collar-bone, and I moaned, this time from my body reacting to his. My stomach gurgled, and I laughed, ruining the moment.

"I'm sorry, but I really need food. It's been a long day."

Elliot let go, raising his hand to stroke my cheek in such an intimate gesture. I was touched. It had been a long day, and I was tired and this felt better than anything had all day.

"Oh. Better get you fed, then. It smells good."

"Go help yourself. It's in the kitchen."

He kissed me again, despite the broccoli I was certain I had stuck in my teeth, and headed in the direction of the food. I watched as he walked away, admiring the way he filled his jeans and smirking at the thought I would soon have him out of them.

Elliot stopped. "Are you looking at my butt?"

I sat on the couch, tilting my head. "Maybe."

"I could feel your eyes on it, like they were burning a hole." He waggled his hips, and I snorted with laughter. "Any day I can make you laugh that way is a good day," he said before disappearing into the kitchen.

LATER, I lay in Elliot's arms, revelling in the sensation of his naked skin against mine. My body was his, but my heart was my own. At least, that was what I kept telling myself.

"What are you thinking about?" Elliot asked, nuzzling my cheek.

"This. What we're doing. It's so freeing to have you as a friend and be able to be this close without any expectation of anything more."

"Hmmm."

I turned my head toward him. "I like what we have. Whatever it is. You make me feel safe."

Elliot kissed me softly, tenderly. "I'm glad I make you feel that way. I don't want to be anywhere but with you."

I smiled. "How about monogamous friends with benefits?"

"Well, it is safer." Elliot's kisses were on the move, down my neck as his hand ...

"You want to go again?" I asked

"That is a bit of a crazy question while I've got my hand between your legs. What do you think?" His dimples told me just how happy he was to be there.

I shifted my hips, raising them to meet his hand.

"I think you have your answer."

8

APPARENTLY IT TAKES three weeks to form a habit. After three months of this whatever-it-was with Elliot, I was as blissfully happy as I had been from the start. He was most certainly entrenched as a habit.

I craved routine. At work I had it; routine was essential for me to keep my head above running the business. Especially with it growing the way it had.

My home life was a different story. I'd never been one for keeping to timetables or doing anything on a regular basis. Having Elliot in my life changed that.

Sort of.

With his odd jobs and the band he occasionally played in, we had to squeeze in time together. That meant late arrivals, or that he'd be gone before I woke. Soon my days became work, Elliot and sleep. Sometimes it was Elliot, work, sleep. When I was really lucky it was Elliot with bacon sandwiches for breakfast, work and then sleep.

It might have been a casual relationship, but I had never been more fulfilled. He met all my needs in the bedroom and out of it? I always did like a good snuggle on the couch. If I'd wanted to commit, he would have been close to perfect. I didn't know how he felt about anything more, but I was still terrified.

On the other hand, now I knew what it was like for Olivia meeting Logan. He'd become her friend before anything else, although with those two that didn't last two long.

I'd dated outside of my social circle, sure, but never anyone as free as Elliot. He never planned, sometimes didn't know what he was doing from day to day, did all kinds of random jobs, and somehow made enough money to keep himself afloat even without his grandmother's help.

She was on a pension and barely had enough for herself. Having Elliot around helped her.

This was the last thing my dad ever wanted for me. The business had been a huge thing for me to take on, he knew how serious I was. But if I was hooking up with anyone for any length of time, Elliot wasn't the type of guy he would approve of.

He wanted me with a career man, someone who would pull his weight financially and emotionally. When I thought I'd found that, it turned out to be a steaming pile of ...

Around Elliot, I could be myself for the first time. I took better care of myself, keeping up the lunchtime trips to the gym and eating well. But, a little bit of that rebellious streak leaked out every time I saw my friends now. I hadn't eaten anything green at Le Grande for months.

Olivia was now waddling like a duck. At six months pregnant, she was huge and I marvelled more than ever at my friend working and managing her home life with her children and Logan.

I pulled into the car park below her apartment, wondering for the millionth time just when they were going to move, their tiny little place cramped with the four of them.

We saw one another at work all the time, but it wasn't the same as spending relaxing time together.

As I knocked, footsteps ran toward the door and it flew open, Thomas standing there with big eyes.

"Rebecca's here, Mum," he yelled at the top of his voice.

Shy little Thomas wasn't so shy anymore.

"Come in," Olivia called from inside. I took a step in the door and surveyed the chaos that surrounded me.

I loved this place. It didn't matter to them that there was barely enough room to swing a cat—they laughed and loved and were all content. Such a warm and loving family, it was hard not to envy them.

Holy crap.

The man who put that glow in Olivia's cheeks stood right in front of me, and I ran my eyes over him, taking in the view. He was tall, well-built with dark hair and stubble. Seeing it made me think of Elliot, his cheek against my thigh, those little hairs scraping and tickling my skin as he ...

I swallowed hard. *Not now.*

"Hey Logan," I said.

He moved his gaze from me to Olivia and a shiver went up my spine watching as her cheeks pinkened. Oh, there was no denying it, she had it bad. Although she welcomed me with open arms, there was no debating the pair of them wouldn't be upset when I left and the kids were in bed. They had better things to do.

Honestly, that guy was gorgeous, and I might have just humped his leg like a horny dog. But he was Olivia's and I was ... *shit.*

"How are you doing, Rebecca?" He wrapped his arms around Olivia's waist protectively. He'd been bad enough before, now he was in mega Papa Bear mode. I was lucky Olivia was still coming to work. Soon he wouldn't want to let her out of his sight.

"I'm well, Logan. How about you?"

"I'm well."

Olivia beamed at him and he kissed her. I stifled a sigh; the love between them was so obvious. There should be more couples in the world like Logan and Olivia.

"I don't even think you have to answer that. Now when are you moving into that house?" I grinned.

Olivia smiled and Logan sighed loudly. "Very close—next week or two. We'll be there before the baby arrives. I've promised Liv."

"Sure. Well, if you need more space, you're welcome at my house. There's plenty of room there."

Logan shook his head. "Thanks. We'll be fine, I'm sure."

Olivia squeezed his hands. "I know you're just teasing, but I will be so damn happy when we're out of this place." She smiled at me.

"I bet. Unless you're planning on letting that baby sleep in a drawer, better hurry up." I raised my eyebrows at Logan, and he rolled his eyes.

"I've got to get to the workshop. I'll leave you two to gossip."

I waved at him. "It was good to see you, Logan. Go on, get out of here so I can find out the latest on your sex life."

He chuckled, kissing Olivia on the neck. "It'll all be in her next book. See you later, Rebecca."

Shaking my head as he left, I kept laughing. "He bites so well."

She picked up a cushion from the couch and threw it at me. "You're terrible at baiting him. He's as frustrated about the house as I am."

I laughed as I caught the cushion. "Well, maybe he needs to stop being a perfectionist and just move you guys. Who cares if it still needs some work? He has perfection right here." I opened my arms dramatically, waving them around as she smiled.

"He wants everything just right. And I do too. The bedrooms are all done, just waiting on the furniture."

Her cheeks glowed with excitement. Oh, this was so good for her, and I loved it. Logan and the house and the baby were just what she needed to plant her feet on the ground. Since the day her shithead husband left her, she'd been unsettled

"I'm so happy for you. I know I give Logan shit, but I love the pair of you. You're just amazing together."

She sat on the couch, and I sat beside her, placing the cushion back down.

"This is good for all of us. My boys ..."

"Where are they? Thomas was here for about five seconds before disappearing."

"He came out for a couple of cookies. They're playing in their room. They were building a tent by pushing the beds closer and draping a big blanket over top. Logan helped them weigh down the ends. I can't wait until they have somewhere to run around and let out all the pent-up energy."

Her jaw dropped. "I am being so rude. Do you want a coffee or something?"

"No, I'm good. If I want one I'll make it myself. Stop you from getting up. I just wanted to come and hang out with you for a bit. I've missed that."

"Me too."

I took a deep breath. "I wanted to share something with you that I've been keeping to myself."

Her brows furrowed in concern. "Is there something wrong? You have this look on your face like you're about to tell me something terrible."

"No. Actually it's pretty amazing." I looked down to avert my gaze. "I met someone a while ago and we've been kind of seeing one another. It's casual, and I'm enjoying it, but it's scaring the shit out of me."

Olivia smiled, nodding. "I get that. Logan was so caring and gentle, but after Evan left me I was scared about starting something new. I'm glad I did, though."

"It's just ... I know my dad won't like it. Alexander was a lawyer; Elliot does odd jobs."

"Does it matter?"

I shook my head. "Not to me. I've just always tried so hard to meet Dad's standards, and this isn't it. But, it's not like we're getting married or anything. Just having a bit of fun." I sighed. "*So much fun.*"

She grinned, patting my arm. "Enjoy it. Your father doesn't have to know—at least not yet. Tell him if it gets serious."

"I just had to tell someone."

"Then I'm very honoured that it's me."

I leaned over, hugging her over that big bump, loving that I could confide in her. My most special friend.

9

I'D GIVEN Elliot a key to my place by the second month. Given that he was coming and going at night, it made more sense than getting out of bed to let him in.

I was almost asleep on the couch in front of the television when the key turned in the lock. It wasn't that late, and I looked up to see Elliot coming in the door.

"Hey," I said.

He leaned over the back of the couch and kissed me. "How was your day?" he asked.

"Did you seriously ask me how my day was?" I laughed.

Elliot looked puzzled, his eyebrows raised. "What's wrong with that?"

"That makes us sound domesticated. I don't think we are."

He sat as I moved over, leaning over to kiss me again. "What are we?"

My breathing became heavy as he moved over the top of me, pressing his hips against mine. His lips grazed my neck, and I became a gasping, groaning mess, feeling him hard against me. He knew exactly how to get me going.

"Elliot," I whispered.

"What are we, Becs?"

"I don't know, but I really like what you're doing."

He sucked gently at my neck while I clawed at his back, willing our clothing to just disappear because the last thing I wanted was to waste time getting undressed.

"Want to watch a movie? There's one on TV tonight that I want to see," he whispered.

I dissolved into laughter as he pushed up and off of me, sitting up as I threw a cushion at him.

"Damn you, getting me all hot and bothered like that."

He grinned. "Before I forget, I brought you a present, something you'll love."

My curiosity piqued, I cocked an eyebrow. "What is it?"

"I dunno if I should give it to you. It's something very special."

I growled, and he laughed. "You are so impatient."

"You know it."

"You would have found it if I'd been lying on top of you for much longer."

What the hell could it be?

Elliot held up one hand, finger up to indicate that I should wait and reached into his back pocket. In a flash he produced a packet of microwave popcorn. "Tah-dah," he announced.

I rested my elbow on the armrest, laughing. "Is that all?"

"I offer you a gift and you laugh at me."

"What's the movie, smart arse?"

Elliot grinned. "*Finding Nemo.*"

"What are you waiting for? Get into the kitchen and pop that stuff. I'll find the right channel."

My eyes weren't on the television as he walked away. My heart warm at the close relationship we now had. That he'd remembered this was one of those movies that had made me emotional made me feel cared for. If our crazy attraction we had to each other ever died off, one thing was clear.

We were friends.

***

"I TOLD one of my friends about you today," I murmured, stroking his shaggy locks, pushing them off his face.

"I thought I was your dirty little secret." Elliot waggled his eyebrows, and planted a kiss on one breast.

I ran my fingers through his hair as he kissed closer and closer to my nipple, making me sigh. "My friend Olivia always told me her secrets. I felt like I could confide in her. If people find out about us, they find out about us, anyway. I'm not ashamed of you. Just a little scared of Dad."

He reached his spot, and I sighed again.

"Elliot," I moaned, tugging on his hair just a little.

"I should let you get some sleep. You have work tomorrow."

I ran my hand down his back, stroking his skin as he snuggled against me. "Unfortunately you're right."

He held me tight in his arms, and I nestled into his chest, feeling safe.

"Sleep," he whispered.

"Yes, Dad."

His chest vibrated as he laughed.

I kissed his golden skin. "I'm sorry. He'd be more 'Why aren't you working?' than telling me to get some sleep."

"He can't be that bad."

I looked up, shaking my head. "No, he's not that bad. It's just how I feel sometimes. I've always tried so hard to make him happy."

Elliot placed his palm on my cheek before running a finger down my neck and across my collarbone.

"Maybe that's why you don't feel fulfilled. Maybe you should work on making you happy," he said.

Smiling, I snuggled back in, resting my head on his chest. "I am."

IT WAS STILL DARK when Elliot gently shook me awake.

"Hey, I've got to get going. I've got an early start."

"What are you doing today?" I mumbled, rubbing my eyes as I sat up.

"I got a few days with a trucking company, filling in while some of their guys are taking holidays. Loading and unloading trucks."

"I'll pay you double to stay in bed with me. You're warm."

He laughed. "Wake up, Sleeping Beauty. I want to show you something."

I yawned and looked at the clock. It was just before five, and I'd be up and out of bed shortly anyway. I liked getting into the office early before everyone else got there. It was peaceful, quiet, and so much easier to concentrate.

"Fine. This had better be worth it."

I pulled a T-Shirt over my head. Elliot wrapped a blanket around me and led me out and into the living room, through the back door and out onto the deck.

"What are we doing out here? It's freezing. Let's go back to bed." I tried my best puppy dog look, but he shook his head, slipping his arm around my shoulder and pointing.

That sappy sentimental man had brought me out to watch the sunrise. And it was beautiful, the sun peeking out above the trees, the sky tinged with pink. *Shepherds warning*. It lasted for just a moment before I realised I'd rather look at him. Why, when I didn't want to give my heart away, was it trying so hard to just be with him?

"Isn't it amazing?" he whispered, snuggling up close to me.

"It is." *You are.*

"Any room under the blanket?"

I laughed, letting go of one end so he could wrap it around himself, and we stood in the cold dewy morning, watching the sky fill with golden light.

His arms were tight around me, as if he didn't want to let go, his nose buried in my hair, and he planted small kisses on my head.

This was wonderful, but call it intuition, something wasn't quite right.

"What's wrong?" I asked.

"Why do you think anything's wrong?"

"The way you're acting. I love watching the sunrise with you, but you're being weird."

Elliot took a deep breath, and I held mine as I wondered what the next words out of his mouth would be. "I'm going to be away for a couple of months."

I swallowed hard. We might be casual, but I'd kinda gotten used to the few times a week late-night rendezvous.

"Why?"

"After I finish the job with the trucking company, I've got some work labouring on a construction site. It's down south and I can't afford to be back and forward, so I'm not going to be around for a while." He bent his head, kissing me softly on the lips. "I'm sorry."

"Don't apologise. You have to do whatever you need to do." I licked my lips, tasting his kiss. "You are coming back though, right?"

"Of course I am. I feel bad about leaving when I said I'd help Nan out, and it might not be the only trip I make. It all depends on how it goes."

I nodded. I couldn't be upset about him earning for himself. What was I going to do? Be his keeper?

Actually ...

No.

"You'd be crazy not to grab the opportunity."

He nodded, kicking his toe against the ground.

"So ..."

What's he holding back?

"If you don't want to wait until I get back, that's cool. I mean, clearly you have needs and ..."

I shrugged. "It's only a couple of months. And you know I have no social life."

"Well, if you get a chance and you want to, don't feel bad about it."

Did he just tell me not to be wait for him?

There it was, the punch in the gut I had to hide because it hurt so much more than it ever should have.

And then he kissed me so deeply I thought he was about to suck my tonsils out. My heart sang as I relaxed against him.

Looked like he was going to miss me too.

———

HE WAS BACK THAT NIGHT, which was good because I'd been thinking about his words all day. Would he really be okay if I went home with someone else? If I brought another man home to sleep in my bed?

I wasn't okay with that. It would just feel wrong. And at the same time, did that mean he thought I wanted him to be able to do that, too?

It was late when he came in, and I was already in bed, stirring as he came into the bedroom.

"Hey," I murmured.

"Sorry. Did I wake you?"

"What do you think?" I sat up and flicked on the light. His eyes were heavy, as if he was really tired. I wrinkled my nose at the sweaty aroma coming off him.

"You haven't been home to shower?" I asked.

He sighed, twisting his mouth. "I just wanted to be with you after this morning. You giving up your warm bed to stand on the cold deck meant a lot to me."

I grinned. "Go get in the shower and throw your clothes in the washing machine."

Elliot's right eyebrow arched. "You mean walk around naked?"

Laughing, I threw back the covers and crawled across the bed to the other side where he stood.

"You could, or you could use a towel. There are plenty in the bathroom, you know."

He grinned. "You could always join me in the shower."

I rolled over, slipping out of bed. "Now there's a good idea."

Elliot wrapped his arms around my waist and kissed me, his lips lingering on mine as he ran his hands up and back down my spine.

"You stink. You know that, don't you?" I chuckled.

"You can wash my back."

"More than your back needs washing." I pulled out of his embrace, took him by the hand and led him to the bathroom, flicking on the shower as he pulled off his shirt.

His hands landed on my waist, pulling at the T-shirt I'd worn to bed, and lifting it over my head. As I fiddled with the water temperature, he had lifted his hands to my breasts, squeezing them gently as he kissed between my shoulder blades.

He let go, hooking his fingers in my panties and pulling them down my legs. I turned around as he ran his hands up my thighs and shook my head as he looked up at me with the expression of a dog begging for a treat.

"Awww." He frowned.

"You're still overdressed." I pointed at his pants, and he grinned as he unbuttoned and unzipped, standing to push them down along with his underpants.

Elliot sprung to attention, in more ways than one, and I grinned as I took him by the hand, taking a step backward into the shower.

The warm water sprayed over my back and I tilted my head to let it hit my neck. Elliot wrapped his arms around me, holding me closer as the drops wet our bodies. He raised his hand to my face, digging his fingers into my hair and bringing my lips to his as I surrendered completely to him.

No one would be taking his place in my bed.

"Do you remember what you said this morning? About me not

having to wait for you?" I asked, gazing up into those baby blue eyes of his.

He nodded, frowning.

"I'll wait."

A smile spread across his face, and he pressed his nose to mine, planting a gentle kiss on my lips.

"I know you want to keep this casual. I just wanted you to know that if it was something you wanted ..."

I raised a hand, running my fingers down the back of his neck. "Keeping it casual doesn't mean I want to jump into bed with anyone else." I pressed my nose against his. This felt intimate, *normal*, better than anything.

And we hadn't even made it to the sex part yet.

10

I HATED ELLIOT BEING AWAY. But this time, the loneliness wasn't the same as it had been before. This time I enjoyed spending time with myself. I had to; it was the only distraction I had.

I danced like no one was looking, until falling into a heap on the floor. I sang along with every song I knew on the radio, loudly and proudly. I thought I sounded good, but I could be tone-deaf for all I know. The temptation to go out for a drink or go partying just wasn't there.

The house was a mess. I let the dishes drain on the bench, the soapy bubbles dripping everywhere. It was with great reluctance that I changed the sheets on the bed, trying to hang onto the scent of Elliot for as long as possible. Maybe he'd never stayed the entire night, but he'd spent enough time for the pillow to smell of him still. So even though I changed the sheets, I left the pillow alone, just to have something to cuddle.

If I didn't know better, I'd think I loved him.

The tradition I did keep was lunch with the girls. It had been the one thing that had helped get me through the bad times in my life, because even if they weren't always supportive of my choices, they could be relied on to be there for me.

I pulled into the restaurant car park, pondering the month before, and how much I'd enjoyed the food. Maybe I'd order the same thing this time; I could do with the satisfaction a big meal could bring. It had been almost as good as sex. But not sex with Elliot.

Stop it. He'll be back when he's back.

My phone buzzed as I got to the door. I pulled it from my pocket and smiled at what was on the screen. Great minds and all that.

> Casual, I know. But I miss you.

He scratched an itch like no one else had, so enthusiastic to please us both. He was never selfish—always kind. Seeing his message brought tears to my eyes, melting me in a way I hadn't been in so very long.

I wiped my eyes before opening the door, smiling enthusiastically at my friends sitting at that familiar table.

"Rebecca," Gemma said warmly.

"Hi, you lot. It's good to see you." I sat, throwing my phone in my bag and placing it on the floor beside me, still warm from the simple text message.

"How are you?" she said.

"I'm doing well. How about you?"

She blushed. "Well, I met a guy."

I grinned. "Good for you."

"It's so good to see you," Katya said, placing her hand on mine, that engagement ring sparkling in the bright light. Nicola nodded assent, smiling at me.

I looked around the table, studying the faces looking back at me. Not that these guys weren't always friendly, but something was just a bit off.

"What's going on?"

"What do you mean?" asked Nicola.

"I can't put my finger on it," I said, studying their faces. I understood Gemma's new-man glow, but the other two were looking at me with what? Sympathy?

"Do you remember that woman we saw Alexander here with a while ago? The one he brought here for lunch?" Katya asked.

I nodded, curious where this was going.

"They just got engaged."

My lips curled into a smile. "Good for him. Hope he can keep it in his pants this time."

Nicola cocked a perfectly shaped eyebrow. "Really? We thought you might be upset."

"He's ancient history. I have bigger fish to fry." I sighed contentedly. "Much bigger fish."

"What is *that* supposed to mean?" asked Katya.

Raising my hand to wave down the waiter, I grinned. "Actually, I'm enjoying some time by myself at the moment. You should all come around one night. We'll drink wine and watch bad television."

Gemma clapped, excitedly. "That sounds like fun."

Even Katya smiled. "Like a pyjama party? We haven't done that since school."

"That would be cool. Just us girls. No boys." I laughed.

The waiter appeared beside me. "May I please have that delicious fatty steak dish?" Puzzlement crossed his face for a moment before he clicked as to which meal I was talking about.

"Can you make that four?" Katya asked.

"Oh, I couldn't," Gemma said.

"Of course you can. Live a little." I winked at her, and she lit up. It was as if she'd been given permission to indulge.

"Well, okay."

"Sounds good to me," said Nicola.

For once, the Lonely and Shallow Club didn't quite seem to match its name.

It was funny how that one little act of rebellion changed things. Now I watched as my friends moaned through their lunch, the taste of the steak and sauce being better than probably anything they'd eaten in a very long time.

And what I really loved? For once, none of them paid any attention to their surroundings, enjoying the food and not caring about what anyone else thought. At least that's what it looked like.

This was unlike any other lunch we'd enjoyed together, and even though we'd been close and knew most of one another's secrets, somehow this bonded us closer than we'd ever been. I hadn't had so much fun at one of these lunches, ever.

We ordered a gateau with four spoons, spending the next hour giggling and gossiping, but not the way we usually did. Instead it was gossip from our school days—every story about me getting into trouble, every memory of how my friends had been there to support me and bail me out.

There was one thing I kept secret. Elliot. I didn't want word to somehow get back to Dad. Not that there was anything to tell.

We were casual. Right?

***

WE HAD our sleepover the following weekend.

I spent a big part of Saturday afternoon at the supermarket buying junk food, popcorn, wine—all kinds of things ranging from slightly naughty to eat to things that might just make us explode.

Despite my independence, I'd never been this free before. I'd still tried to live within the constraints I'd put on myself, trying to live up to my father's expectations. Trying to be the professional that I wasn't.

There was one more person I needed to have with me—that was if her guard dog would give her leave.

I pulled into the car park of Olivia's building and made my way up the stairs. Mama Bear didn't get a lot of time to herself; I hoped Papa Bear appreciated that.

Jack flung the door open when I got there. "Muuuuum, it's Rebecca," he yelled.

"Thanks, buddy," I said with a smile.

"Come in," Olivia called from somewhere inside that crazy, busy flat.

I stepped in the door. Logan sat on the floor with Jack scampering back to sit on one side of him, Thomas on the other. They all had controllers in their hands and were playing some game, whooping and screaming as they went.

"Welcome to the madhouse," Logan said.

Olivia sat at the table with her laptop in front of her, no doubt working on her next book. She looked up at me with that warm smile of hers. "Come and sit down."

I sat opposite her. "What are you up to?"

"Just got some ideas for a story and making some notes. What are you up to?"

I grinned. "I thought I might take you away from all of this for the night."

Even without eyes in the back of my head, I could tell Logan had turned his head to look at me. Might have been that prickly heat at the back of my neck.

"What do you have planned?"

"I'm having a few friends over. We decided to turn it into a sleep-over and I thought you might like something different to do. We're going to eat crap, watch television, do girly stuff and drink wine. But of course I have plenty of juice and soft drink as well."

She looked over at Logan. I didn't want to turn around and meet his no doubt angry glare.

"You should go, babe. I'll be fine with the kids. We'll just order a pizza or something."

"Are you sure?" She chewed on her bottom lip, switching her gaze between us.

"Go for it. It'll be so much harder when the baby arrives. Make the most of it." He moved toward her, leaning over and kissing her softly.

She lit up. "Thank you."

"You don't have to thank me, Liv. That's what I'm here for." He kissed her again, this time lingering on her lips.

With Elliot on my mind, and seeing the way Logan was encouraging her to have some time for herself, the emotion began to build. If I hadn't been in someone else's house, surrounded by people, I might have cried. Maybe in bed by myself, later.

"You're so good to me." She snuggled against him.

"That's the easy bit," he said.

I sighed loudly. "Can we get the lovey-dovey stuff out of the way so we can get on the road?" I curled my lip to give off that sarcastic look.

"I'll go and pack a few things." Olivia sounded excited. At least I wasn't pushing her into something she really didn't want to do.

She stood, giving Logan one last little snuggle before disappearing off to the bedroom. He leaned on the chair she'd been sitting in and gazed down at me.

"Thanks for doing this. I've been trying to convince her she needs me to take over more of the load. Especially now."

I nodded. "It's my pleasure. I did think you might be a bit more protective of her, considering the baby."

He let out a loud breath. "I'd wrap her up in cotton wool if it helped, but that's almost as bad as neglecting her. She needs time with her friends."

Olivia came back out with a small pack. "I just threw a nightgown and toothbrush in. I'm ready."

"Cool," I said. "We'll just take my car and I'll bring you back in the morning."

Logan moved toward her, lifting her chin with his finger so she could look into his eyes. It was sweet and a bit sexy all at once. "You need anything, and you call me. We can be in the car and over at Rebecca's in fifteen minutes."

She nodded. "I'll be fine. Bit weird being away for a night, but I think I'll cope."

"Tell me about it." He bent his head to kiss her, and I looked away this time. This was bound to be a little more intimate. It would have to be their first night spent apart since getting together.

"Hey boys. Want to camp out in the living room tonight? We'll order pizza and play games."

There. That was his coping mechanism for an empty bed.

Olivia hugged him. "Have fun."

"We will." He let her go to say goodbye to the boys, and finally I had her all to myself.

We climbed into the car, and I backed out of the car park, turning and pulling onto the road.

"So, what's this in aid of?" Olivia asked.

"Just celebrating some me time. I wanted you to meet my other friends, too. It'll be a nice fun evening, I think."

"What are they like?"

I laughed. "Very different from me, but I don't know if you'll see that tonight."

"Huh?"

I glanced at her. She had confusion written all over her face from her raised brow to her open mouth.

"I have had a recent breakthrough in discovering what makes me happy. And I'm kind of hoping it's rubbing off. I'm just glad you're along for the ride."

Olivia leaned back in her seat, relaxed and happy. I didn't know if I'd provided her with any answers.

Tonight would be fun.

11

OLIVIA HELPED CARRY the grocery bags inside, despite my protests. The last thing I wanted was for my pregnant friend to be running around after me. This was supposed to be a break for her.

"Sit down on the couch and put your feet up, young lady." I wagged my finger at her.

"Make me." She poked her tongue at me and I laughed.

This took me back to the earlier days of our friendship, the evenings we'd spent together between the two men in her life. I'd been with her through her worst times and watched her find what she had now. I loved this lady so much it was crazy.

We tipped bags of chips into bowls, covering the table in food, and I hauled in a big plastic bucket, filling it with ice for drinks.

Finally we sat on the couch, each with a drink in our hand, and we toasted one another for our efforts.

"It's a damn shame you can't drink with me on your night off," I said.

Olivia patted her stomach. "I know. Maybe once this one is a little older."

"I'm so happy for you, you know that? I was sure Logan was

going to be all 'Stay away from my pregnant wench', but he was really very good."

She sighed contentedly. "He is good. I don't know what I did to deserve him."

"You're you. That's what you did."

Olivia rolled her eyes.

"I mean it. Sometimes we go through these really shitty times in our lives, but they're worth it for the amazing times on the other side. Good things come from bad."

She cocked an eyebrow. "You weren't drinking before you picked me up? We've had this conversation before."

She smiled, and I moved a bit closer on the couch, reaching out to hug her. "Having you in my life has been a big part of that. Seeing you get your happy ending ... I mean, I'm not ready to have a full-on new relationship with anyone, but I'm feeling better than I have in forever," I said.

"I'm so glad to hear that."

Could I tell her about my conflicted feelings regarding Elliot? That he meant more to me than just sharing my bed sometimes.

I bit down on my bottom lip. "Actually, there's something ..."

Tap-tap-tap-tap-tap-tap.

"Damn it. Sorry. That'll be one of my very impatient friends at the door."

I leapt up, opening the door to Katya, who stood there with a bottle of wine in her hand. "Rebecca," she said warmly.

"Katya, come in."

She hugged me as she stepped through the entrance, and there was more warmth in her embrace than there had been in forever. Not because our friendship was ever strained—she'd just never been a naturally huggy person.

"Katya, this is Olivia. Olivia, Katya." I waved between them by way of introduction.

"Let's open the wine. Where are the glasses?" Katya asked.

"On the table. Just two glasses though. Olivia won't be having any."

"Why not? We're celebrating. Exactly what I don't know, but—"

"Olivia's pregnant."

I swear I've never seen a transformation as complete as Katya's at that second. Her face softened as she moved around the couch and saw Olivia's bump. "Oh. That's wonderful."

Olivia looked at me with a *what have I gotten myself into* kinda expression. It was subtle, so Katya wouldn't see it for what it was, but I'd known her long enough to see it.

"I managed to pry Olivia away from her big protective Papa Bear for the night. I'm going to spoil the shit out of her."

Katya laughed. "Big protective Papa Bear?"

"Get her to show you a photo," I said. "He's gorgeous, and completely in lurve with this one." I nudged Olivia's shoulder. Olivia blushed, and rolled her eyes.

"It is a girl's sleepover. It's compulsory to share photos," Katya said, completely deadpan.

As if either of them could resist sharing photos of their men.

I don't have a photo of Elliot.

Maybe because he's not *my* man.

WE HAD SNACKED ALL EVENING, watching *Sleepless in Seattle*, a good old romance movie. By the end of it, we were all blubbering messes, going through tissue after tissue.

"I love that movie," I said, sniffing and sounding as if I was about to spit something out the back of my throat. Everything was streaming—my eyes, my nose, and all I could think about was Elliot.

"Let's talk about something that will make us laugh. How about our sex lives?" Katya said.

I rolled my eyes. "As if your sex life is anything to laugh about. I bet you and Tim go at it hammer and tongs."

She giggled. "Is it that obvious?"

"I think I've got cobwebs growing," Gemma said.

"I thought you met someone?" I poked her leg with my index finger.

"I did, but I'm keeping him guessing."

I studied her closely as she grinned back at me. "Good for you." I slid my arm around her shoulders and squeezed her tightly.

"So that's no sex for Gemma, lots of sex for Katya. What about you?" I asked Nicola.

Nicola scanned the room, her cheeks growing redder by the second.

"Well, I met someone."

"Who?" I asked.

"He's older. Quite a lot older. I had a crush on him a long time ago, but we ran into one another and something just clicked." She sucked in her lower lip, meeting my eye with a look that said she wasn't sure whether to continue.

"So? Tell us all about him." Gemma leaned forward.

"There's not that much to tell. We're enjoying spending time together."

Gemma rolled her eyes. "No. Tell us about the sex. You know, for those sad sacks who aren't getting any. Right, Rebecca?"

I swallowed. "Yeah, right."

"Oh. That's amazing. I was really worried that the image I'd built in my head would turn out to be a load of crap and that the sex would be boring, but that is not the case." Now she was coming out of her shell. It was strange for her to be in one in the first place. She'd never had any trouble talking about her sex life before.

"Really?" Katya's eyes grew wide.

"He can go for hours, and he's huge—like crazy big."

"Lucky girl." Katya smiled, and I clamped my lips together tightly.

"Sounds great, Nicola. I'm really happy for you." I raised my glass to toast her. "To amazing sex and good friends."

Katya looked at Olivia. "What about you?"

"Olivia has lots of sex with the lovely Logan," I said, waggling my eyebrows.

Olivia went a brilliant shade of red, but nodded and giggled. She'd been a bit quiet compared to the others, but she seemed to be enjoying herself.

"What I love is that he's so completely and utterly in love with her, and he dotes on her, he really does." I shared a look with Olivia that I hoped showed just how happy I was for her. And I was. Logan was everything she could have ever needed.

"The sex is amazing."

I laughed out loud. Olivia opening up spoke volumes for just how comfortable she was.

As I looked around the room, the women I loved the most all had smiles on their faces, really enjoying our time together, and I felt a pang of regret that we hadn't done this more often. We'd sat in that snooty restaurant so many times talking crap but not like this—this was a truly bonding experience.

"What about you, Rebecca? Are you really getting none? I mean, I know your relationship with Alexander was really sexed up. Do you miss that, or do you have someone who rocks your world from time to time?" Katya asked.

"Ooooh like that gorgeous guy cleaning the cars that day. You know I might have wandered past a few times trying to get another look, but I haven't seen him back in the car yard again."

Gemma's words were like a knife to the stomach. *Elliot's mine.*

No damn it. He's not.

"He was pretty hot alright," I said. "No, there's not really anyone permanent in my life right now." I met Olivia's gaze, one of her eyebrows raised at my response.

She smiled. Olivia had her secrets in the past, and I knew she'd keep mine. I hadn't exactly lied.

"That was so funny that day," Nicola said. "Alexander's reaction —if he hadn't stuck his dick in someone else, you two would be still be going at it like crazy. I'm glad you found out and dumped him, he'd still be doing it behind your back. I bet you'd even be married with babies on the way."

"Yeah, but he did. And that's that." I was so sick of seeing him, hearing about him, listening to these theories of 'what if' when he had been the bad guy in our relationship.

"Why don't we watch another movie?" Olivia suggested. I could have kissed her for changing the subject.

I got up and walked to the cabinet beside the television to pick another movie.

"What do you guys want to watch?" I asked.

"Something funny after that weep-fest," Nicola said.

I pulled out a copy of Shrek, holding it up.

"You've got kids movies? Let me look," Gemma said, moving behind me. She grabbed hold of a DVD, pulling it out. "*The Lion King*. Let's watch that."

I'd had that sitting in the cupboard for a while, but now it had new meaning. Seeing it made me think about Elliot. Damn him for going away.

No. He has to do whatever he has to do. He's coming back.

"I want something funny. How about this?" I pulled out *Men in Black* and she nodded.

"I enjoyed that. Besides, Will Smith."

There. Done.

I popped the DVD in the player and we started all over again.

Sitting at one end of the couch, I pulled my feet up and hugged my knees in the corner. My mobile sat on the armrest and buzzed as the movie started.

I picked it up and smiled.

> Saturday night and I'm thinking about you.
> What are you up to?

Elliot was thinking of me. I couldn't begin to describe how good that felt.

Sleepover with the girls. What are you doing?

There was no watching the movie now, but the others were glued to the television, laughing at all the funny parts and not paying one bit of attention to me.

Watching some awful film on TV and wishing I was in bed with you instead

I laughed, out of sync with the others, and Olivia cocked her head at me before spotting the phone in my hand. She smiled and went back to the movie. Of all of them, I could rely on her not to bring attention to what I was doing.

I could do with some of that too. I've been a bit itchy.

I sent back

If I was there I could scratch that itch.

I bet you could.

Holy crap this was hot, sexting away while the rest of the room was oblivious.

It's getting tough being away from you. I wanted to come back this week, but I've got to see this through.

I gazed at the phone for a moment, not knowing what to say. He missed me. Just like I missed him.

"Earth to Rebecca." Katya was looking back at me from her spot on the floor.

"Sorry, what?"

"I said, do you want me to throw some more popcorn in the microwave?"

I shrugged. "If you want some, go and help yourself. You know where everything is."

She grinned. "This was such a great idea, doing this."

"I'm glad you think so."

Nicola stretched, pulling the lever to put the footrest up on the recliner she sat on.

"This is the life. We should do this more often." She yawned.

Katya stood, making her way toward the kitchen. "Are we keeping you up, Nicola? Or is that what your older man does for you? Pretty sad if he's got more energy than you." She paused and looked back, poking her tongue out.

"He does wear me out, but no. I'm just comfortable and relaxed and happy sitting here."

That summed up how we all felt. I hadn't been so happy in years.

We all camped out on the living room floor rather than split up to sleep in the bedrooms and I pulled the bedding off my bed and from the spare room. Olivia was the only exception; I made sure she got the couch. No way was I going to let my very pregnant friend sleep on the floor. Besides, the couch was warm, soft and insanely comfortable.

I'd spent a lot of hours with Elliot on that couch.

Elliot.

Shit.

I grabbed the phone from where I'd dumped it on the coffee table, and pulled it with me under the blanket. There was a text on the screen that was only a few words long but it made me warm all over.

Sleep well. I miss you.

I sighed. Damn it. So much for not getting too involved in anything new.

I miss you too. Goodnight.

It wasn't the first time he'd said he missed me, but it really was harder to deal with. How do you get so tangled in someone it almost becomes an obsession? My resistance to getting in too deep was slowly being eroded by his thoughtfulness. It didn't help that my poster child for happy endings was sleeping peacefully on the couch nearby.

I closed my eyes, hugging my phone close. No more messages for the night, but I was surrounded by friendship and love.

I should have done this a long time ago.

12

THERE WERE some very bleary eyes and lots of yawning in the morning. Tired, I dragged myself into the kitchen and flicked on an element on the stove.

"What are you doing?" Olivia asked. Of course, she was the one out of all of us with no hangover. She certainly looked a lot better than I felt.

"Cooking breakfast." I rubbed my face with my palm, still half-asleep.

She smiled. "Let me do that."

"Uh-uh, pregnant lady. I said I'd take care of you and that's what I intend to do. Go and put your feet up. I'm making bacon and eggs."

Nicola stood in the doorway, rubbing her eyes. "I don't know if that's such a good idea."

"It'll be fine," I mumbled. "We all just need something to get us going."

"Are you sure about that?" Gemma said, leaning on Nicola. The pair of them clung to one another as if they needed the support. Maybe they did.

"I'm positive. I discovered bacon sandwiches one morning when I was hungover. I'm going to teach you just how amazing they can be."

Katya walked past Gemma and Nicola standing near the door and sat at the table. "Sounds good to me. I'm ravenous."

I smiled sweetly, opening the fridge and pulling a carton of eggs and packet of bacon out. They had become a staple of my kitchen; I never knew just when I might need them.

As soon as the bacon began to sizzle in the pan and that familiar aroma filled the air, Gemma and Nicola joined Katya and Olivia at the table.

"That does smell good," Gemma said.

"We should do this again," Katya said. "And not wait so long this time. We could have been doing this instead of all those lunches at that snobby restaurant."

I gaped at her, one eyebrow raised. "Wasn't it *your* idea to go to that snobby restaurant?"

She shrugged. "Maybe. I don't know."

"Whatever we do next, Olivia has to join in." Gemma said, smiling across the table.

"Doubt it. She'll be way too fat for the next one." I winked at Olivia and she laughed, rolling her eyes.

"I hate to say this, but I think you're right." She nodded.

"Besides, one night alone and Logan's probably going to chain you to the bed or something." I poked my tongue, flipping the bacon.

This was so much fun.

I'D NEVER BEEN SO glad to have bought both bacon and eggs for the occasion. Despite some initial protests, all five of us wolfed down our breakfasts. Gemma even asked for seconds. Gemma never asked for seconds.

One by one they went home, leaving me with Olivia and a living room full of blankets and pillows.

"Want me to help tidy?" Olivia asked.

"Over my dead body."

"Well, the sleepover has finished."

"Until I deliver you to your family, you're not doing a thing. Speaking of which, I'll drop you off and then come home and clean up."

She got that dreamy look on her face she always did when she thought of Logan. They hadn't spent that much time apart, but she would be missing him.

And I was missing Elliot.

Damn it. I didn't want to think about that.

"Are you okay?"

Damn her for knowing me so well.

"I'm fine. Just the guy I've been seeing is out of town at the moment."

Olivia's lips curled into a smile.

"What?" I asked.

"Is that what all those text messages were about?"

Grinning, I nodded. "No one else said anything."

She tilted her hand, her index finger pointing to her chin. "Completely sober."

I chuckled as I opened the front door. "Should I take you home, Cinderella?"

Olivia rolled her eyes, grabbing her bag as she walked past me and out the door. "Yes, but I want the full story. And you are going to tell me one day."

I unlocked the car remotely, and we climbed in. She gasped as she sat down, and I stared at her, terrified in case I'd broken her.

"Olivia?"

"I'm fine. The baby just kicked really hard. It's just been butterflies until now."

She glowed with excitement, a completely different woman to the one I'd met all those months ago.

I turned the key in the ignition and the engine roared to life.

Slowly, I backed down the driveway. I had precious cargo in my passenger seat, and I would get my butt kicked if I wasn't cautious.

Almost as if she read my mind, Olivia patted my arm. "You know I'm not made of china, right? I've had this conversation with Logan too."

I laughed. "I know. You're the toughest woman I know."

Pulling into the traffic, I started the short journey to her place.

"You think I'm tough? I think I'm just a giant marshmallow. Particularly big right now."

I slowed as we reached a stop sign, checking thoroughly before driving through the intersection. She'd been so strong through her marriage breakup. I'd admired her for that.

"You are a big softy inside, but you dealt with so much crazy stuff. That's what I admire about you. I know you had the boys to put first, but you got through that horrible marriage break-up, and you started again. That's kinda what I want."

"With neighbour boy?" I knew the question was coming before she asked it.

"Maybe. I mean I found it so hard to trust people again after Alexander. He was my whole world, other than the business, and not only did he screw around on me, he didn't even attempt to put things back together."

"I was kinda surprised the girls banged on about him so much," Olivia said.

I nodded. "Yeah, but he's part of a wider groups of friends. You know that phrase 'Don't screw the crew'? Yeah. Although in my defence, we were in love, and it was all very lovey-dovey for a long time. It's just because I haven't had anyone serious in my life since then that they show so much interest. And because he'll be at Katya's upcoming wedding."

We slowed again, this time for a red light, and I tapped my fingers on the steering wheel, not due to impatience, but to not really wanting to discuss my past.

"Trusting again is hard, but it can be worth it." Olivia said the words so softly, I could barely hear them over the hum of the car engine. She was right. It had worked for her. Why couldn't it work for me?

The light went green and I drove the half a block to her apartment building.

We pulled up outside her place and I stopped the car, smiling. "Maybe you're right. Thanks so much for coming over. I really enjoyed it."

She nodded. "So did I. Your friends are fun."

I swung my head from side to side. "Sometimes."

Olivia laughed. "Well, I had fun. Suppose I'd better get inside and make sure Logan is alright. The boys can be a bit full on. I can't wait to hug them."

Rolling my eyes, I smirked. "Logan will be fine. I'm sure he'll want to make up for the *one whole night* you spent apart."

I stayed until she climbed the stairs, a little envious of the homecoming she'd receive.

Hurry up and come home.

13

IT WAS a boring two months while Elliot was away.

I'll be home today.

I must have looked at that text message a million times, tension pooling in my stomach at the thought of seeing Elliot again. I'd missed him more than I could have ever imagined. Despite my insistence that we were casual, his absence had left a much bigger hole than I'd thought it would.

Work dragged. I loved my job. Work never dragged. But, by four I couldn't sit still any longer.

"Grace, I'm going home."

She smiled, a warm genuine smile, which left me wondering what I'd done to get that. It was pretty rare.

"Good. You should relax a little more. Take some time to stop and smell the roses."

I backed out of the building, a little weirded out. She'd never been quite so nice, though I had to admit she had her moments.

Maybe she'd just read Olivia's last book. That always put her in a good mood.

"Thanks, Grace. Bye."

I jumped in the car. I'd recently bought the Nissan 350Z, and the leather interior smell filled my nostrils. Damn I loved this car. Maybe I could go for a little drive before going home, take it out of the city and onto those long country roads ...

Whatever. You can't wait to get home.

That would have to wait for another day. I wasn't afraid to admit to myself at least that rushing home to see if Elliot was there was right at the top of my list. I needed his arms around me, and other parts of our anatomy to join multiple times, and ...

Oh holy crap, I need to get home.

His car wasn't in the driveway next door, and I frowned as I drove into the garage. Damn it.

Entering the house, I threw my car keys on the coffee table, sighing as I flopped down on the couch. *I guess I could keep myself entertained?*

The problem was that knowing that he was so close to being home, I just didn't feel like playing alone.

Tap-tap-tap.

Oh holy shit, don't let that be a delivery guy or something. I might jump him.

I ran to the door, pulling it open, my heart racing.

Elliot stood on the other side of the door, running his fingers through that shaggy hair and grinning with those damn dimples that made me clench my girl parts and ache for him to touch me.

"Where did you come from?" I looked around.

His brows furrowed. "Next door. Where else would have I have been?"

"Your car's not there."

He grinned. "It developed an oil leak on the way home. I dropped it off at a garage nearby to be looked at."

"Oh." I tilted my head. "How did you know I was home? Are you stalking me?" I asked.

He laughed. "No. Not intentionally anyway. I heard the car, thought you might like some company."

"By company, are you meaning roll-around-on-the-bed-naked company?" I asked, raising my eyebrows hopefully.

Elliot grinned again, making me hotter than the middle of summer. "Doesn't just have to be the bed."

That did it. I grabbed him by the shirt, pulling him in the door and pressed myself against him. Grinding my body to his, I could have just done him in the doorway, but I was way too classy for that.

"Come on."

It would have been one of those really sexy moments if he'd been wearing a tie. I could have just grabbed it seductively and pulled him gently toward the bedroom. Instead I grabbed the waistband of his jeans and practically sprinted to where I wanted him.

"Someone's in a hurry." He sang the words, following right behind me.

I just wanted him on top of me, in me, all around me. Our dirty little secret. Olivia could keep her big brown bear with the puppy eyes. I had my bronzed musician who turned my legs to jelly whenever he smiled.

On a strictly casual, no-strings-attached basis, of course.

I had half my clothes off in the gap between the bedroom door and the bed, stripping off my jeans along with my underwear as I lay down and holding out my arms while Elliot laughed at me, taking his time as he slowly lifted his shirt over his head.

"Hurry up," I grumbled, only half serious. Him making me wait had to be half the fun.

Naked, he climbed onto the bed, sliding himself over my body until he was on top of me, his bare skin against mine. My breathing grew ragged at the sensation, and he laughed as he kissed me, his body shaking as he chuckled.

"I missed you, Becs. Tell me how much you missed me."

"I need you inside me."

"That's not what I wanted to hear."

I paused. The grin on his face was a mile wide and he had the erection to match.

"I missed you, Elliot."

His mouth claimed mine as soon as I'd said the words. I wanted this man so damn much. The taste of his mouth was like coming home.

He trailed kisses between my breasts and down my stomach, before grabbing hold of my thighs and plunging his tongue into me. I squealed as I thrust toward his face, loving the contact, needing him as much as he seemed to need me.

"This, I missed this," I moaned, running my fingers through his hair, his head nodding in a rhythm I matched with my thrusts.

"I dreamed about this," he murmured, his tongue going about a hundred miles per hour.

I hit my peak in record time, tumbling over the edge as he moved up and into me in one swift movement. He'd never felt so good as he did right at that moment, filling me, kissing my breasts, his hands caressing my sides, my back, pulling me up to meet him.

Gladly, I gave my whole self, surrendering to the warmth of his skin, wanting more, needing everything.

And for the first time, I didn't ever want to let him go.

14

THERE SHOULD BE a law against anyone making loud noises on a Saturday morning. At least until midday.

I might not have been hungover, but I was still half-asleep when the pounding on the front door started. I staggered out to answer it, in my track pants and baggy T-shirt. The phrase "bed hair" could have been invented for me. In the mornings I could be a bit of a disaster area.

It had worked to my advantage sometimes. Staggering out of bed to answer the door with bleary eyes, my hair sticking up like I'd stuck my finger in a light socket—I was sure it had scared off unwanted visitors more than once.

Not this one, but then he wasn't unwanted.

"Hey, beautiful."

Elliot was far too chirpy for this time of the morning. It was, after all, 10.32 am. On Saturday and Sunday, it might as well have been dawn.

"What are you doing here? Don't you need to sleep or something? It's daylight."

He grinned. "Get dressed. We're going out."

"Where are we going?"

Elliot hooked his finger in the loose waistband of my track pants. "It's a surprise."

I sighed, trying so hard not to show my delight and failing. He always had a way of making me smile. With our 'friendship' renewed, it'd be so good to go and do something out of the house.

"Fine." I pecked his lips and turned to go to the bedroom. "What am I wearing?"

"Just jeans and a shirt. It's nowhere fancy, but I bet you'll like it."

"Hmm." I tried my best to sound suspicious, but inside I was excited. I was ready for that, if not a little more.

My life was so confusing. Elliot's absence and return was making me see casual wasn't all I wanted.

I pulled on a pair of jeans and changed my T-shirt, then ran a brush through my hair and tied it up in a ponytail, off my face but still a bit messy. That'd have to do.

Elliot stood in the doorway, shuffling from foot to foot, twisting his mouth.

"Are you okay?" I asked.

He looked up, and for a moment his expression was really serious, as if he was seeing me for the first time. I didn't know what it was, but this was something new, something stronger than we'd had before.

Baby steps. One thing at a time.

"Is this a date? I just ... well, it feels like one to me."

His question caught me by surprise, especially when I didn't know the answer. Going out in public with him was a first. Asking me that made it kinda weird.

"I don't know. Can't we just be two friends spending the day together and see how it goes?"

Now he grinned, tilting his head to look at me. "Can't even commit to the word date."

I laughed, grabbing him by the waist and kissing his nose. "Is that what you're calling it?"

He shook his head. "Not if it makes you feel uncomfortable."

"I don't think I've been on an actual date in years."

Elliot reached out his hand for mine. "Come on then. Let's go on a non-date date."

"I like the way you think."

He laughed as we stepped out of the door. I squinted in the bright light.

"I know it's hard being outside when the sun's up. I'm sure you'll manage to get through the day without disintegrating, or whatever it is vampires do."

"Oh, ha ha ha." I poked my tongue out at him.

"Have you got sunscreen on? You'll need it. I've got some in the car if you don't."

I rolled my eyes. "I didn't put any on. It's hard to plan when you don't tell me where we're going."

"Big day outside with lots of fresh air. Sound good, Rebecca, vampire queen?" He stuck out his top teeth over his bottom lip, doing some lame vampire impersonation. All I could do was shake my head.

I followed him out to his car. It was a beaten up old Toyota Corolla that had seen better years, but it suited him somehow. He opened the passenger door for me, and I grinned at him as he closed it behind me.

"You are being a gentleman, aren't you?" I said as he opened the driver's door.

"Just making sure my lady is taken care of."

His lady.

He got in and turned the key in the ignition. The car croaked to life, and spluttered a bit.

"Is your car okay? We can take mine."

Elliot grinned. "Nothing major. One day I'll learn to take care of the small things myself."

"So where are we going?" I asked.

"I told you. It's a surprise." He backed down the driveway and out onto the road. "Ready?" he asked.

"For our non-date date? Sure."

Elliot laughed as he accelerated, and we drove halfway across town to a very familiar-location.

"The zoo?" I burst out laughing as the big outer building loomed. There were cars everywhere, children being pushed in strollers, and holding hands with their parents. And us.

"I used to love coming here when we visited Nan. Mum and Dad would bring me and we'd spend the day. I haven't been in years."

"What made you decide to come here today?"

He pulled into a park, the engine coming to a stop as he turned the key and paused to look at me. "I thought it was time for us to spend the day together."

I grinned.

"I also thought it would be good for you to get some fresh air. What have you been doing while I've been away? Working or staying in the house, right?"

Puzzled, I tilted my head, as if asking what he was on about.

"I know you, Rebecca. If you're not at work, you're at home. Unless something's changed dramatically in the last few weeks, you don't get out a lot."

I shrugged. "I spent time with other friends. It was at home, though."

Elliot pulled out the keys. "Come on then. Let's go."

He took my hand in his as we got out of the car, and he led me toward the gate, squeezing my fingers.

"This is such a great idea," I said.

As we reached the ticket booth, I reached into my bag for my purse.

"I'm paying." Elliot pushed in front of me.

"Yes, boss." I snuggled in closer, squeezing his butt.

"Two adults please," Elliot said, handing over the money.

He took my hand in his as we walked through the gate together, heading toward the enclosures, stopping when we got to the lions.

"These are what I came to see," Elliot said. He put his arm around my shoulder, pulling me in close.

"Are you getting all sentimental about that movie?" I asked.

"Is that a crime?"

"No. I think it's kinda sweet."

I turned, and he moved his arms to around my waist as I kissed his cheek.

"So, I drive you wild with hot sex, and now you think I'm sweet? Must be winning."

"Winning what?" I hooked my arms around his neck.

"You."

I thought my heart was about to explode, and for once I didn't have any kind of comeback at all.

I COULDN'T SLEEP despite the day out in the sun, and our big dinner full of carbs, and all the physical exertion after that. All I could think about was what Elliot had said. Was he seeing this as more than just a casual sex thing?

I didn't want to ask him. As much as I wanted to know, I didn't.

If he wanted some kind of commitment, the idea still scared the hell out of me. As much as I wanted to trust him, the memory of throwing ice-cold drinks at Alexander still played on my mind, seeing him pull out of the woman he was screwing behind my back when that morning he'd told me just how much he loved me.

Elliot and I had never exchanged those particular words, but the thought of him being with anyone else tore a hole in my gut. Sometimes I just wanted to curl myself around him and never let him go, but the threat of being as hurt still seemed to hang over me.

I turned onto my side to watch Elliot sleep. He was always so scruffy, even when he smelled soapy and clean. I'd never been with anyone quite like him before. Our lives were almost complete opposites, but we connected on a deeper level than I had with anyone else I'd ever been intimate with.

He made me laugh, and he laughed with me. He hadn't made me cry. Yet. Being with him was so easy, almost too easy at times.

It scared me. He scared me.

Falling in love with him could be the best thing that ever happened to me, but that couldn't happen. At least, not yet.

Baby steps.

Elliot stirred as the phone screeched beside the bed.

He opened one eye, looking at me as I fumbled to get hold of it.

"Who is it?" he mumbled as I flicked on the bedside lamp

I grinned at the name on the screen. "Olivia! It's midnight, what's going on?"

"You did tell me to call you when the baby was born."

Elliot groaned as I squealed loudly. "Rebecca."

"Who's that?" Olivia asked.

"A friend."

"Sounds like a *very* sleepy friend."

I laughed. "Only just gone to sleep actually. But enough about me. The baby is here?"

"Yes, I've just been moved to a room. She's beautiful, Rebecca. Logan and I are totally in love with her." She sounded tired, content, and I wanted to jump out of bed and get to the hospital to see her, but it'd have to wait.

Elliot rubbed my leg, and I grinned down at him. His face was full of questions.

"Olivia had the baby," I whispered, holding my hand over the phone.

"Who *are* you talking to?" Her tone told me she knew exactly who.

"You weren't supposed to hear that." I giggled, running my fingers through Elliot's hair. He stroked my thigh and I blew him a kiss.

"We are catching up when I get home. You need to come and see our little girl."

"Sounds wonderful," I said.

"Good night."

I sighed as I lay back down. Elliot wriggled closer and flopped his arm over me.

"Good news, then?"

"I'm so pleased for her. She's got everything she could have ever needed. A loving boyfriend, a big house for them all to live in, and now they've got their first child together."

He raised his hand to my breast, stroking my nipple. "Come here."

I grinned, rolling toward him. He leaned forward, kissing me softly.

"I thought you wanted to get some sleep," I whispered.

"Well, now I'm awake. You weren't exactly celebrating quietly."

"Whoops." I grinned.

Who needs sleep?

15

AT THE END of the following week I stared at the ceiling, Elliot's hands roaming my body. So many things were going on in my life, the best one of all was in bed with me.

I closed my eyes, wriggling down the bed to get more comfortable.

The hands stopped. "What are you doing?" Elliot said in a teasing tone.

Oh. It wasn't that I didn't enjoy what he was doing. My head was in some other space. But I couldn't tell him that.

"It's just so relaxing," I said, as seductively as I could.

He laughed, moving over on top of me and pushing my hands above my head, pinning me to the bed.

"Got you."

He'd been more caring since our non-date date, less of the *wham, bam, thank you ma'am* kinda deal we'd always had. More gentle. More loving ...

Snap out of it.

His knees parted my legs further and he entered me, inch by

inch, ever so slowly, all the while maintaining eye contact. This was weird and good and weird.

I sighed, thrusting my hips toward him as much as I could, restricted by his weight on top. We lost eye contact as his gaze swept across my face, and he dipped his head, latching his lips to my neck and gently sucking.

"You're not really into this, are you?"

He'd lifted his head and was looking at me again, his eyebrows twitching as if he was unsure whether to be concerned or not. His thrusts slowed to match the mood.

"It's not that. I just have a lot of distractions at the moment."

"Are you going to tell me that you've met someone and this is it?"

I smiled, reaching up to touch his face. "No. I wouldn't be in bed with you if that was it." Running my finger down his cheek, I tilted my head to the side. "I went to see Olivia during the week. What she's been through has been life-changing. She's struggled for so long, but now everything has changed for her."

"Meeting you changed my life." His words touched me, and my insides melted as he turned his head to kiss my hand.

"It's been pretty good for me, too."

"So you're not pulling out of our arrangement?"

This time, his choice of words made me giggle and I pushed him off me and onto his back, straddling his hips and lowering myself back onto him. "No, no pulling out going on here."

"Do you know why I like you so much, Becs?"

"You get sex on demand and I'm insatiable?"

"That, and you make me laugh. It's pretty damn hot."

Right at that moment, I just wanted to chain him to the bed and keep him. I wiggled my hips and he let out a loud moan, all the while with a big cheesy grin on his face.

"Was that for real?" I asked.

"Do it again and maybe I'll tell you."

I laughed, leaning over to kiss him. With him I always felt

comfortable in my own skin, never needing to watch what I said. I could just be myself.

What have I been doing with my life?

"Do you know what else I like?" he whispered, nipping at my neck as I lay flat, pressed against him.

"What?"

"I like that I can just be myself with you."

I wiggled my hips again and cried out as he rolled us both over, claiming the top spot once more.

"Come and see me play?"

My mind went blank as he said it. He'd managed to get me on such an angle I was about to ...

"Holy shit, Elliot."

"What? Is that a yes?"

I nodded franticly, wiggling my hips and letting out a grunt that started him laughing and he came shortly after me with a guffaw in my ear.

"Well, that's never happened before," I said.

Elliot rolled off me, and I turned my head toward him, meeting his eyes as we both dissolved into fits of laughter. He slid his arm under my neck and I wriggled closer to him, my heart as warm as my body.

"You're my best friend, you know? I don't know what I'd do without you in my life."

"You're not so bad either. For an old chick."

I gaped, slapping him on the arm as the grin on his face grew bigger.

"So, are you coming to hear me play?" he asked.

"Where and when?" Right at that second, I would have done anything he asked.

"Tomorrow night at the Capitol Club. We're on stage from nine until ten."

I took him in, the pleading in his eyes, the smile on his lips. He really wanted me to hear him play. I hesitated, for a moment unsure of what to say. All this time we'd been screwing and we'd only once left the little bubble we'd put around us. Our relationship barely existed beyond the front door.

"What's your band's name?" All this time, and I didn't even know. There was so much I didn't know about Elliot, so many things we'd never discussed. Hell, I knew one day he wanted children, but I didn't even know what his parents did, anything about his childhood, or the name of the band he'd played in since before we met, even if it was off and on.

"Oblivion."

I screwed up my nose. "That's a bit morbid."

"So will you come and watch me play?"

"Maybe."

"That'll do." He kissed me, his tongue pushing into my mouth with so much urgency it might have been possessed. Maybe he was just excited.

THE FABRIC WAS soft against my skin, the satin glinting in the bedroom light as I turned from side to side. I'd get away with not wearing a bra with this top. The shoestring straps and low neckline made me feel almost naked, but there was enough fabric to cover up the bits I didn't want to show off.

"Not bad for an old chick," I said, grinning at my reflection.

I grabbed my handbag and pulled my cash card out of the purse, shoving it into one pocket, my phone in the other. That should be enough to get me through the night without carrying too much crap around. Olivia teased me all the time about carrying around the kitchen sink with me; tonight I travelled light.

As I drove closer to the city, the crowd thickened. People were everywhere, some already staggering out drunk from bars, most just having a good time. It had been forever since I'd done anything like this. I was much more of a homebody, quite happily curling up with a bottle of wine and watching television until I fell asleep.

The closest park I could get was a block away, and as I stepped out of the car, the cool night air hit me, the light fabric of my shirt rippling in the slight breeze. I'd never been more glad to have worn jeans in my life; at least the bottom half of me was warm.

I shivered, pulling at the shirt to stop it from clinging to me. The last thing I needed were random strangers in the street seeing that the cold had made my nipples stand up straight. What I really wanted was a cardigan.

It would have been easy to get back in the car and go home, but instead I took a deep breath and headed toward the club.

Thump, thump, thump.

The beat was pounding from halfway down the block, and I forced my eyebrow down as I took in the girls with skirts up to their navels, and tops with much lower necklines than mine. If anything, it made me feel far less self-conscious as I approached to pay the cover fee.

I pushed my way into the building, pondering the legality of just how many people were inside. I looked around for some indication of their fire limit and ...

Stop acting so old and responsible.

I found a gap in the hot, sweaty bodies dancing around me, and spotted Elliot on the stage already. They must have gone on early.

If I'd ever thought he was hot before, he looked crazy sexy now. His muscles flexed as he put all his effort into playing his guitar, slapping it into submission as it wailed.

I couldn't move. I was stuck to the spot, mesmerised by this rock god on stage. It was a beautiful sight, and as I slipped my hand into my pocket to grab my phone to take a photo, I noticed someone watching me.

He was tall with a bushy dark beard, and wore jeans with a flannel shirt. *Oh great. Attract A Hipster night.* He swaggered toward me, his eyes firmly focused on my chest, and I sighed, shaking my head. All this effort for Elliot—I hadn't thought of the unwanted attention my plunging neckline might bring.

Ignoring him, I raised my phone, lined up the photo and clicked. Somehow it captured him perfectly, that scruffy hair flying just as he threw his hand down to hit the next note. Whatever happened between us, I had this moment when my best friend, my lover showed his skill to a very excited, primarily oestrogen-filled audience.

"Hey," Mr Hipster said, still not raising his eyes to my face.

"Not interested."

He stood there as the song finished, and I looked past him as a little blonde thing in a barely there skirt jumped up on the stage. She grabbed hold of Elliot, and she had to be a surgeon the way she started performing a tonsillectomy on him. With her tongue.

Pains in my chest grew as I stood there, unsure of my next move. Go closer and let him know I was there? Find out he wanted it?

It was easier just to leave and pretend I'd never been here. He didn't owe me anything. I'd been a fool to not think about his life outside my house. I fought back the tears as I turned to leave, not helped by the twat who had approached me grabbing hold of my arm. He had a strong grip, and the panic rose in me as he pulled me closer to him.

"Not running away, are you?" Now he was this close, I could smell the alcohol on his breath. His eyes were red and glazed, and I yanked my arm away from him, scared of what might happen if I didn't get out of there.

"Get off me."

"Come on." He grinned.

I shook my head, rolling my eyes, and pushed my way past the people blocking the exit. Pausing as I got to the door, I gulped the cold fresh air that punched my lungs as I tried to make sense of everything.

What an idiot.

"Are you alright, miss?"

I jumped as the bouncer beside me spoke. I hadn't even seen him, but he was pretty hard to miss, just a big ol' wall of muscle.

"No. Some dickhead grabbed me in there. Wouldn't be surprised if I have a freaking bruise from it."

"What did he look like?"

"Tall, jeans and a red flannel shirt, big long beard."

"Shit. That describes half of the guys in there."

I shook my head. "Sorry, that's about the best description there is." I looked back over my shoulder, only to spot him. "That one there."

The security guard turned and spoke to another man behind him, who nodded and disappeared into the crowd.

"He won't be doing that to anyone else."

I swallowed hard, grateful, but now was a good time to disappear back to my car and not linger while the dickhead got thrown out into the same street I stood on.

"Thanks. I'll be going."

The guard nodded, winking at me as I turned on my heel and set off down the street at a stiff pace.

When I got to my car, I sat for a moment taking deep breaths, and I leaned back in the driver's seat, looking at myself in the rear-view mirror.

"What were you thinking, Rebecca? Those girls are all ten years younger than you." I shook my head as I spoke to my reflection.

Time to go home.

16

THE SOUND of the shower woke me a little after two in the morning. It could only be one person, and I slid out of bed, stumbling toward the faint light showing under the en suite door.

Elliot grinned when he saw me, sliding back the shower door just a little.

"Wanna join me?"

I shook my head, lowering the toilet lid so I could sit on it, just wanting to go back to bed and away from him. But at the same time I wanted to be near him, as he seemed to want to be near me.

"You okay, Becs?"

I shrugged, rubbing my eyes. "Half asleep. Why are you here?"

"I had an amazing night," he said. He lifted the shower head from the cradle, running it over the last of the soap bubbles, which ran down his body and into the drain. He pulled back the shower door and grabbed a towel from the rail beside it. "I wish you'd been there. The crowd went nuts."

Leaning forward, I buried my face in my hands rather than answering, his hands landing on my shoulders as he stood over me. I looked up. He'd wrapped the towel around his waist and was standing there, all dripping wet and smelling of *Johnson's* baby soap. My favourite.

"You look tired."

I feel about a million years old compared to the girls throwing themselves at you.

"I'm just glad it's Sunday. At least I get to sleep in," I grumbled. I stood, catching a glimpse of myself in the mirror, my hair tousled from sleep, probably with a million little tangles to brush out. What a sight.

"Come on, beautiful. If you're up for it, I could do with a little tension release before sleep. I'll make you bacon sandwiches in the morning."

My eyebrow crept up. "You want to stay the rest of the night?"

"It's two in the morning. Where else am I going to go?"

"Home?" I shrugged.

His eyebrows drew low as he looked at me, scanning my face for something. "Do you not want me here?"

"I'm half-asleep. I don't know what I want."

I pushed past him, exiting the bathroom and flopping onto the bed, face down.

"Is that an invitation to something new?"

No matter how tired, annoyed, and frustrated I was, that made me laugh, and I rolled onto my back as he lifted the towel to dry himself off.

Articulating my emotions was too hard, so I lay and watched this beautiful, naked man in my room as he dried himself before climbing into bed beside me.

"What are you thinking?"

That this is the weirdest night ever? That I feel further from you than ever, but all of this is just so intimate?

"Nothing. I just want to go back to sleep."

His right arm slipped under my neck, pulling me to him.

"I was there, okay?" I mumbled.

"What?"

"I came to see you play. Took a photo, saw you with a girl, got harassed and left again."

"Rebecca, look at me."

He had to be serious for him to use my full name. He was the only one who called me Becs, and that was all he usually called me.

I met his gaze. For a change his expression was so serious. I fought the urge to just close my eyes and go to sleep.

"You saw me with a girl?"

"Yeah. You looked like you were playing tonsil hockey with her." I said.

"And now you're here, letting me climb into bed with you." His expression didn't change. No joking, no sign of any humour.

I shrugged. "It's better than being in a cold bed."

There was that earnest look again. "Are you jealous?"

Yes.

I rolled my eyes. "No. I'd just appreciate it if you are putting your penis anywhere other than in my lady bits that you tell me so I can make a choice whether to keep doing this or not."

He nudged my head to one side, brushing his lips down my neck

"We decided on monogamous friends with benefits. Just the way you wanted it. My penis only goes near your lady bits, no one else's. I'd tell you if I was even considering that. I'm not about to disrespect you, Rebecca."

There it was again, my full name. What was up with him?

"Oh, there was no performing tonsil surgery on her with your penis either?" I didn't want him inside me if he'd been inside anyone else, but I didn't stop him touching me.

"She grabbed me, kissed me, and I told her thanks but no thanks. That was it. I wanted you with me. Are you sure you're not jealous?"

His hand was inside my panties now, his fingers stroking my clit, driving me insane. It took everything in me not to make more noise, cry out as my climax approached. I didn't want to give him the satisfaction.

"No," I yelped as he thrust his fingers into me.

"It's okay if you are. I like it."

The bedside drawer opened and he pulled his arm out from under me as he fiddled with the condom. My head swum with a mix of emotion. Could we have an actual relationship? This friends with benefits thing had been fun, oh, so much fun. But there had to come a point where we worked out where it was going.

It was easy to come home and sink into a warm bed with an eager man, rather than chase after anything else. And it wasn't just that he wanted this too—he was sweet, charming, had the biggest heart of anyone I'd ever known, and had been willing to keep this whole thing a secret. Not that I was ever embarrassed by it.

Having Elliot to love was the icing on the cake. Not just the sex.

I gazed at him in a new light as the revelation hit me.

"What?" he asked, his lips twisted into a confused smile. He was probably wondering about the way I was looking at him, as if I'd never seen him before.

Elliot was this beautiful angel who had given me what I needed whenever I needed it. He was everything I'd ever been taught was wrong, and yet he felt so right. Being with him was just so easy, as if he was a part of me that was missing.

"Nothing, just tired." At least I could have tonight in his arms and wake with him, maybe even tell him how I was feeling after I'd had my morning coffee and could speak coherently. Staying was a first—maybe there would be many more sleepovers.

As he moved over me, I ran my hand down his chest. We'd been intimate so many times, but this was different. At least for me.

"I'm sorry if seeing that upset you," he whispered. "I wanted you to be there so you could share another part of my life. One you haven't been a part of until now."

"I know, I'm sorry."

"Although, I'm kinda glad you didn't stick around. Some big fight broke out as the bouncers tried to take out some guy who'd harassed a girl or something."

He slid into me, cocking his head as he began to thrust slowly.

Leaning over, he kissed my shoulder before looking at my arm, his brows dipping in concern. "That's an impressive looking bruise coming up. What did you do?" He bent his head, touching his lips to that same part of my bicep, kissing me better.

"That's probably where I got grabbed. Freaking dickhead decided that I might want to do something with him. I got out of there as fast as I could and set the bouncer on him."

He nodded, knowingly. "So it was you behind the big fight?"

I shrugged. "Guess so."

"Trouble-maker," he whispered. He picked up the pace, pumping in and out of me like a man possessed. "I'm glad you weren't hurt. Don't know what I'd do if anything happened to you."

The words made me want to cry, but I held it in. For him to have come back to me. Could this really turn into ...?

I couldn't even think the word it was so far out there.

And as he came, groaning in my ear, kissing my cheek, the cool night air filling the gap between us as he pulled away to dispose of the condom, there was only one question circling in my head.

Could he just be the one?

IT WAS NEARLY ten before I woke, and while the bed was cold, the smell of bacon through the house brought me comfort, familiarity. What would I do without Elliot and his bacon sandwiches?

I stumbled out of bed, grabbed a big T-shirt from my chest of drawers, and followed the aroma.

Elliot stood at the cooktop, just the same way he had the day I met him, dressed in a T-shirt and boxers.

I wrapped my arms around his waist, leaning my head between his shoulder blades.

"So you decided to wake up? I thought you were going to sleep all day."

"It's not *that* late." I let go, and he turned around to face me, leaning in to give me a kiss.

"I did wake you in the middle of the night. I thought about waking you for some early morning fun, but I figured you needed the sleep."

I grinned, giving him a quick kiss before turning toward the table. It was set with two plates, the buttered bread just waiting for the bacon. "I'm always up for fun, you know that. Especially of the *your penis* variety."

He shook his head and laughed. This was nice—just two people who cared about each other sharing time together. My belly ached wondering how to even suggest we try anything more. This was just all too hard.

"So, is this going to be a regular thing?" I asked, sitting at the table.

"What?"

"You staying the whole night."

He laughed, lifting the bacon from the pan and dropping it onto a plate to carry to the table. The days of bacon grease on the floor were long gone.

"I don't know. It is kinda nice not to get out of bed and go home. You're quite cuddly."

Cuddly? Was that a compliment?

"I still woke up alone," I said, stabbing a bacon slice with my fork and lifting it onto the slice of bread.

"Is that a hint?"

I shrugged. "I also like the bacon. What can I say?"

Taking a bite, I closed my eyes. Damn, that was a good start to the morning.

"Good?"

I nodded, unable to speak with my mouth that full of food.

"You're going to hate me," he said, as I took another big bite.

"I doubt it." I mumbled the words.

"I'm going away again."

I swallowed the food, aware my breathing had accelerated. Having him invite me to watch him play was a huge step, him staying most of the night an even bigger one. Now he was leaving again? We'd settled back into our routine as if he'd never gone away, I didn't know if I wanted to go through us being apart again. Not for weeks or months.

"Do you have to?"

He nodded. "I've made the commitment. I'm trying to get some more stability in my life, and it might be far away, but this doesn't have to stop. I'll be back."

"Elliot, I hated you being away last time."

"Does that mean you want it to stop?" His eyes were so full of emotion, his heart right out there for me to see.

"No." I got up and walked around the table. He pushed out his chair and pulled me onto his lap. "I just missed you a lot. How long is this trip for?"

"I don't know."

"How can you not know?"

"It's open-ended. There's a lot to take care of, and I want to be there right until the end. Prove that I'm reliable. It might just turn into a permanent thing."

I gulped. "Permanently not here?"

He shook his head. "After this, there'll be other opportunities closer to home. This is all about proving myself."

Those were the words that won me over. I still didn't like the idea of him going away, but I'd spent so many years trying to prove myself to Dad, I understood that need more than anything else.

"Can I come and visit you?"

"We'll see if we can work something out. There's no spare room where I'm staying, but there's a motel nearby. We can talk on the phone as well. I'll try to get to the spot where I have decent coverage more often."

I raised my hand, stroking his chest. "I'm going to miss you. You know that, don't you?"

"I'll miss you too."

He pulled me down for a kiss, each one between us growing more tender. I tingled from my toes to the top of my head.

"I get that you're scared, Becs. You don't need to be scared with me," he whispered.

When he stayed for the rest of the day, it was the longest time we'd spent together since we'd started sleeping with one another.

This was so confusing. I wanted more, but didn't know how to say it despite him seeming to be open to it. Being with Elliot was one thing—committing to him was another. Not that he was going to be around for a while. He made me want to break my promise to myself that this was not going to get serious.

Deep down, I knew it was way too late for that.

17

HE WAS GONE for all of winter. And that old adage 'absence makes the heart grow fonder'? Holy crap that was true.

It was next to impossible to get hold of him, he was often out of coverage range, and we played phone tag a lot. At least I had voice-mails full of affection.

He always sounded so tired too, and I wanted more than anything to tell him to forget it and just come home. But then, I remembered his words, the way he was looking to prove himself.

At least work was busy which helped keep my mind off the time.

I didn't want to be with anyone else. I wanted him—his arms around me, holding me day and night. His gentle kisses that set me on fire. I guess I'd known from the beginning it was destined to be him. We were just a perfect fit.

I loved his scruffy hair, his stubble, that beautiful toned, tanned body. And I loved his mind, his humour, and his sensitivity. No matter how hard I fought it, I loved that crazy man.

He'd brought spontaneity to my life, more than I'd ever had before. He'd brought friendship and love. Now all I needed was to know if he loved me back.

The last message I got he thought he'd be back in a week, maybe two, and I knew I'd count down the days to him coming home.

After all this time, I had it bad. And the whole while I fought the doubt about us.

When did I turn into an angsty teenage girl? Even when I was a teenager, I hadn't been like this. I was the type of girl who could take it or leave it. If a guy wasn't interested, or lost interest, there was always the next one.

But then I'd fallen in love. It hadn't ended well, but it had changed me, and even though I'd thought I could just go back to being the old Rebecca, all it had taken was for the right man to come along.

I knew more than ever that the right man was Elliot.

If I'd told him, maybe he would have stopped going away.

Deep in thought, I stirred as the phone rang and despite adoring my friend, I was a little disappointed to see it was Olivia calling. Part of me just wanted Elliot to call me. "Logan and I are finally getting married."

The words tumbled down the phone at me, and my heart was warmed at just how happy Olivia sounded. This had been a long time coming, and I couldn't be more pleased for her.

"Good to hear it. I'm glad someone has tamed the wild Olivia."

She laughed. She laughed a lot these days, and it was a sound that was great to hear. So different from those early days when even when what she said was positive, she'd sounded miserable.

"I want you there. It'll be a quiet thing with just our family. My mum and Logan's mum. Logan's friend Maddy and her husband Andrew. And you. Maybe you can bring Elliot."

I bit down on my lip, unable to verbalise all I'd been feeling.

"Maybe," I said.

"I need you to help me find a dress. Nothing too over the top. We just want to go across the road to the park, get married under a tree and come home for a barbecue."

She kept talking, but I wasn't really listening. Would Elliot want to come with me? Was I overthinking it? I have always been really good at overthinking things. At least, I think I have been.

"Rebecca?"

"Sorry. Yes, sounds great. Anything I can do to help, just let me know."

"I'll just be glad to see you there. You've done so much for me, I don't know if I can ever repay you."

I closed my eyes, smiling at the words. "There's nothing to repay. You've been such a good friend to me. I'm just glad to see you happy and getting some."

Olivia laughed. "Come and see me soon. I miss your face."

Since she'd left work to raise her family, I didn't see her very often. She'd brought so much fun and excitement to my life for such a short time, but I could never resent her for finding the man of her dreams and settling down with him.

Was that what I wanted?

Was I mature enough to actually have an adult relationship without screwing it up?

You're overthinking it again.

"I miss your face too. Let's have lunch and go shopping one day. Bring that beautiful baby of yours with you."

"How about Wednesday?"

"Sounds good. See you then."

I sighed as I hung up the phone. That beautiful baby of Olivia's, little Chloe, had the biggest blue eyes and those gorgeous rosebud lips. She was so precious that my ovaries begged me to do something every time I saw her. That was another thing I'd never thought would be possible for me.

But maybe it was.

I had to put my big girl panties on and do what I wanted with my life. That was the only way to get it going in the direction I wanted it to go. Not Dad's direction—I'd played his game for long enough.

It was time to do something for me.

ON FRIDAY AFTERNOON I had my lunch booked in with the girls. Katya was getting closer to her wedding date, and I grimaced as I climbed into the car, knowing the afternoon would be full of wedding gown talk, reception talk, and Tim talk.

You have no idea what you've taken on, Tim.

None of us had been invited to be bridesmaids; Katya had sisters. It was a relief, if I was being honest. I didn't want to be too involved. But I'd received my invitation, including a plus one.

Wonder if Elliot will be back in time to take me.

Argh, what was I thinking? Katya's father and my father were friends. Dad would be there too. The last thing I needed was to deal with Dad meeting Elliot.

I wasn't ashamed of my relationship with Elliot, whatever it was, but Dad had certain expectations of me, and Alexander was the epitome of perfection to him. The last thing I wanted was to drag my best friend and lover into a situation that wasn't fair on him. I wanted to ease Elliot into a meeting with Dad, if there was going to be one.

I walked through the door at the same time as Gemma, and I went through the routine of greeting them—Gemma with her air kiss which I couldn't even be bothered screwing up, Nicola unusually quiet, Katya more bubbly than usual. That wasn't surprising, given how close we were to the wedding.

"I don't know what it is with all these weddings. I've got yours and then I've got Olivia's the week after," I said.

Gemma laughed. "How is Olivia? You should bring her to lunch sometime."

"She's well, but busy."

"I know you've told me this, but I forget. She had her baby, right?" Gemma asked.

I nodded. "She did. A little girl, bringing the total number of babies in her house to two. The little girl and the big tattooed man."

The three of them all giggled. They'd seen the photos of Logan, but none of them did him justice. That big, tough-looking baby. Thinking of him made me think of Elliot again and I pushed the feeling down.

"I hope her wedding goes well. What's she doing?"

"They're getting married in a park across the road from their house. Just a handful of guests. It's the second time she's been married and Logan wanted to do whatever Olivia wanted. I don't think he wanted much of a fuss."

Katya smiled. "That's lovely. It's so good when your partner wants whatever you do."

If Elliot and I got married, I wouldn't want a big fuss either. All that would matter was him and me promising to love one another forever and ...

What are you doing?

18

BLOW JOBS.

Maybe not the best topic to be distracted at work by, but it was Monday morning, which was never easy, plus, I couldn't stop thinking about Elliot. I was also about to get the recent audit results delivered by Dad's Chief Financial Officer, the man who taught me all he knew about blow jobs.

I'd been eighteen and had just upset my father by changing my mind about what I wanted to do at university. He'd wanted me to study Business, but I'd wanted to study English Literature. I did do some business papers too, but I loved books and words and it was so much more appealing to me.

Instead, on the days I had no lectures and in the holidays, I interned at Dad's business under the guidance of his CFO, Lance Patterson. Lance was a very attractive older man, not quite the same age as my father, but not that far off it. His hair didn't have any hint of grey like Dad's had; he was stylish and refined. The man also loved oral sex like no one else I've ever met.

I spent an entire summer learning how businesses ran and honing my blow job skills. And more than once my father nearly caught us.

It was the thrill of it back then, tucked under Lance's desk as he worked. Oh, he would make it up to me later—that man gave me some of the biggest orgasms I ever had. Over time, we settled into a friendship, still playing when neither of us had partners. Today he would arrive to go over the audit results, and I looked forward to seeing him.

"Rebecca," he said warmly as he entered the office, closing the door behind him.

I stood, moving toward him, embracing him as he kissed my cheek.

"So, what's the verdict?"

He cocked an eyebrow. "You want to go straight to the audit results?"

I shrugged. "Isn't that what you're here for?"

"I wanted to see you too. It's been a while." His face was so open and honest. I knew he wouldn't lie to me. That was how he felt.

"It has."

I held a hand out toward the couch to indicate that he should sit. "Coffee?"

"Maybe afterward, though you know you don't have anything to worry about with this audit." He sat, watching me with steely blue eyes as I sat alongside him.

"They still make me nervous."

"They do, or I do?"

I laughed. "You never make me nervous. I've seen you naked, remember?"

His eyebrows wavered. "As if I could ever forget. Seem to remember seeing you too."

This was how it always was, this flirty conversation. A shiver went down my spine at the intense look he gave me. Twelve years and the man still had this affect. There had been times when I'd have gladly given up everything and been with him, humping him seven days a week.

"Well, I kind of have someone else seeing me naked at the moment."

He grinned. That was also how it was between us. No sadness or jealousy, just care and support. Lance had been with me through the best times in my life and the worst. He'd held me when I'd split with Alexander with no expectation of anything sexual.

The audit temporarily forgotten, he reached for my arm. "I hope this is a good one, not one who is going to dick around on you."

"We're keeping it casual, but he's a nice guy. There's no one else in the picture."

I was taking that one for granted. Elliot could have a harem of women out there and I wouldn't know about it. But given his reaction to the way I touched him, I doubted it.

"Good on you, Rebecca. I mean, I'd be happy to offer my services any time." His eyes drifted downward as he sighed.

"I should get on with the results of this audit." He reached for his bag, pulling out a file and opened it. Passing me a copy of the checklist, he started talking, pointing at all the ticks. This time there weren't any crosses.

"Your father is so proud of you, Rebecca. Just keep on doing what you're doing."

They were words I wanted to hear from my father, but from someone who worked as closely with him as Lance did, they still meant a lot. I wiped the tears from my eyes, and he looked back up from his papers and smiled.

"Are you okay?"

"I just ... I'm being silly."

"No you're not. I know what a big thing it was for him to trust you to run this part of the business. He didn't undertake it lightly, but he has faith in you. More than I think you realise sometimes."

I nodded, just knowing that in a second snot would dribble out my nose and I'd have to sniff or wipe it.

He pre-empted it by fishing a tissue out of his pocket. "Here. It's clean."

"Thank you," I croaked.

"How about I take you out for coffee? We can celebrate the results and you can tell me all about this young man. He is young, isn't he? Not an old fart like me."

I laughed through my tears, shaking my head. "No, he's not an old fart. Neither are you. I bet you can keep up with men half your age."

"I've always kept up with you, haven't I?" He smiled that dazzling smile which in other times would turn my stomach to jelly. Today it wasn't the smile I wanted to see, the memory of Elliot's face when I went down on him hammering away in my brain. I wanted to see that face again.

"Come on then, old man. Take me out for coffee." I stood, grabbing hold of his hand and pulling him to his feet.

"Anything for you, Rebecca," he said, leaning over to kiss my cheek.

LATE AFTERNOON MEETINGS SUCKED, and Grace had managed to slip one into my schedule.

This one dragged as the client went on and on making promises to repay finance that I knew he couldn't afford. I almost felt sorry for him. His company was in its dying moments, but I wasn't about to lose mine to save him. Not because I'd be letting my father down, but because I'd be letting myself down. This was the part of the job I hated.

Instead of going home, I climbed into the car and drove to the nearest bar. Being tough was hard sometimes and I needed something to drink.

It was quiet. Some rugby game played on a television in a corner with a group of guys all hanging around watching it.

I sat on a barstool, and the bartender pulled himself away from the end of the bar where he could see the TV, smiling as he approached.

I'd grabbed the wine menu and flicked the pages aimlessly. "Something sparkling, please," I said, pointing at the line on the sheet.

He nodded and poured the drink, filling the glass to the brim. Handing him a ten dollar note, I took my first sip as he cashed it up in the till and gave me my change. Just one and I'd get going.

Not that there was much to go home to.

I closed my eyes and took a second sip. The bubbles fizzed in my mouth, and I swallowed, the liquid warming my stomach.

Gets too hard and you drink. Too much like your mother.

The thought scared me and I put the glass down. I wasn't a big drinker, but I knew how to have a good time with it. Still, the thought of ending up like her turned that warmth into pain.

I pulled my phone out of my bag. It had been on mute during the meeting and I hadn't switched it back.

"Shit." I'd missed Elliot calling me. I put it to my ear as I pressed the message button.

"Hey, Becs. I guess you're at work. Sorry, I'm so useless at times. I know I haven't called much, not because I don't miss you. I miss you like crazy. Things have just been really full on here. I'll tell you all about it when I get back." He paused, the rush of words ending.

"I'm not going away again. This is just too much. I'll call you again soon. Call me or text me and let me know you're okay too."

I put my hand to my mouth, choking back the tears. He missed me enough to stop travelling? More than anything I wanted him back, wanted him with me.

Jumping off the barstool, I left the wine glass on the bar, still filled halfway. The bartender looked at me with one eyebrow raised as I took a step back.

"Thanks so much." I waved brightly, turning and trying hard not to skip out of the place.

I climbed into the car, and dialled Elliot back.

"Hi, you've reached the voicemail of Elliot Franklin ..."

Damn it.

I let the words play and when the message tone sounded, all I could say were four little words.

"I miss you too."

THE HOUSE WAS dark and cold when I got home, and I sighed as I threw my car keys on the coffee table and flopped on the couch.

What was I doing? I could have had the warmth of a man for the evening, one who'd stay for the night if I wanted, but I'd kept him at arm's length because of Elliot.

Elliot who'd told me that he understood I had needs and not to feel bad about filling those needs. And yet, there was no one else I wanted but him.

You love him, Rebecca. Just admit it.

I plucked my phone from my bag on the couch beside me, and scrolled through my messages but there was nothing new.

If you're trying to make me miss you more, you win.

The mobile rang in my, and my heart was in my throat as I scrambled to answer it.

"Becs." Elliot sounded tired.

"Hey. I keep missing you."

"I know. I'm sorry I haven't been better at keeping in touch. This whole trip has been really crazy. I just wanted to let you know I'll be back soon, and I really need to see you."

I hiccupped up the sob in my throat, the words I wanted to hear so badly.

"I need to see you too," I whispered.

"Man, it's been forever." There were sounds in the background, like a distant crowd. A party?

"Sure feels like it." I sighed.

"Umm, anyway, I'll be back next week."

"No chance of you coming back for the weekend?" I asked.

"No, babe. I'll be home soon after. A friend of mine needs some help."

A friend. Why did those words pinch at my gut?

"Oh? Anything I can help out with?"

"Just ... just be there when I come home."

Home. Now he had me worried as his voice cracked.

"Elliot, what's wrong?"

There was some noise in the background that I couldn't quite make out, and I lost him to it.

"Sorry, Becs. I gotta go. I'll explain everything when I'm home. Miss you."

"Miss you too."

I held onto the phone for a while afterward, as if there was magically going to be more, but he was gone. Gone to deal with whatever he was dealing with.

Whatever he didn't want to tell me about.

CHAPTER NINETEEN

SAY THE WORD, *Rebecca, and I'll stay. I'll always be here for you.*

They were the words I'd dreamed about, the option I'd always wished I'd had with my father when my parents split. And I'd tell him that I didn't want him to leave, that I loved him, that I needed him. And we'd all be playing happy families, even when we weren't.

Now they were the words I heard when I dreamed of Elliot.

I couldn't take him going again. Whatever it took, I'd say the words and make him stay. He had to. I had a cold bed, and a lonely heart and there was only one man who could fill them both. More than ever I knew how I felt about him.

But before that, I had to get through the weekend.

Katya's wedding.

She'd been planning it well before she'd become engaged, she had the most amazing organisational skills of anyone I knew. Every little detail had been planned to a minute degree. We had our ups and downs, but I loved her and I was so proud to be her friend today.

She'd planned it for a Sunday evening. It wasn't a conventional time for a wedding, but it wouldn't be Katya if she didn't do something different.

I pulled up outside the church and took a look at myself in the rear-view mirror, wondering for the millionth time if I couldn't have found someone to come with me. Preferably Elliot, but in his absence, maybe I could have brought Olivia. She knew Katya now and would have enjoyed myself.

Then again, I could have 'borrowed' her boyfriend. Logan, that soft-hearted oaf, would have helped me out. The thought of that made me giggle. I was sure Olivia would have laughed at the suggestion.

But no. I was by myself, which wasn't unusual, but it wasn't fun. Not when I missed Elliot so much.

I climbed out of the car and looked at the building in front of me. It was beautiful—very old, very traditional, and very much like Katya to find somewhere dramatic to hold her ceremony.

"Rebecca." Dad's voice carried on the breeze and I looked in the direction the sound came from, my eyebrows raising at the sight of him with my mother.

"Dad." I reached back into the car, grabbing my bag and pushing the door closed. The alarm beeped as I set it and walked off to see my parents.

"Mum," I said, as she opened her arms and I went into them.

"I'm surprised to see you both here. Together."

Dad smiled. "Your mother and I were both good friends with Katya's parents. I wanted to make sure she could get here."

In one piece. Without being off-her-face drunk.

I nodded. Mum smiled at me, then hugged me tight. "It's been ages since I've seen you, sweetheart. How are you? Are you here by yourself?"

"Just me."

"Oh, that's a shame."

Dad's mouth twisted into a faint smile. Some things never changed. She wasn't trying to get at me, but the way she said things often left me feeling that I'd disappointed her.

"Yeah. It just worked out that way. Never mind. I get to see you, and Dad."

Mum nodded, smiling sweetly at Dad. Now there was no part of me that wanted them back together, even if they were my parents, and I knew my father well enough to know it didn't matter how sweetly she smiled, today would be a one off for a friend.

"It's good to see you too, pumpkin," Dad said.

Mum let go and I went into Dad's embrace. It didn't matter how many times I'd let him down, he always made me feel safe.

He let go enough to look at me, his eyes full of affection.

"Let's go inside and see everyone." He looked at his watch. "Not much time to go and I'm sure Katya will want a big entrance."

I nodded. "I'm sure."

Watching as they walked toward the church door arm in arm, I wondered just how different things would have been all those years ago if they hadn't broken up. If we'd kept on being that happy family tucked away in the recesses of my memory. Before things went bad.

For today though, they seemed happy to be in one another's company. They might drive one another a little batty, but they'd made an effort for people who were very dear to me, and I loved them both for it.

"Rebecca."

I turned to see Alexander walking toward me, a willowy blonde on his arm. His fiancée.

"Oh, hey."

"Clarissa, meet Rebecca."

Clarissa looked down her nose at me, wrinkling it as if I smelled of dog poop. "Nice to meet you, Rebecca."

"It certainly looks like it."

"Pardon?"

I smiled sweetly. "Nothing. I'm just anxious to get on in there and see my friend marry her Prince Charming."

At that she softened, smiling at Alexander. "It's wonderful when that happens."

And then they end up with their dicks covered in orange soft drink.

"I'm sure it is. I wouldn't know. Oh well, better get going.".

Who introduces their fiancée to their former lover?

I couldn't judge. If Elliot was there, I'd be showing him off to anyone watching. Including my ex.

As the time was drawing closer to the ceremony, I turned and made my way toward the church door and stood for a moment just watching everyone filing in.

I moved out of the way so people could get past me, taking in the beauty of the surroundings. It was amazing, very peaceful, with large pews on a polished wooden floor, and huge stained-glass windows that refracted the light giving the room an tinge of colour.

And then I heard them on their way through the door. Alexander and Clarissa arguing.

I clamped my lips together, trying to shut out the noise. I had no idea if she realised just how loud she was, but in the still of the church the sound carried.

"Why is she even here?" Clarissa hissed the words.

Alexander took a deep breath. "Because the bride is one of her best friends. Look, babe, I'm not walking out on a friend's wedding because my ex is here. We share a group of friends and that's not changing."

They came through the door, completely oblivious to my presence. I tried desperately to turn away, but I found myself drawn to the conversation, meeting Clarissa's steely glare as she turned to look for seats. She sat down, her arms folded as Alexander sat beside her, pleading with her to stop being so crazy.

"Rebecca." Gemma waved, and I made my way to the front, just behind the family seats. She pointed at the very good-looking man beside her. "This is Justin."

The hunk waved at me and I nodded. "I'm so glad to see you. Nicola is here somewhere; I heard her before. God knows where she's got to," Gemma said.

"I'm sure she'll turn up later."

I tipped my head toward Tim, standing nervously, waiting for the ceremony to start. "Wonder how he's doing."

"Oh, he'll be fine I'm sure. Katya will have him organised. He just has to stand there."

I giggled, and Tim raised his head, winking at me. I gave him the thumbs up, nodding, and he grinned.

"I can just picture the timetable. Reception until ten pm. Sex between ten and midnight."

Burying my face in my hands, I shook my head. "Stop it. I know she's organised, but ..."

"Do you remember high school? There was the school timetable and the Katya timetable."

I looked at my watch. There were two minutes until the ceremony was supposed to start and people were still filing around. Maybe it was tradition for the bride to be late, but this one wouldn't be.

As the music stated, the guests scrambled to their seats and Tim stood up straight. He'd played very little part in setting up everything, of that I was sure, but he did look beautifully dressed and ready to meet his bride.

We stood.

The flower girl came first. Tim's niece made her way up the aisle, led by Katya's elder sister. The other two sisters followed, all of them dressed in this wishy-washy beige colour.

I knew when Katya had appeared from the look on Tim's face. His jaw dropped as his beautiful bride made her way toward him, wearing a figure-hugging white dress which sparkled in the rays of the fading sun shining through the stained-glass windows. Katya was like a glittering rainbow as she moved toward him, and I fished in my bag for a tissue before Gemma handed me one.

"She's beautiful," Gemma said.

"As if she'd be anything else." I leaned on her, and she rested her head on my shoulder. Her date forgotten, the two of us stood, clinging to one another as Katya drew level with her groom and the ceremony started.

"Shove over." Just as we sat, Nicola appeared, squeezing into a spot that didn't exist, cramming the three of us into a space for two. "You can sit on his lap," she said to Gemma, pointing at Justin.

Justin looked pretty pleased with himself as Gemma snuggled closer.

"Where did you get to?" I whispered.

"I got tied up talking to someone. I'm here now." Nicola squeezed herself against me.

The ceremony was beautiful. Katya had everything planned with the military precision she was famous for, and I wiped my eyes as she exchanged vows with Tim.

My phone buzzed in my pocket, and I resisted the urge to look at it right away.

Please let it be Elliot.

Distracted, I lost concentration, but stood and applauded as the minister pronounced them married and introduced them to the congregation.

I hugged my friends, walking arm in arm with them out of the church. Justin trailed in Gemma's wake like a puppy. It was kind of adorable.

"You'll be next," I said to her.

She giggled. "We'll see. I decided to follow in your footsteps and let go a little. Just enjoy it all instead of being so wound up about what everyone else thinks."

"Good for you." I grinned.

Gemma let go of me, hooking her arm through Justin's. "What was it you said? Live a little?"

I laughed as she disappeared off toward the car park.

Good for her.

THE RECEPTION WAS at a beautiful old house with a huge veranda around the outside. There was a huge garden where the photos were being taken, and a large marquee with a buffet table for the feast that was about to happen. Outside the tent was a pig on a spit, and the smell of roasting pork made me drool and think of bacon.

Bacon.

Crap.

Pulling my phone out of my pocket, I flicked it on to check for messages.

I need to be home.

That was all it said, but I clutched my phone to my chest, warmed by thoughts of Elliot being with me again. This time I'd hold onto him and never let him go. Maybe I didn't want the big princess wedding, but he was my Prince.

My stomach rumbled as I tapped out a reply.

Good. I need you.

And I did. It wasn't even about the sex, even though after all this time our physical reunion would be earth-shattering. His arms around me would do. I'd snuggle down and go to sleep for days, as long as I was with him. No more of this half-a-night crap.

I barely heard the speeches, sipping wine and eating food until I was floating, quite happily and bloated. When the music started, I let out a loud burp, Gemma laughing beside me as we sat back to let our stomachs settle.

As day turned to night, I decided to get up and move. The car would have to stay here for the evening; I'd already had too much to drink.

"Rebecca." Katya ran straight at me, wrapping her arms around my neck, her half empty wine glass slapping me in the back.

"Hey, wifey."

She giggled, sitting down next to me.

"I love you," I said, leaning on her shoulder.

"Love you too. Thank you for being with me today."

I raised my head, smiling at her. "I wouldn't be anywhere else. We've been through some crazy times together, haven't we?"

She nodded. "Crazy, fun, sad ... everything really." Katya pursed her lips, nodding toward Gemma, now dirty dancing in the middle of the marquee with Justin. "What do you think of that?"

I shrugged. "She's having fun. He seems to hang on her every word. Maybe she just needs a fairy-tale ending to sort her out."

"She needs a good hard screw against the wall, that's what she needs."

I laughed. "At the rate she's going, it'll be happening in the middle of the dance floor. Who needs a wall?"

Katya spat out the wine she'd just sipped, snorting as the liquid went flying through the air. "You know, I might think you were being bitchy if it wasn't so true."

I hadn't laughed so hard in ages. Elliot hadn't been on my mind for all of five minutes, but the thought of Gemma and Justin, and Katya and Tim brought all those feelings to the surface again. In that moment, I'd have given anything to have him there with me.

"I should stop drinking so much or my big sexy night isn't going to go that great." Her eyes widened. "I should go and check on Tim. If he drinks too much, he'll never get it up."

Without thinking, I waved my hand at her. "As if you're ever going to notice."

She stiffened beside me. "What's that supposed to mean?"

I was too far gone to even realise for a moment what I was saying. "It's not like he's hung like a horse, Katya."

She stood, her nostrils flaring as she stared me down. "How would you know?"

Shit.

"I didn't mean anything. I'm sorry. Come and have another drink. I was just being a dick."

"No. What would you know about how well Tim is or isn't hung?"

I put down my glass, holding out my hands to her. Stupid me drinking stupid alcohol. "Years ago, before you two got together, we had a little thing. And I mean really little. I'm not talking about his penis, but it was one tiny blow job."

She just stared at me. "When?"

"When we were at university. Before he even met you. We took a class together and one day we had a bit to drink ..."

"All this time you two were, what? Laughing behind my back? Oh ha ha, Katya doesn't know."

I shook my head. "No. It was never like that. Hell, in all the time you two have been a couple, he's never mentioned it to me."

She leaned over me. "Well, screw you. I thought you were my friend. Instead you're keeping dirty secrets."

What was left of her wine splashed my face. She'd drunk most of the glass, so there wasn't very much, but it was what triggered her actions that hurt. All this time I'd managed to keep quiet, not upset her. Even when she drove me nuts with her holier-than-thou crap, I'd respected and loved her enough to not hurt her with something that was a non-event.

What have I done?

THE SKY CONTINUED TO DARKEN, and I sat in the dim light of the marquee, not knowing what to do. I dabbed at my face with a napkin, even though the wine had long since dried.

Mum appeared out of nowhere, grabbing my arm. "Sweetheart, do you know where your father is? I'm a bit tired and he said he'd take me home when I wanted to go."

"Haven't seen him, Mum."

"Can you take me?"

She must have been completely unaware of my intoxication, and even I noticed I was slurring words.

"I can't, Mum. I've had too much. Want me to see if I can find Dad? You sit down and I'll go for a look."

She nodded, sitting at the table. "If I can't find him, I'll sort you out a taxi. Okay?"

I moved away, looking around. Alexander stood by the door, his fiancée nowhere in sight. "Hey, have you seen my dad? Mum wants to go home."

"I think I saw him inside a while ago. Talking to Katya's dad."

Making my way inside, I spotted Katya's father deep in conversation with some woman I didn't know. No sign of my father. I scoured the room, but he was nowhere to be found. "Where the hell are you?" I muttered under my breath.

Turning to go back outside, I nearly collided with Clarissa. Oh joy.

"Rebecca. I'm so sorry." The way she said it sounded like she was one of those snakes speaking in Harry Potter, hissing the S at me. I didn't have time for her crap.

"Nothing to be sorry about. I'm just looking for someone."

"Maybe I can help." I looked at her sideways. This was the woman who had been all pissy about me being here, but now she was being helpful?

"I'm looking for my father. Mum wants to go home, but I can't find him to take her."

She smiled, a sly smile that sent shivers up my spine. I didn't know what it was about her, but I trusted her about as far as I could throw her.

"Oh. I saw him heading that way." She pointed toward a corridor with rooms either side. Maybe he was looking for a toilet. Who knew.

I made my way down the corridor, trying the doors. There was either no one in them, or they were locked, and no sign of a bathroom down there.

There was one more room, right at the end and I placed my hand on the door handle, tapping as I turned and pushed it open.

There was my dad, balls' deep in Nicola. Her hand was fisted, and she bit down on it, muffling her cries as he pushed her up against the wall.

"I don't think I can actually take any more today," I said.

With a resounding bang, Dad stepped back, dropping Nicola, and she fell to the floor.

"Rebecca?"

"I came to see if you were ready to take Mum home, but I can see you're busy."

I just couldn't deal with it, my head already swimming from Katya knowing one of my dirty secrets. Now I had to deal with knowing Dad's. And Nicola? Since when had she been screwing *my father?*

He zipped up his pants, put up his hands, palms visible, and nodded. "Now, darling, it's not what it looks like."

Why do people say that? Why do they even bother? It very clearly was what it looked like.

"Well, it looked like you had your penis in my friend. Which if I wasn't drunk I might be a bit more upset about, but I'm beginning to think this kind of thing is par for the course today," I said, flatly.

Nicola picked herself up, pulling up her panties.

"Dad. Just do up your pants. And tell me if you can take Mum home or not, because the last thing I want is her getting drunk now. If you're busy, I'll organise a taxi."

He blinked, as if he was waking up from a daydream. "Uh, sure thing. I'll be out in just a minute."

I turned, closing the door behind me. There was no way for me to even process this right now, so I went back outside, sitting with Mum until Dad came and took her away without a word.

What a great night.

I NEEDED to get some fresh air. Most of the wedding guests were still in the marquee, so I went back outside and onto the veranda of the house.

The sobs built inside me as I looked up at the sky. What a crappy night. One stupid off-the-cuff comment to Katya. She was far too smart for that to go unnoticed.

I took a deep breath of fresh air. It was sweet with the jasmine that surrounded the balcony, and I held my hand across my face as I sneezed, wiping it on my dress.

"Still ladylike, then." An unmistakable voice came from behind and I sighed.

"What do *you* want?"

Alexander drew level, gripping the railing beside me.

"I was just with Tim. And then I heard Katya found out about you and him. On today of all days. Are you okay?"

"There was no me and Tim. You know that."

He nudged my shoulder with his. "Come on, Rebecca. There was for about thirty seconds."

I suppressed a smirk. "That might be funny if her finding out wasn't such shitty timing. I never tried to hide it from her, I just always thought it better that she didn't know."

The warmth of his arm around my shoulders felt good. Too good. I could close my eyes and pretend everything was how it was back when we were together. Before it all went to crap.

Elliot.

I wriggled away from his grasp, and he gave me a half-hearted smile.

"Sorry, old habits."

I shook my head. "That hasn't been a habit for a long time. Think you'll have to come up with some other excuse."

"Do I need an excuse to be a friend to you?"

Our gazes were locked as I processed the words. It was difficult in my inebriated state.

"I don't think it's a very good idea."

Footsteps coming closer broke our stare, and I turned my head to see Katya approaching. Even if she had a whole bottle of wine to throw at me I'd take that over this uncomfortable moment with Alexander.

"Katya," I said, forlornly.

"I'm sorry for being a jerk," she said, the corners of her mouth twisting into an uneven smile.

"I'm sorry I blew your husband," I replied.

She snorted. "I'm glad no one heard that and got the wrong idea."

"I'm right here." Alexander waved at her.

Katya rolled her eyes. "No one important."

"I didn't want to keep anything from you. By the time I realised you two were going out, it was serious. You were so nauseatingly happy, and the last thing I wanted to do was throw some historical spanner in the works."

She laughed. "I was happy. Am happy."

"Tim wouldn't have wanted to hurt you either. I think we both just figured it was best to forget it ever happened. That man freaking adores you."

Katya flung her arms around my neck, and I hugged her tight. "Love you," I whispered.

"Love you too, my crazy friend. Now to find you someone to love. Someone who's going to treat you like a princess." She let go, giving a pointed look to Alexander.

"Actually, I think I might have found someone. Only I don't know yet. But I really hope so."

She pursed her lips, studying my face. "Spill the beans."

"Not now—not here. It's your wedding day. Go and spend the night doing sexy stuff with your husband. Plenty of time for us to catch up later. Maybe I'll know for sure by then and not just be having a drunken rant."

Katya hugged me one more time before kissing me on the cheek. "Good night. Get home and get some sleep. Lord knows you look like you need it. We'll be going soon."

With that she turned, and I sighed as she disappeared among the crowd. I didn't look that bad, did I?

The hairs on the back of my neck were standing on end, and I just knew Alexander was still there. "Don't you have a fiancée to go and find inside?" I asked.

He drew level with me, gazing at me again with that intense stare I knew so well. The one that had gotten me into trouble in the first place.

"I just wanted to say you look good. Really good."

I looked side to side, up and down, anywhere but into his eyes.

"Thanks. You too."

"I mean it. You're just glowing. I haven't seen you like that in forever. It's so good to see."

I gritted my teeth with no idea where this was heading. In those early days when we'd split up, I'd have given anything for him to say something like that, to give me a reason to forgive him and move on with out lives.

"I was wondering if you wanted to have dinner sometime."

At that I cocked an eyebrow. I'd felt so alive since I'd started screwing around with Elliot and had realised just how dead the relationship with Alexander had been. Sure we'd had a lot of passion, but I hadn't laughed as much as I had with Elliot in so long, literally crying with laughter at times. I felt safe and even if it wasn't love, there was more affection in my relationship with Elliot than there had been with anyone else. I knew he genuinely cared about me.

"Let's just count all the reasons that's a bad idea. Apart from the fact that you're engaged."

"Rebecca, I know things went bad, but I've been thinking about you a lot lately. Everything happened so fast when we broke up and …"

I took a deep breath, and attempted to flare my nostrils. With no idea if it worked, I interrupted him. "We didn't break up; I kicked you out. After you and your dick went wandering. I'm not interested in dinner with you; I had dinner a million times with you. If you really gave two shits about my feelings, you would never have cheated on me."

He took a step back. When I was with him I wasn't whole. Now I felt whole. Having people like Olivia and Elliot in my life had done that for me. I knew what true friendship was, and even love, and it wasn't what was standing in front of me.

"I never meant to hurt you,' he said.

"Well if that was your goal, maybe you should have kept it in your pants."

We stared each other down for a moment. "You know that drink you threw at me was damn cold. I had to replace the couch too. Fanta stains are hard to get out." His lips twisted into a smile, and I couldn't help but shake my head and laugh.

"Good. You deserved it."

He grinned. "I'm sorry. I really thought I'd end up spending my life with you, but I did something stupid. I hope one day that you'll find it in your heart to forgive me."

I shrugged.

"What you said to Katya. Are you really seeing someone?" he asked.

It was my turn to grin. "That would be none of your business. Goodnight Alexander."

As I made my way back through the crowd to the door, I looked around for my father, hoping that he hadn't quite left yet. Maybe he could give me a lift home. No such luck.

I had Corporate Taxis on speed dial, so pressed the button and waited for them to answer.

"There's an hour-long wait." The call centre operator sounded bored.

"Fine."

I sat out on the lawn at the front of the house, fiddling with my phone. I sent a text to Elliot.

I miss you.

The words made me sniff, and before long I had tears rolling down my cheeks. Not just for Elliot, but for Dad, for Katya, for Alexander. Everything at once piled on top of me and the stress came streaming out as I sat on the grass and wept.

I dialled Olivia. She always made things better.

"Rebecca?" She sounded concerned. *Shit.* It must be eleven pm by now. Late for her these days. "Rebecca, are you okay?"

I hadn't said anything, just sniffed and made bleating sounds from crying. What a loser.

"I just wanted to hear a friendly voice," I whispered.

"Where are you? What's going on?" Now the stress was clear in her voice. Just what she needed, me to stress her out.

"I just ... I think I'm in love with Elliot, and I caught my dad screwing Nicola, and Katya found out I gave Tim a blow job."

"Wait. You blew Tim? Her fiancé?"

"They're married now; it's their wedding day. She found out on their damn wedding day because I couldn't keep my mouth shut."

A deep voice in the background told me Logan was hovering. Of course he was. The first hint that something was wrong and he'd be all over her.

"Do you want me to come around? You sound so upset."

"I'm at the reception waiting for a taxi."

"Want me to come and get you?"

I sniffed into the phone, not wanting to make her come out this late at night, but needing the comfort.

"Where are you? Tell me where you are and I'll come and get you." The voice behind her rumbled. "Logan will come and get you."

"I'm at the Rose Gardens. You know, that big house they have wedding receptions in." I was tired, slurring my words, and all I wanted to do now was sleep.

She muttered in the background. "He can be there in about fifteen minutes. He's on his way, and he'll bring you here or take you home."

"Thank you," I whispered.

"That's what I'm here for. We love you, Rebecca."

I clutched my phone to my chest as I hung up and took a deep breath. At least I could get home safe and sound and not have to wait around. My friends were amazing.

A cool breeze caught my breath, and I inhaled deeply. It lulled me into a false sense of sobriety for just a moment, and the guilt at calling Olivia washed over me.

She was probably exhausted with that small baby, and I'd called her to cry down the phone. I buried my face in my hands. What a mess I was; what a mess I'd always been.

I tucked my knees up, and sat in a foetal position as I waited. Damn it, Logan would probably be cranky and I'd have to deal with him being pissed at me for upsetting Olivia.

A car pulled up on the street nearby, rumbling beside me as someone got out. I was in my own little world, barely noticing when big hands landed on my arms, pulling me to my feet.

Soft brown eyes took me in, full of sympathy. "Hey you," Logan said. "Let's get you out of here."

I flung my arms around his neck. "Thank you for coming. My car's parked here, but I'm in no state to drive."

"You call us any time you need help," he said.

I shivered, and he held me at arm's length to look at me. "Where's your jacket?" he asked.

"I didn't think I'd be standing out on the street."

He laughed, slipping his from his shoulders and wrapping it around me. It was soft black leather, and so warm.

"You're such a cliché, Logan."

"Huh?"

"Your big noisy car, black jeans, white singlet and black leather jacket."

He shrugged. "It's just me."

"Don't ever change," I said.

"Come on." He took hold of my arm to lead me to the car when out of the driveway nearby, Alexander and his fiancée were making their way out of the complex.

In the dim light, I waved. I must have looked a sight. Only moments before I'd been in there alone. Now I was being led away by a six-foot-something tall hunk with big arm muscles and tattoos that were visible now his jacket was off. The nearby streetlamp gave off enough illumination that the little spot we were in was well lit, and I wasn't about to waste this opportunity. I snuggled in tight against Logan, leaning my head on his shoulder.

"What the hell are you doing?"

"Just play along for a minute." I looked at him, trying to plead with my eyes. Besides, having him help me walk was a lot better than a drunken stumble to the car.

He opened the door, holding my hand to steady me as I sat. Closing the door, he bent, rolling his eyes. "What am I playing along with?"

"That's my ex and his fiancée. Just one of the reasons I'm so screwed up tonight."

"So what are you trying to prove?"

"That I'm not alone. I mean, I was there alone tonight." I tilted my head. "But now I have you."

He laughed, that deep chuckle that resembled Elliot's, making me miss Elliot even more. I sighed.

"You smell amazing by the way. Do you and Olivia share soap or something? She always smells of coconut. I've never been close enough to you to smell you before."

To Logan's credit, he suppressed most of the smile that swept his face. Being drunk and babbling always seemed to impress the boys.

"Are you okay, Rebecca?"

I nodded.

"Don't you dare vomit in my car." With that he stood, walking around to the driver's side and climbing in beside me.

"Where are we going? Our place or yours?"

"I just want to go home." To my own bed, to recover for Elliot's return. That was all that mattered now.

The car roared to life, and I settled back in the car seat. We drove away from the train wreck that was my night.

At least Katya was happy.

It was a quiet ride home. All I wanted to do was sleep, and Logan didn't ask me any further questions about the night. I guess he knew I'd catch up with Olivia in the next few days and he'd get all the gossip from her.

As we turned into my street, I squinted into the distance at the house next door to mine. Elliot's car? That beat up piece of crap was parked next door, and my heart sang as we pulled into my driveway.

"Do you need me to take you to get your car in the morning?" Logan asked.

"I'll just grab a taxi over, though if Elliot's home I'll ask him to take me. I'll call you if I get stuck."

"Elliot?"

"My. Um. Well."

He laughed. "Never mind. You can tell me all about him later."

He got out and walked around the car to open my door, taking my arm to lead me to the house. "I'll make sure you're inside and okay before I go," he said.

"You are so good to me. What did I ever do to deserve you?"

"You have always been so good to my lady. I'll always love you for that."

I laughed. "Aww that's so sweet. I should have recorded you saying you loved me."

"Becs?" From the dark alcove at the front door came Elliot's voice.

"Elliot?"

He moved forward, and I squealed, throwing myself into his arms. "I didn't know you were home yet."

"Obviously." I looked up at his face. He wasn't looking at me, more over my shoulder at Logan.

"I've been at Katya's wedding. I had too much to drink so Logan brought me home."

"Is that right?"

I nestled my face in his chest, so warm, and his familiar scent filled my senses. I'd missed this man so much.

"I'm so glad you're here."

"Ahem." Logan stood behind me.

"Oh. Logan, this is Elliot. I thought he was back next week, but he's here early."

"You've still got my jacket."

I clapped my hand over my mouth. "Oh, I'm so sorry. I promise I haven't got too many girl germs on it." My head was light now. Nothing could stop me washing away the wave of crap from this night.

Slipping the leather off my shoulders, I let go of Elliot to pass the jacket back to Logan.

"What are you doing, Rebecca?" Elliot said. I hadn't noticed the pain in his tone until then.

"Just giving Logan back his jacket. He can go home and we can go inside. I have a lot I want to say to you."

"Have you been screwing him too?"

The words hit me like iced water. Did he really think I would do that?

"No, I ..."

"I have just been through the worst time of my life and couldn't talk to you about it because I was terrified you were going to walk away from me." His voice wavered as he spoke and I had no idea what he was talking about. Worst time of his life?

He shook his head, clearly emotional. "Are we still a thing, Becs? Is he what you want instead?"

Holy shit. With those words I had just about had it with all the men in my life. Apart from Logan. But that lasted about thirty more seconds.

"Elliot, I haven't ..."

"Have you already fucked him? Or was that coming after you told him you loved him?"

I had no idea Logan could move so fast, but in an instant he had Elliot pinned to my front door, held by the throat.

"What did you just say to her?"

"Logan. Stop it. I just need to explain." I grabbed hold of Logan's arm, trying to pull him back, but I might as well have tried to move a really freaking big rock.

"You don't need to explain. If this is the guy you've been losing your shit over, he should know you wouldn't do anything behind his back. And if he bothered to ask, he'd know I'm marrying one of your best friends."

Elliot glared at Logan before shifting his focus to me. "Becs?" His arms were down; he didn't even try to fight against Logan's hold. They were comparable in size, but maybe he realised it would just make things worse.

"Let him go, Logan."

Logan nodded, dropping his hand. "Sorry, man. She didn't deserve what you said to her."

Elliot kept his eyes on me. "I'm sorry. I'll go."

"Don't. Stay and tell me what's going on and I'll tell you about what's happened with me," I pleaded.

He shrugged. "I can't stay anyway. I just wanted to see you."

"Why can't you stay?"

"I've got to get back to Nan's place."

"See you in the morning, then?"

Elliot moved past Logan, bending to kiss my cheek. "We'll see. I've got other priorities now."

"What's that supposed to mean?" I asked.

"Goodnight, Rebecca." He looked back over his shoulder. "Logan."

I watched as he walked away, the earlier tears returning as he disappeared into the darkness.

"What a dick," Logan said.

"I thought he'd give me a chance to talk to him," I whispered.

Logan wrapped his arms around me, giving me a big bear hug. "Let's get you inside. Liv'll call you in the morning." He kissed the top of my head in a father-like gesture that just made the tears worse.

Fishing my key out of my bag, I trembled as I slid it in the lock and pushed open the door. I flicked on the living room light, and sighed. It felt so good to be home, but my heart ached for Elliot. Too drunk to even think about going next door and talking him into coming back, I flopped on the couch.

"Are you going to be okay?" Logan asked. He slid his jacket on over his arms and stood in the doorway as if unsure about coming in.

"I'll be fine now. I'm just going to go to bed and sleep this off. I'll have to tackle Elliot tomorrow."

"Rebecca, for what it's worth, the way he spoke to you wasn't acceptable and I'm not sorry for what I did. But I think you mean a lot to him from the way he reacted to me. He's gone off half-cocked, but his heart is in the right place."

I nodded. "I know."

"Don't let him speak to you like that. Ever. If he does, he'll have to answer to me. Okay?"

I sniffed and nodded again, forcing a smile.

"Call us if you need anything. Even if it's three in the morning, we'll be here."

"Thank you," I said. I sounded hoarse from the combination of alcohol, crying and needing sleep.

He winked and closed the door behind him. A mix of emotions swirled inside me as I sat there, unable to grasp everything this day had brought.

Time for bed.

WHEN I WOKE, I pulled myself up and out to the bathroom. I was still wearing the clothes from the day before, and my eyes were still red and swollen from crying. *I am such a wreck.*

I swear the jackhammers in my head had multiplied since the last time I'd been drunk. And to my utter joy, the smell of bacon permeated my senses. Relief that Elliot must be back drove away the noise in my brain as I pushed the mop of unruly hair back out of my eyes and stumbled down the hallway.

The kitchen was a mess. Beeping its head off was the fridge, the door hanging open the way I'd probably left it. Drops of bacon fat were everywhere, and a half-eaten sandwich sat on the kitchen counter.

I groaned at the sight. *Don't drink and fry.* Ignoring safety information was nothing new, but this was just stupid. I'd risked my house and my life for the sake of a memory. Thank God nothing had caught fire.

Worse still was that Elliot wasn't there, and I couldn't even remember eating the damn sandwich.

MY MOUTH WAS LIKE SANDPAPER.

I am never drinking again.

I wandered to the front window, taking a look next door. Elliot's car was gone from the driveway. *Shit.*

Picking up the phone to send him a text, I closed my eyes when I saw there was a message waiting. *Please let it be something good and not more crap to deal with.*

> I'm sorry. I have been through so much these past months and I really need to see you.

My heart was in my throat as I read it. I wanted to see him so badly, but at the same time my irritation at his behaviour still grated.

> We need to talk.

I pressed send on the text. I nearly followed it up by telling him I loved him, but that might be a bit much for him to deal with right now and doing by text didn't feel right. I'd get him back to talk and then I'd explain everything. He had to understand. Maybe then he'd open up and share whatever he had kept from me.

Elliot had secrets.

I hated secrets.

I hadn't heard from my father either. Memories of seeing him and Nicola weren't helping the nausea situation.

I guess after all this time I couldn't blame Dad. He might have had other women in his life since Mum, but he'd never made a big deal about it. Of all the people for him to be with.

Oh God. What if this is serious and Nicola becomes my stepmother?

Laughing out loud, I wished I had someone to joke with. Katya would be honeymoon humping, and Gemma was probably doing something similar with Justin.

I picked up the phone and called Grace.

"I'm not coming in today. I'm sick."

She snickered. "Your father is looking for you. That kind of sick?"

Urgh. "Something like that."

"I'll tell him you're not coming in. If he wants to come looking for you then it's up to him. He just showed up here with flowers. Is someone in trouble?"

"Thanks, Grace." I hung up.

I sat on the couch, hugging a cushion to my chest. Hell, if he wanted to screw someone younger then good on him. Without his identity, I'd cheered her on to pursue him. Did it really make that much difference knowing it was my father? Oh crap. It was my father.

Lost in thought, a knock on the door startled me, and I held my hand to my heart, begging it to stop racing. Dad or Elliot?

Please be Elliot, please be Elliot, please be—

Dad stood in the doorway, a big bunch of geraniums in his hand and a pleading look on his face.

"What are you doing here?"

"I just wanted to make sure we were okay."

I stepped aside so he could come in, his arm brushing mine as he walked past.

"Dad, I don't know what to say."

He looked me over, standing there in my daggy old track pants and sweatshirt, my hair unbrushed and tangled, and gave me a smile I hadn't seen in years—the smile that said that no matter what had happened, he loved me. Sometimes, that was all I needed.

I wrapped my arms around his waist, snuggling into his chest. He sighed, bringing in his arms for a hug, and we just stood there for a while. *My daddy.*

"Do you want a coffee?" I asked.

He kissed the top of my head. "That sounds good. Got a vase I can put these into?"

I let go, nodding and taking the flowers from him. "They're gorgeous, Dad."

"Just like my girl."

I shook my head with a grin, and left him to sit on the couch while I went into the kitchen. Moments between us like this had been few and far between for so long. Mostly our meetings were about business, and even when they weren't, they inevitably turned that way.

"I've only got instant," I called out. Most days I grabbed take-out coffee, and my coffee machine sat on the kitchen counter unused. I couldn't even remember the last time I'd bought anything for it.

"That's fine."

It didn't take long to boil the water and mix it all together, and I took two cups back into the living room, passing him one and sitting on the couch beside him.

"I'm sorry," he said.

I cradled the mug in my hands, taking a deep breath of that coffee scent and closing my eyes.

"I should never have put you in that position yesterday. It was thoughtless and impulsive," he said.

Sighing, I opened my eyes, meeting his. "Dad, I don't even know what to think."

"Not hating me would be a start."

"I could never hate you."

The silence hung between us as if we hadn't just had the warmest hug in so very long.

"You have always come first, Rebecca. No matter what. I loved you from the moment I laid eyes on you, and the thought that our relationship could be damaged by this is killing me."

Tears sat on my cheeks as I took another sip to try to get my head together.

"I just wish you'd told me. Finding you like that was the worst part."

"Would you have understood?"

"I think I would have tried."

I was tired, just wanting to crawl away and sleep the day away. Not just because of the after effects of my drunken night, but I wanted my brain to stop working, thinking about what I'd seen, thinking about what Nicola had said.

Oh. My. God.

"Now I know who she was talking about."

He cocked an eyebrow, his lips turned down. "What?"

"We had a girls' night a while ago. A sleepover."

He nodded.

"Nicola told us all about this older guy she was seeing. How amazing he was and how he ..." I stopped as I remembered her words.

"Yes?"

"Dad, it was a girls' night. We were talking about $S\,E\,X$."

His eyes widened. I'd never seen my dad blush before, but there it was, his cheeks blazing as we stared at one another.

He lowered his gaze, and I could see his indecision as he clearly struggled with asking me what Nicola had said.

"I don't know everything, Dad, but she told us a lot. Enough to know that she was very obviously impressed."

He grinned before blanking his face, but it was too late. The size of his smile told me volumes about how he felt about her.

"You love her."

He swallowed hard, his Adam's apple bobbing as we looked at one another.

"Well, I don't know about that."

"I do. It's written all over your face."

He sighed. "Say that's the case. How would you feel about that?"

"I can't pretend it's not weird, but I'm not going to be a bitch and stop you from being happy. Not after all this time alone."

His face softened as he took another sip of coffee. "She makes me feel alive, Rebecca. I buried myself in everything when your mother and I separated, and I know I haven't always been the most attentive of fathers, but I want to change that."

I ran my finger around the rim of the cup. "So. Have you told her parents yet?"

"We haven't told anyone. It's going to be a lot tougher for her than me, I suspect. You're being very reasonable. But then, I wouldn't expect anything else from you, my big-hearted girl."

He reached for my hand and I grabbed hold of him, squeezing his fingers in mine.

"I love you," he said.

"I love you too."

"I had hoped you wouldn't be too mad. Not after your dalliances with Lance."

There was no mirror required to tell me that any colour in my face was gone. I sat there, stunned, unable to say anything.

"I'll never forget when I worked it out. We were talking in his office when I spotted your shoes beside the desk, tucked under but not well enough. And then I saw a glimpse of foot with that bright red polish that you had spent hours on the night before."

I gulped. "All this time, you never said anything."

"What would I have said? You were an adult, and we weren't that close at that time. Raising a girl was so hard, I had no idea how to connect with you and have the kind of relationship where I could talk to you about your sex life."

"Dad," I croaked the word, fighting back the overwhelming feeling of helplessness. Back then I could have reached out to him, but had no idea how to connect with him either. It could have all been so simple.

He smiled. "Tell me what else is going on in your life now." He didn't let go. I think he just wanted to the contact, wanted to know that he still had me despite my reassurances. I didn't want him to let go.

"Katya's wedding was such a screwy day. She found out about something I never told her from my uni days and got all upset with me, I found you with Nicola, and Alexander asked me out for dinner."

Dad's lips twitched at that last bit. "Isn't he engaged to someone?"

I nodded. "He was there with his fiancée."

Dad screwed up his nose. "I hope you said no."

"As if that's ever going to happen again. Besides, I have someone else. I think."

He cocked an eyebrow. "You think?"

"I've kind of been seeing someone. It wasn't serious, but I wanted more. But the night of the wedding things got all screwed up."

"You didn't take him to the wedding?"

I shook my head. "He's been away working."

"Oh? What does he do?"

I bit down on my bottom lip. *Here we go.* Closing my eyes, I took a deep breath.

"Elliot doesn't really have a career as such, he does odd jobs and picks up work where he can find it. He's away labouring on a construction site at the moment."

Slowly, I opened one eye, peeking at Dad, who didn't look half as horrified as I'd thought he might.

"Does he have any career plans?"

Might as well lay it all out there. "Not really. I think he has to work out what he wants first. He plays in a band sometimes, too."

One side of his mouth appeared to be trying to smile. "So my girl has found herself a musician?"

"It's been pretty casual so far."

"But you want it to be serious."

I shrugged. "I guess. I mean he treats me better than most other guys have. This whole him being away a few times like this has hit me harder than I thought it would." I lowered my gaze, unable to look Dad in the face anymore. His expression still wasn't giving too much away.

"You love him."

"I don't know about that."

"I do. It's written all over your face."

I let out a choked laugh. Using my words against me—what was the world coming to? Dad grinned, his eyes sparkling like I'd never seen before, letting go some mischievous little imp inside.

"I'm glad you're happy," he said. "I hope you've found someone who will love you forever. Maybe I'll end up with grandchildren after all."

Who was this man and what had he done to my father?

"I thought you wanted me to concentrate on the business, on my career."

Dad shook his head. "I love what you've done with the business. You're the best performing subsidiary I have and your company is doing well, too."

I gaped, putting my coffee on the table to slap his arm. He slopped coffee everywhere, laughing as I took his cup from him and continued my assault, gently slapping him until he put up his hands in surrender.

"Rebecca, stop." He grabbed hold of me, wrestling me into another embrace while I laughed. "All I ever wanted was for you to be happy. You've worked so hard, and I can't even begin to tell you just how proud I am of you. How proud I've always been of you. If this is the man you want, just be with him."

Tears sprang up as he rocked me. Even at my age it was comforting. My whole life I'd had this internal battle going on, torn between being the good girl he wanted and the rebel, desperately trying to get his attention.

After all this time, I finally realised he needed my approval.

Now to sort things out with Elliot.

22

SECRETS. Secrets can destroy you, no matter how small they are. Sometimes it's easy to protect someone with a little white lie, but if it comes back to bite you? Well, I'd had enough of secrets. Telling Dad had taken some weight off, even if it turned out to be nothing I had to worry about.

Now I'd put my heart on the line and if Elliot wanted it, it was his. I could only hope I wasn't too late.

He missed me.

He needed me.

After Dad left, I went back to bed and slept until mid-afternoon. When I woke, I showered, washing away the gross feeling, standing under the shower until there was no hot water left.

I dressed, slipping on a pair of jeans and a T-shirt, and pulled the sheets off the bed. If there was any chance of having a guest, I wanted the bed to be clean. Even if it would just end up being all hot and sweaty anyway.

My stomach grumbling, I headed out to the kitchen, cracking a couple of eggs into a pan and toasting bread to stop the achy, hungry feeling I now had.

Shower, food, coffee. Now I could take on the world.

I picked up my phone. No further message from Elliot.

> I need to talk to you. Please call me.

I pressed send and waited. And fidgeted. And waited.

Staring at the ceiling for what seemed like an eternity, I looked back down at the phone. Two minutes had passed.

You need something else to occupy your time.

I went back to the living room, flicking on the television and opening the laptop on the coffee table. There were a couple of work e-mails, and I wasted a bit of time on Facebook.

Elliot and I aren't friends on Facebook.

I typed his name in the search and pressed enter, my heart pounding as I saw his photo. His profile was pretty closed up, but there were a few photos of him, and I clicked the request friend button.

My phone beeped as he accepted it.

The message tone sounded.

> Aren't you working? What are you doing
> mucking around on Facebook?

The words were followed by a big poking tongue emoticon. Talk about mixed signals.

> I'm at home. Can we talk?

> Oh. Go out on the deck.

I stood, moving back through the kitchen and out the back door.

Elliot stood on his grandmother's deck, with that affectionate look on his face I knew so well.

"Hey," he said.

"Hey, yourself."

He reached the fence first, beckoning me closer.

"I'm sorry about being a complete douche. I was going to come over after dinner to apologise. I missed you so much," he said.

My heart skipped a beat as I looked at him, and I had no doubt he meant it. "I missed you too."

"I'm also sorry I didn't call you more often. Things have been a bit crazy."

My heart wavered as I looked at him. He'd just said he missed me, but he'd not called me, clearly too busy with something else. Alarm bells raged in my head. Not my Elliot—he couldn't do anything bad. *Could he?*

"Like what?"

"Some stuff I need to talk to you about. I should have at least sent you a text, but I was so damn anxious to get home and see you. When I say I missed you, well, I didn't think it was possible to need someone around so much."

I exhaled the breath that felt on hold forever, his soul open to me for the first time. We'd shared so many intimate moments, but right now, on opposite sides of the fence, we felt closer than ever.

"There's someone I want you to meet," Elliot said.

"What are you up to?" I asked, aching for him to jump the fence, to jump me.

"I'll bring her around the front door. Be over in a minute."

Her? He had a 'her' for me to meet? His mother? I already kind of knew his grandmother.

Curious, I walked back into the house and through to the front door, opening it. Moments later he appeared, walking up the driveway, a small child by his side. She was at a guess about four, with blonde pigtails and the cutest little pink dress. *Who is this?*

Elliot spoke to her as they walked. I couldn't hear it, but she held his hand tight as our eyes met and she slowed her step to walk slightly behind him. Whoever she was, she was adorable and shy.

When they reached me, he looked at me so earnestly I wanted to cry for some reason. What was this all about?

He kissed me tenderly, producing from behind his back a single red rose. Very obviously clipped from his grandmother's garden.

"I'm sorry about last night. I was such an idiot. I missed you like crazy and then seeing you draped over that guy ..."

"It wasn't just a guy, it was Logan. Olivia's partner."

He twisted his lips, looking sheepish. "I worked out it was something like that afterward. I'm so sorry, Becs, I hope you can forgive me. I let my emotions run away with me."

I grinned, running my finger across the soft, silky petals of the rose. "I think I might be able to do that. Hope I'm not going to be in trouble for having this." I swung back and forward, raising the flower to my nose and taking a deep sniff of the gentle perfume.

"Nan cut it for me. She felt sorry for me moping around, and I confessed what I'd done. If it means anything, she told me I was an idiot, that she'd never seen any other men around here."

"Because there haven't been. Apart from my dad this morning. And Logan, who helped me out when I was far too drunk to drive for myself."

He cocked an eyebrow at me. "Why were you that drunk? All the time I've known you, you haven't been like that. Not since the night before we met."

"It's a long story. Want to come inside and catch up?"

Elliot looked down at the little girl beside him. She was yawning, and kicking her feet into the ground, very clearly bored. "Shall we go inside and sit down?"

She hid behind him, poking her head around his leg at me. I grinned. "Boo," I said.

With a giggle she came out a little, and I stood aside while Elliot led her into the house. She had big blue eyes that took everything in. What a little heartbreaker.

"Who's this?" I asked.

"That's what we need to talk about."

They sat on the couch and Elliot stroked her head as she snuggled up against him.

"Do you want a drink or anything? I think I have some juice in the fridge."

He smiled. "We just had a snack. Rebecca, I'd like you to meet Ruby."

Slowly I sat in a chair opposite them. "Hi Ruby. It's nice to meet you."

She grinned and I looked back at Elliot curiously. "What's going on?"

He took the deepest breath I think I'd ever seen him take, never taking his eyes from me. "Ruby's my daughter."

I swallowed hard and looked again at the little girl. Her gaze was fixed on Elliot and in profile I could see it more than anything.

"I know I need to tell you the whole story, but I wanted you to meet her. She's going to be living with me now."

My head swam as he reached for my hand. This was huge and unexpected. My chest began to hurt at the thought that something had obviously happened for him, for both of them and I had no idea what it was.

"That's why I came over. I wanted you to know everything. I tried to come over this morning before work, but you didn't answer the door."

"I was asleep. You could have let yourself in."

He looked sheepish. "After turning up on your doorstep and jumping to some really big conclusions, I didn't want to make any assumptions about being welcome."

I nodded. He smiled at Ruby.

"I should have brought over some of her toys. Keep her busy while I tell you everything."

"I've got some pens and paper if she wants to draw?" The ache in my heart made me want this story, no matter how painful it might turn out to be. If Ruby was there, where was her mother?

"That'd be great. What do you think, Rubes?" Elliot asked, tickling her under the chin.

She giggled and twisted her head away. "Nooooo," she said, with a laugh.

"No to being tickled, or to drawing? Want to draw, baby?"

Ruby nodded, her pigtails flying. I couldn't help but smile; she was so precious.

I stood and moved to my desk, opening the drawer. There were always plenty of pens in there, highlighters, the works. Grabbing a pile of paper, and a handful of random pens, I placed it on the surface and motioned for her to come over.

She ran over, hopping on the chair, and ran her fingers across the pens, carefully selecting the first one.

Once she'd started scribbling, I made my way back to the other side of the living room, sitting in a chair opposite Elliot. Despite his earlier words, the need for some distance, to put a barrier between us was necessary. What if after all his words he still broke my heart?

"Ruby's mother and I were together about five years ago. Not for long. We broke up after six months because it just wasn't working. Anyway, I get this call a few months ago and Toni's dying. Twenty-five years old and she has cervical cancer. Wasn't picked up early—she was never very good at keeping appointments. Anyway, she tells me that I have a kid."

I turned and looked back over my shoulder. It really was clear as anything looking at her. She frantically scribbled on the paper, looking up to check on Elliot and smiling at me before returning to her drawing.

"She's amazing. Bright as a button and very artistic. She starts school next year."

Turning my head back to face him I nodded. "She seems very sweet. Why didn't you tell me?" I didn't mean the question to sound as if I had to know for my own benefit. I just thought that with him sharing my bed often, he might have shared this with me.

"I didn't know how you'd deal with it. Here we were in this casual relationship, and I didn't even know for sure that Ruby was mine. The last thing I wanted was to lay all this on you and then find that she wasn't mine after all. Toni didn't have any family support so I went and stayed with them to get to know my daughter and to say goodbye. I stayed until ... we buried her last Friday."

Tears stung my eyes as my heart broke for that little girl behind me. She'd lost her mother, and only just discovered she had a father. What an upside-down world she must be living in. And yet she was so good, sitting quietly and colouring while the father she'd just met spoke to me. Another stranger.

"Elliot, I'm so sorry."

He shrugged. "I wish I'd known earlier. Maybe I could have made things easier for her, stayed and taken care of Ruby. I don't know. Anyway, I'm home now and not going anywhere else. Ruby needs me. I need you."

I stood, moving to the couch beside him and wrapping my arms around his neck.

"You're not upset?" he whispered.

I leaned back, cupping his face in my hands. "I'm hurt that you didn't tell me what was going on, but that kinda pales in comparison to what you two have been through."

"I know. I was scared to tell you. This wasn't part of our deal."

"Maybe not. But it's your deal now. You need to do what's best for her."

Elliot's brow wrinkled as he frowned. "What about this thing we've got going? What about what's best for us?"

That brought a grin to my face. I'd missed him so much, just having him back in my house was enough for me right now. We didn't have to be rolling around naked to enjoy time together.

"We'll work it out. You can bring Ruby over for dinner some nights maybe."

He snuggled into my shoulder, leaning against me and watching her.

"I'd like that. This whole thing is so scary, Becs. I have no idea what I'm doing trying to be her dad."

I kissed the top of his head, squeezing his shoulder. "Looks to me like you've gotten off to a great start."

He gulped. "I was worried that you wouldn't want for us to ... well, you know."

"Why wouldn't I?" I asked.

"I know how you feel about children."

The words stung, stabbing at my heart like pinpricks. "I don't know if you do."

"You said you didn't want any. I mean, I know we're not *together* together, but with Ruby in my life I thought things might change between us."

Ruby slid off the chair, and held her picture up for us to see. "Elliot, look what I drew," she said.

That did it. I burst into tears at the sight of her picture, very clearly a family. At a guess it was her in the middle, Elliot on one side and her mother on the other.

She frowned, tucking the picture behind her back and slipping around the coffee table to stand beside Elliot.

"Ruby, it's beautiful. I'm sorry I'm crying, but it's just such a lovely picture," I whispered the words, unable to force my voice above a murmur.

A little smile appeared on her face, and Elliot reached for her, pulling her closer. "It is very lovely, sweetheart. What is it?"

"Me and Mummy and you."

"She'd love it." His voice cracked, and I squeezed his shoulder even harder. "We'll put it on the fridge when we get home."

"When can we go home?"

"We'll go and see Nan in a little while. I just wanted to come and say hi to Rebecca so you could meet her. She's a special friend of mine."

Ruby tilted her head to get a better look at me, and I winked, making her giggle.

She had her father's dimples, and that same mannerism of

swaying back and forward looking at the floor. On him it was endearing, on her, cute.

I didn't know just how much room you could have in your heart until that moment. Elliot needed me; Ruby needed me. Nothing in my life had ever been so important.

23

I SAT in the silence when they left, consumed by thoughts of the future. This was the moment I had to make a choice.

Elliot would need help, support. He might have his grandmother, but she wouldn't be around forever. Could I make the type of commitment he needed? Was that even what he wanted at all?

Elliot had made it really clear he wanted to see me. What if he just wanted to keep me on as a booty call? After the weeks I'd missed him, been faithful to him even though he'd never asked me to, and all the feelings of longing—how would I feel if he made that decision?

Ruby had to come first now, of course. Some selfish little part of me wanted him to myself, but that wasn't going to be. I had to share him in some form. I couldn't resent her, especially after all she'd been through.

The thought of her made me smile. She was shy, but composed. Unsure of herself, but Elliot's cheekiness shone through her. She'd grow up to be a lot like her father. Beautiful and creative.

Lost in thought, I jumped as my phone vibrated across the table, rattling the cups that still sat there from Dad's visit. The text message made me laugh. It was from Elliot.

> There's a lot more I want to say to you. But not for little ears. See you tonight.

I clung to the phone, holding it against my chest with glee. My body grew warm at the memory of his touch. It might have been months since we'd had sex, but every second we'd spent together had been unforgettable. My dirty little secret. I'd told Dad about Elliot, but now I had more to talk with Dad about.

So much to think about.

And yet it seemed to be the easiest decision of all.

My stomach churned as I pecked at my dinner later, unable to concentrate.

I love Elliot.

There, I'd thought it. Now to say it out loud.

I ran at the sound of a gentle tap on the door. Elliot waited on the other side, and didn't stop to say hello. He grabbed me in the doorway, pulling my body to his, and kissing me with the intensity I craved.

Backing away from the door, he pushed it shut with his foot as we moved down the hallway toward the bedroom. He grazed his lips down my neck, guiding me toward the bed before running his hands down my back and pulling my legs up as I jumped. He twirled me around, and I laughed as he growled.

"I feel like I've been waiting for this forever," he said.

"Me too."

I fell backwards onto the bed, reaching for the button on my jeans and wriggling out of them while he pulled his T-shirt over his head. Sitting up, I pulled off my shirt, his hands on my back as he unclipped my bra. Those big, warm hands stroked my skin.

"I missed you more than anything, Rebecca Wallace."

"Sex now, talk later." I grinned, leaning back.

He smiled, hovering over me and kissing me, stripping off his jeans. Nothing had ever felt as good as his flesh on mine, together as we needed to be. This was never meant to feel this serious, be this real, but it was, and I gladly gave my heart to this man.

Elliot slipped his hand between my legs, rubbing my clit and moaning just as I did. "This is home." He said the words, nuzzling my neck, making me sigh and shudder as I gave myself to him, body and soul.

I'd spent all this time thinking about him, dreaming about him, and now neither of us had to wait. He slid on top of me as I spread my legs, pulling him in, wrapping around him as if I never wanted to let him go.

"I'd almost forgotten just how good you feel," he murmured.

For my part, I was so lost in sensation that I could barely respond. This was where he belonged, on top of me, in me, all around me. I couldn't be apart from him like I had been these last few months.

"Don't ever go away again," I whispered.

His eyes were so sad. "I don't plan to. Not now."

He thrust slowly, scanning my face as we moved together. I lowered my legs a little, not needing to hold him there. He was where he wanted to be; I felt that more than ever.

His biceps flexed as he moved, and I steadied my hands on them, feeling his muscles, trying to find distraction from the intense gaze I was under. It wasn't uncomfortable, but it was as if he were seeing me for the first time, his eyes boring through me.

"Rebecca," he cried as his body stiffened before he flopped down on the bed beside me. He turned toward me, leaning over and kissing me so tenderly I thought I would cry.

"Sorry that didn't last as long as I wanted it to. I was just so damn anxious to be with you. I wanted to get Ruby off to sleep before I came over here; she doesn't know Nan very well and all I could think about was being inside you, smelling you, getting you naked under me. I need to get back in case she wakes up."

I stroked his face. "I've missed you so much. I don't mind at all."

He licked his lips, as if there was something he wanted to say but held back.

"What is it?" I asked.

"I didn't know if you'd want this. I mean, I know we talked about it earlier, but you've had a few hours to think about it. This whole thing with Ruby, well, I wasn't sure if that was going to put you off me."

That brought tears to my eyes. Did he think that I would turn my back because of his little girl? His words stung like a knife to the heart.

"Why would it put me off?"

"You said you didn't like children."

I sighed. "No. *No.* I just never thought bringing any of my own into the world was such a good idea. Ruby is gorgeous and sweet. Olivia's kids are adorable. It just scared me to think of having children and then subjecting them to what I went through."

Elliot squeezed my hands in his. "You wouldn't do that, though."

Shrugging, I pulled away. "I don't know that. My mum is an alcoholic; I like drinking sometimes. My dad is a workaholic; I work hard at my business. What if I'm too much like both of them?"

I looked out the window to the sky outside. It was 7.30 pm, and the spring sunsets came later and later. Any remnants of light were disappearing and the sunset was a glorious orangy red. Seeing it like that reminded me so much of my childhood. The times I'd still be waiting for Mum to cook dinner as the sun went down, the times I'd sit and watch the sunset while waiting for Dad to come home from work. He worked such crazy long hours.

That was the last thing I would ever want for any child of mine.

Elliot's hand landed on my shoulder, and I looked back at him with tears in my eyes. "You're not them, Becs. You'll never be them because you know how it feels to go through that."

"Ruby's lucky she has you. You'll do whatever it takes to look after her, and you'll be there for her."

He nodded. "I just want to help her get through this. It's so much to deal with—her mother dying and some strange man turns up to take her away. Toni had talked to her about me; she kind of knew who I was, but it's such a huge adjustment."

I turned, and he wrapped his arms around me, hugging me tightly. "Whatever you need from me to help her, I'll be here. I want to be here for both of you."

"You're amazing. You know that? I hid the truth because I didn't want to lose you just as I found Ruby." He stroked my arm, and I closed my eyes for a moment, enjoying his touch.

"I would never have turned my back on you. We've come too far for that. Do you really think I'd give up this? Us?"

"What are we, Rebecca?" His eyes searched mine, looking for an answer to a question that was stuck in my throat.

I shrugged. "We'll work it out." I smiled as he nuzzled my cheek. This was serious for me, I knew as much now. But we needed time to work through that together.

He had a small smile on his face. "I'm sorry I didn't keep more in touch. I didn't want to tell you the news over the phone; I had to see you face to face. It's awful enough that I dropped all this on you, but I just couldn't do it at a distance."

There he was, being all sweet again.

"I'm really sorry I can't stay the rest of the night. I want to, but I need to get Ruby settled. She's been through so much."

I stroked his face with the palm of my hand. "It's okay. It'll take time for her to adjust. Sounds like she's just getting used to you."

I love you, Elliot.

Opening my mouth to speak, I still couldn't say the words. Instead I just closed my mouth again.

"So we have plans for Saturday. I'm going to take Ruby to the movies and then we're going shopping because she needs some new clothes. I thought you might want to come with us? I have no idea about little girl's clothing."

"Saturday I have a wedding to go to. Olivia's. You know, you met her boyfriend the yesterday when he grabbed you by the throat?"

Elliot frowned. "I can't say that was fun."

"He was just defending my honour."

"Maybe we can go shopping on Sunday?" He looked at me, hope in his eyes.

"Sunday will be fine. Now ..." I stroked his chest. "How about some more you and me time before you have to disappear?"

He grinned, and I just wanted to poke those beautiful dimples in his cheeks. "I accept your invitation."

"Repeat after me. 'I'm sorry for being an idiot. Only Elliot gets anywhere near Rebecca's vagina'."

He roared with laughter. "I'm sorry."

"No. I want to hear the words." My eyebrows were raised as I looked at him expectantly. I needed to know that he understood I didn't want anyone else.

"Fine. 'I'm sorry for being an idiot. Only Elliot gets anywhere near Rebecca's vagina'."

I smiled sweetly. "See? Was it really that hard to say?"

He rolled on top of me, pinning me to the bed. "No. Right now I'd say anything if it made you happy." He grinned, kissing me.

I ran my hands down his spine, his smooth skin underneath my fingertips. "I could spend a week in bed with you after all this time away," I said.

"Only a week?"

I laughed. Having him back was good for my soul.

"Maybe two."

24

SOMETIMES, two people find one another and it's as if they were just destined to be together. That was Olivia and Logan. Two halves of a whole, slotting together as if they'd always been there, side by side.

I stood in the park, waiting with the other guests for Olivia to come across the road. She and Logan had opted for a wedding venue that was close to home, before we would go across the road for a barbecue dinner. The low-key occasion suited them; they didn't care about anything else but being together.

Logan fiddled with his tie and I caught his eyes, smiling and nodding. *You're fine*, I mouthed. He gave me the thumbs up, smiled, and started sliding the fabric between his fingers again, grinning as I rolled my eyes.

Olivia's friend Maddy stood nearby with her little girl, Carly, beside her. The girl was the spitting image of her mother, and seeing her made me ache to have Elliot and Ruby with me. Maybe I should have spoken up about wanting him to be there. Then again, he needed the time with his little girl too. Sharing him might be tough.

"There she is," Maddy whispered, nudging me.

Tears welled in my eyes as I watched my dear friend approach on Maddy's husband's arm. Here Olivia was, about to marry the love of her life, wearing a stunning cream dress, which brought out her dark colouring. She'd never looked so beautiful. Andrew smiled proudly as he gave her away.

And Logan? Well, Logan's jaw dropped as she approached. The love they had for one another radiated from the two of them, and I was very glad to have brought a packet of tissues as I wiped my eyes.

My mind drifted back to Elliot as they exchanged vows. I didn't know if we could have the type of relationship Olivia and Logan had, dedicated to one another, raising a family together. Seeing little Chloe again brought all those baby feelings to the surface. Could I risk having a child of my own one day? Would I screw them up, or could I be better than that? And what about Ruby? I couldn't replace her mother, but could I be a mother figure to her?

Still deep in thought when we made our way back across the road, I watched as Olivia and Logan shared a moment with Chloe. He kissed the little girl goodnight, and Olivia made her way up the stairs to tuck her into bed.

I approached, tapping Logan on the shoulder.

"Hey, Rebecca." He wrapped his arms around me, hugging me tight. "I'm so glad you're here. I'll always be so grateful for the way you helped Liv out when she really needed it."

I wriggled to get him to ease up his bear-like grip. "Thank you for inviting me. I'm glad she found you, Logan. You are just what she needed."

"I hope so." He grinned.

"Anyway, I'm going to get out of here. It's been a wonderful day, but I think I'll be going sooner rather than later so you two can get going with your sexy times."

Logan laughed. "Are you sure? Andrew cooks a pretty mean barbecue. It'll be a while before everyone else leaves."

"I'm just a little tired, and I don't want to be that one annoying person who hangs around that you struggle to kick out at the end of the night. Besides, Elliot and I are working through everything. He'll be over at my place later."

Logan let go of me, cocking his head. "Just make sure he's good to you. And you're always welcome here. You know that."

"I know. But tonight I'm going to leave you all to it. Have a great wedding night. Give that girl some hot stuff to write in her books. I could do with something good to read."

Logan roared with laughter, and leaned over to give me a peck on the cheek. "Fine. But Liv will want to catch up with you, so you'd better come and see us soon."

"It's a deal." I took a deep breath and smiled. "Love you guys. Don't do anything I wouldn't do."

"Doesn't leave us with a lot then, does it?"

I slapped him on the arm and he waggled his eyebrows at me. "Say good night to your gorgeous wife for me."

———

ELLIOT WAS in the living room when I got home, sitting on the couch, flicking through the television channels, with his feet on the coffee table as if he owned the place. All I wanted was to sink into a bottle of wine. I didn't feel like just jumping into bed with him.

"Hey Becs, what's up?"

He'd cleaned up, the stubble gone for a change, his hair trimmed short. He looked almost respectable.

"Nothing. Just need some time with a bottle of wine."

He cocked his head. "What's wrong, babe?"

"Elliot, I'm tired. I'm not in the mood for rolling around. Maybe tomorrow."

I sat beside him as he patted the couch, and he hooked his arm around my shoulders. "You never say no. What's going on?"

"You wouldn't understand."

How could I tell him how happy I was for my friend and miserable for myself? That I wanted someone to take to me to a damn wedding, wanted someone on my arm?

"Try me." Now I was close to him, he smelled so good. As if he'd made the effort and had just showered, his skin musky from the shower gel I kept for him in the bathroom.

"I don't even know where to begin."

He studied my face, casting his eyes over me with this look I'd never seen before. "The start would be good."

I rolled my eyes, fighting back tears. I never cried. What the hell was wrong with me?

"Becs, if you can't talk to me, who can you talk to?"

He was right. I'd been monogamous with him for all these months, not just because of the promise we'd made one another, but because he was there and comfortable, like an old pair of slippers. Being with him was easy, and I'd never felt any pressure for it to be anything else than what it was.

It suddenly occurred to me that I didn't know if he'd slept with anyone else in that time. He'd told me that if he was ever thinking of going there he'd tell me, but would he? Not that it should bother me. I knew he'd be safe; he was far too smart to do anything that stupid. But the idea of him being with anyone else made my skin crawl. As if

...

"Olivia got married today."

"I remember you telling me. That's awesome. I'm pleased for her."

I leaned back on the couch, pulling away from his grasp. "She deserves all of the good stuff that's happened to her. Her ex was such a douche, and Logan adores her. I love seeing them together, but it just makes me realise how empty my life is. I have my business and that keeps me busy, but it's not the same as having someone to share your life with."

As I spoke, I looked past Elliot, staring at nothing on the far wall. We sat in silence for a few moments.

"Shit. Maybe I just need a drink."

I stood, and he grabbed my hand, pulling me back down beside him.

"You want to know what I'm doing here?"

I shrugged. "Your grandmother fell asleep in front of the television and you want to fool around? I'm assuming Ruby is already asleep."

His dimples moved as he grinned. Something was going on with him, and as tired as I was, I had to admit to being curious.

What if he's changed his mind about us?

The thought stung and I frowned. This had always been casual, but I didn't know what I'd do without it. I couldn't see myself finding anyone else like Elliot—ready and willing to make me scream like a damn banshee as I came. No man had ever done that for me, or to me before. And he made me laugh like no one else. Like laughing until I started hiccupping, and then Elliot would mimic me, making me laugh harder. That and my heart had kind of fallen for him without my permission.

"Becs?"

Let's get this over with.

"I give up. What are you doing here?" I tried to pull my hand away, but he wouldn't release it.

His grin died a little as he grew serious, and he squeezed my hand in his so hard I yelped.

"Sorry. I just ... well ..."

Holy crap, he just blushed.

"I'm over this whole friends-with-benefits thing, fuck buddies, whatever you want to call us."

Here it comes.

"It's not what I want anymore. I've been thinking about this even before finding out about Ruby."

Axe falling in three, two ...

"I love you, Becs. I want more than to just be the guy who comes over for a booty call. I want to stay the whole night every night, make you bacon sandwiches in bed for breakfast. What we have isn't enough for me; I need the whole thing."

Did he just …?

I wanted to cry. Here I was ready to be dumped from my non-relationship and the exact opposite had happened.

"I'll get my shit together. I'll be whatever you want me to be, but let me in. Let me in to that part of you that's been shut off from me."

All I could do was stare at him.

"Uh, anything? Nothing? Am I wasting my time here?"

"No," I whispered, searching his face for some sign that this was a joke, that he was teasing.

Here I was about to drown my sorrows because I wanted a love like Olivia's so badly and it really had been right under my nose all along.

I don't think Elliot had ever wanted to keep it casual.

He leaned forward, smiling again, kissing me more tenderly than he'd ever kissed me before.

"We've played it by your rules—now I want to play by mine. I love you," he whispered.

"Kiss me again?"

"Is this what you want? Do you want more? If you want things to stay the way they have been, I'm not going anywhere. I'm way too addicted to you to walk away. But I want you just for me, all for me."

My heart was in my throat as he kissed me again, firmer this time. This wasn't like any of the other kisses we'd shared in bed. It was full of love and promise for the future. It was amazing what you could read into a kiss.

"Yes. Yes I want more." I did want more, and I wanted more with only him.

"Good, because if I don't get you into bed soon, I'm gonna punch a hole in my pants."

I laughed, pulling him closer to kiss me again, his chest against mine, feeling his warmth that belonged to me. I shook with fear. This was the biggest step I'd ever taken, but I was ready. More than ready.

"Becs?" he whispered as he kissed his way down my throat.

"Yes?"

"I'm really glad you left your door open that drunken night."

I laughed, pushing him off to look at that happy puppy expression of his again. "So am I."

"Do you want this? You're not just saying it to get a piece of all this?" He waved his hand in the air, pointing towards his chest, and I pulled him close to me again, laughing.

"Yes, I want this. I want you. I love you."

"I even got dressed up for the wedding, but clearly I got the timing wrong."

I looked at him curiously. "What are you talking about?"

"You said you were going to the wedding, and for some reason I thought you said it was at five and turned up but you were already gone. I thought if it was okay and you wanted, I might come with you, meet your friends. And apologise to Logan."

His words touched me, and even though I wanted his hands to be touching me too, this was a moment to cherish. He wanted me, really wanted me. He didn't just want to be the guy who shared my bed when we both needed release, he wanted to be mine.

"I'm sorry. I would have loved for you to have come with me."

Elliot's lips curled into a sly smile. "Plenty of time for that tonight."

Laughing, I rolled my eyes at him, sure I was grinning like an idiot.

Now for both of us to try to keep it together.

25

IN THE MORNING, I looked down at my phone as it vibrated in my hand. I hadn't heard from Nicola since the wedding, but she must have spoken to Dad.

> I really need to talk to you. Are you at home today?

Sighing, I tapped back.

> Everything's fine. Don't worry about it.

Elliot and I were serious, and all was good with the world. As much as I knew Nicola and I needed to talk, I really didn't know if I could deal with this right now.

> Tell me when you're home and I'll come over. I really do need to talk.

Okay, whatever.

> I'll be home after lunch I think. I'll text you.

Elliot had gone home in the night to make sure Ruby was okay and brought her back over now. She was warmer this time, more familiar with her surroundings.

"Do you want to go shopping today?" I asked her.

The plait in her hair went flying as she nodded. It was scruffy, and at best guess I'd say Elliot was responsible.

"Want me to tidy up your plait?"

She grinned. "Elliot did it."

"I can see."

We shared a look that exasperated Elliot, judging by the sighing sound he'd made. "I tried my best. I never plaited a girl's hair before and Ruby specifically asked for it."

I laughed, rubbing his shoulder. "You didn't do too badly. I'll just tidy it up."

"Girls." He grumped, but the grin on his face told a different story.

"You love it," I said.

Steering Ruby to the couch, I sat her down with her back to me. Elliot hadn't done too bad a job, but the plaits were uneven with wisps of hair sticking out.

"Your dad didn't do too bad a job, really."

"My mummy does it better."

I opened my mouth to say something, maybe divert the conversation to something else, but the words caught in my throat. As I met Elliot's eye, he seemed to be struggling too.

"I bet. Let's see if I can get it almost as good as her." My voice was croaky, but at least the words came out.

Ruby seemed happy, sitting still as I tidied her hair and bouncing up as soon as I patted her shoulder to let her know she was done. She studied her reflection in the television.

"That's how you do it," she said to Elliot, completely deadpan.

And with that little comment, the tension broke and he smiled. Somehow we would all get through this. We'd keep the memory of Ruby's mother alive while creating new memories.

RUBY'S EYES were like dinner plates as we made our way around the shopping mall. There was nothing like this in the small town she'd come from, and there were so many different clothing shops, we could try on a whole bunch of stuff for her.

She'd clung to Elliot at first, but now she and I walked together, hand in hand. From the first store, it had been really clear that Elliot was in way over his head. He didn't know how to deal with little girls and buying dresses and underwear, so I'd taken over.

"Becca, look." She already had her own name for me, after hearing her father call me either Rebecca or Becs. It was too cute, and she giggled as I squeezed her hand when she said it.

By the side of a food store was a ride-on Thomas the Tank Engine. I let go of her hand, nodding, and she ran to it, jumping in and frowning as she pressed the buttons and no sound came out.

"Hang on, sweetie," I said, fishing in my purse for coins. I grinned as I pulled out a two-dollar coin, sliding it into the slot. The machine came to life, growling and grumbling as it rocked gently back and forward, hissing and tooting as Ruby pressed the buttons.

Elliot slid his arms around my waist from behind. "What are you two doing?"

"She's having fun. This place has been a little overwhelming for her I think. Maybe it's good for her to enjoy this."

"Softy," he whispered, planting a kiss on my neck.

"Becca, Becca," Ruby called, waving at me. I waved back, nodding to acknowledge her as she tooted the horn again.

Elliot chuckled, his chest vibrating against me as he did. "Someone's popular."

"She's awesome. Such a sweetheart."

"I'm glad you two are getting along."

I pulled his arms tighter around my waist. "It's easy. She's so much like you."

He took a deep breath. "I honestly think you being part of my life is going to make this easier on her. It's been a tough few weeks."

I reached up, hooking my arm around his neck. "I can't imagine what you and her have been through, but I can be here for both of you."

Elliot pressed his nose to mine and despite us being in the middle of the shopping mall, people milling around, it was like no one else was there.

It might have lasted if a little someone hadn't started tugging on my jeans.

I looked down. "Did the ride finish?"

She nodded. "Can I go again?"

"How about we go and find you some new clothes instead? We can come back another day," Elliot said.

Her lower lip wobbled as she looked up at him with the biggest puppy-dog eyes I have ever seen. Elliot reached for his pocket, and I didn't have to ask to know he was going for another coin.

"How about we go and get some clothes and then go for ice cream? Would you like that, Ruby?" I asked.

The ride forgotten, she pulled at my arm, slotting her hand in mine when I lowered it.

"But. I just ..." Elliot looked bewildered, his eyes flicking between the two of us.

"Shopping and sugary stuff. Two key elements to a girl's heart. Sometimes one isn't enough." I smiled sweetly.

Elliot's eyes looked upward. He looked as if he was fighting an eye roll. "I'm completely outnumbered, aren't it?"

"Uh-huh."

He sighed. "Come on then, let's get going."

Shaking his head as he walked a little head of us, I looked down at Ruby, sharing a conspiratorial smile.

We were going to get along just fine.

RUBY HAD a whole new wardrobe of clothes, Elliot telling me off for taking over buying them when he ran out of money. But she had months of day-care to go to, different seasons to dress for, and then he'd have to think about school uniform. I liked to plan ahead and her mother hadn't had a lot of money to buy clothes for her, a lot of her things were second hand.

I unlocked the door at home, Ruby running past me and into the living room, pouting as she realised the pens and paper weren't still out for her.

"You can come and draw another day," I said. "You've got to get home and unpack all your new things."

Elliot grabbed me by the waist, pulling me tight against him. "Thanks for being there today. I would have gotten lost in the skirts and shirts and underwear."

I rubbed his biceps, squeezing them gently as he waggled his eyebrows. "I enjoyed it. Shopping for her was fun."

He release me from his embrace. "Ruby, let's go. We've dropped Rebecca off. Now we have to get your things packed away."

Ruby's bottom lip dropped.

"Come on then, pumpkin," I said, nudging her arm.

"I'm not pumpkin, I'm Ruby." Ruby laughed loudly. "And your name is Rebecca. Like Rebecca Rabbit in *Peppa Pig*." She laughed so hard I thought she was about to puke, and I bent over, tickling her ribs.

She squealed, trying to tickle me back and failing miserably to reach me. Two large hands landed on my waist, fingers wriggling as Elliot paid me back on behalf of his daughter.

We all fell about until we couldn't breathe for laughing, and I lay flat on my back on the floor, panting to recover.

"We've got to cook Nan dinner and Ruby has to get some sleep," Elliot said, reaching down to stroke my hair.

I nodded.

"I'll come back over after she's asleep. Unless you want to come over for dinner too?"

Pulling him down for a quick kiss, I shook my head. "I promised to text a friend when I got home this afternoon, and she sounds pretty anxious to see me. Next time?"

He frowned. "Everything okay?"

"When you come back later I'll tell you all about my dad and his girlfriend. The one who is half his age and went to school with me."

His lips formed an *O*. "Come on Ruby, let's get going. Give Rebecca a cuddle."

I didn't even manage to get up before she rolled over me, giggling as I hugged her, kissing her face. "Thank you for spending time today with me, Miss Ruby."

She snuggled in, and for just a moment I wanted to tell Elliot to forget about ever going back next door.

"I'll see you soon, sweetheart."

Nodding, she jumped off me and I sat up, taking Elliot's hand as he helped me stand.

Waving goodbye, my heart sank as they walked away. We'd known one another five minutes and that little girl was already under my skin. Could I do this? Could I be what she needed?

NICOLA APPEARED on my doorstep fifteen minutes after I sent her a text. She looked scared, her eyes downturned as if she was afraid to come in.

"If you think I'm going to yell at you, I'm not. Did you talk to Dad?" I stepped back so she could come inside, and she made her way to the couch, still very downcast.

She nodded. "I spoke to Neil. He said you were fine with us. I just wanted to be sure."

I sat beside her. "I'm not going to cause a fuss. You're both adults. Who am I to even try to interfere?"

"I love him, Rebecca. Really love him. I spent so long worrying about what this person and that person thought of me. Starved myself to be thin, ate to put on weight. When I'm with him, I just feel like I can be myself."

"You don't need to justify yourself to me."

She exhaled loudly, her face twitching as she looked at me. What was she so nervous about if she'd just told me all that?

"Nicola, what is it? Clearly there's something else going on."

She licked her lips slowly, scanning my face as she seemed to struggle with knowing whether she could tell me or not.

"I'm pregnant."

Holy shitballs.

"It's your father's. He's been the only man I've been with for months, but I know this could put extra pressure on us." The lilt in her voice grew as she picked at her fingers. I'd never seen her so nervous.

"What do you think I'm going to do about it? Make you get rid of it? Tell him to leave you? If you know him that well, you'll know he'll not want to walk away. He tried so hard with my mother because of me, and then he tried without her to take care of me." I loved both my dad and Nicola, and as much as I wanted to be pissed with them, all I could do was let them be happy without my interference.

Her shoulders slumped, I guess in relief at my reaction. What was the point of being upset about it? If they were together, it would have only been a matter of time, especially with him seeming as serious about it as she now seemed to be.

"The day of the wedding—I am so, so sorry you walked in on us like that. I just have these wild, crazy raging hormones and when I want it, I have to have it. Neil is so accommodating like that."

Oh holy shitballs times a million.

"See, that's the bit I don't want to know. If you love him, fine. If you have sex with him, fine. But I don't want to know about it. That's all I'm going to ask of you. Please don't tell me more stories about how big my father's penis is and how well he uses it."

The nervousness disappeared as she burst out laughing.

"For him to sneak off like that with you in that kind of place speaks volumes for your sex life. I really don't need any more details."

She lunged at me, wrapping her arms around my neck and squeezing so tight I was sure she was about to break something.

"Thank you. I never wanted to hurt you. And when we were kids I never thought your dad was hot. But oh God, Rebecca."

"There's a line, Nicola ..."

"Sorry. I keep saying sorry. Shit. How am I going to tell him about the baby?"

I gave her a gentle push to get off me. "What? You haven't told him?"

"I found out last week. I keep trying to, but I'm so scared in case he doesn't want it."

I sighed, taking her hands in mine. "I saw his face when he told me about you. He loves you. He'll probably want to do the right thing and whatever you want. Just be good to him."

She grinned. "That's the easiest thing to do in the world." Her face softened, like she was in a dream. It took everything in me not to do the standard Rebecca response of pretending to put my finger down my throat. It was nice she'd found a man who would treat her well.

Besides, if he didn't, I'd kick his arse.

26

DINNER WITH DAD. That was the next step. He wanted to take us somewhere swanky to meet Elliot and Ruby, and I let him just so they could have a nice night out.

It wasn't as posh as some places he'd taken me too. Elliot was in dress pants and a button-up shirt. I'd bought him a tie along the way to wear and even tied it for him because he hadn't worn one since school. Ruby giggled as she stared at her father.

"You look weird," she said.

For her part, I'd bought her a new dress. Any excuse to go shopping. It was a pretty little pink frilly thing as pink was *the* colour of choice, and she'd spun around in the little tutu skirt.

"Table for Wallace, please," I said as we entered.

Ruby fussed as she sat, looking around at the opulent room. It was elegantly decorated, but for her, she might as well have been in a palace about to meet a king.

"Here he comes," I murmured. Dad walked toward the table, dressed immaculately as always. His greying hair stood out as a stark contrast to the dark suit he wore.

Elliot squeezed my hand under the table. "It'll be fine, Becs. You'll see."

"I know, I'm just on edge. You don't know my father."

"No, but I know you. He can't be that bad if he raised you."

His confidence was reassuring, but my father had been known to scare people into resigning with that damn glare of his.

I'm a grown-up. I'm a grown-up.

We stood as he approached, and he came around my side of the table to give me a kiss on the cheek, barely looking at Elliot.

"Dad, this is Elliot," I said as we sat.

"Elliot." Dad's gaze was fixed on him and my breath caught in my throat as I shifted my focus from one to the other and back again.

"It's a pleasure to meet you, sir," Elliot said.

"It's good to meet you too. Rebecca has told me a little about you, but not much."

"And this is Ruby."

Ruby waved from across the table and it was as if my father transformed from his poker face into the doting grandfather.

"Hi Ruby. I've heard about you too."

I nudged him with my elbow. "Oh, so you're just acting all cool toward Elliot then?"

"I was just trying to be the caring father, my dear." He shifted his focus to Elliot. "Rebecca told me you haven't settled on a career and you play music. Does that sum it up?" The poker face was back.

"Stop it." I laughed. "Play nice."

He shrugged. "Tell me some more and then I'll have more to talk about."

"Well, I haven't really settled into a career. I do odd jobs around the place, work when there's work around, and spend a lot of time helping my grandmother. She's getting on so I do what I can for her until she's ready to go into a home," Elliot said.

Dad nodded slowly.

"And I'm in a band. But it's a fairly casual thing. Like most things in my life." I cringed as Elliot tried to joke.

I swear my father's eyebrow rose so high, it nearly took off into orbit. Just what he wanted for me. An unemployed musician. I had warned him, but I guess Elliot saying it just emphasised it.

"Dad, Elliot has plans, dreams. He's looking for something permanent now. With Ruby being here, we're hoping to be a lot more settled."

Dad's other eyebrow joined his first. I tried to plead with my eyes, and Dad shifted his focus from Elliot to me. Changing that unimpressed look to a concerned look, his brows now furrowed as he locked his gaze with my own.

"It's okay, Rebecca. I'm sure Elliot will work out what he wants to do with his life. Sometimes it takes a bit of time."

I opened my mouth to speak, I was so surprised at his words.

"Becs." Elliot's hand landed on my shoulder. "Your dad gets it. I'm prepared to do whatever it takes to be with Rebecca, Mr Wallace. I'll take whatever job comes up. Anything."

Dad nodded, his eyes fixed on Elliot's hand. And I was sure I saw a glimmer of a smile.

"Find something you like doing. Don't waste your life working in a job you hate. I spent so many years just working to get ahead and it was never enough. My wife and I split because of it. Rebecca bounced between us, and I never got to spend the time with her I wanted to. It was always about working to make sure she had the best."

"I love Rebecca very much, Mr Wallace. Have since the moment I first saw her."

That was news, and I looked at Elliot, who was looking at me with so much love in his eyes I wanted to cry even more. I was trapped between two men I loved, both of them looking at me as if I were the most important person in the world, and I had no idea which way to turn.

Elliot made up my mind, shuffling his chair over and draping his arm around my shoulder, pulling me in tight for a hug.

I turned my head toward him, smiling through the tears that

threatened. "Love you too," I whispered, unable to speak with any voice. He kissed my forehead and I leaned against him, looking back at Dad.

"Then I'm very happy for you two. Shall we order a bottle of champagne to celebrate?"

"I'm more of a beer guy." Elliot nodded as he spoke.

Dad grinned, loosening his tie and leaning back in his seat. "I haven't had a beer in I don't know how long. I think I'll join you. Shall we make that three?" He looked at me, a gleam in his eye that I wasn't sure I'd ever seen before. He was usually so serious.

"I think I'll stick to orange juice."

Elliot looked at me sideways. "Are you feeling okay?"

"I'm fine. I just don't feel like drinking."

"You're not pregnant, are you?" Dad said. Part of me wanted so badly to laugh out loud, knowing Nicola's news. Somehow that grin on his face had gotten even bigger and I wondered what sort of answer he was expecting. But I was either dreaming, or had ended up in some kind of random parallel universe where my life was back to front. This was unnerving, my father having an almost 180-degree behavioural flip. Would that make him happy?

"No, Dad. I just don't feel like a drink. And I'm driving."

Was that a glint of disappointment in his eye?

"Ruby, what would you like? Juice or maybe lemonade?" Dad asked, smiling warmly at her.

"Juice, please." She said it so quietly, blushing and snuggling behind Elliot

"Two beers and two orange juices then. I'll call the waiter over." Now Dad's smiled widened, and he looked at me with all the pride in his eyes that I'd always wanted to see.

This had to be one of the most bizarre days of my life. He'd never shown that warm side of himself in public, and although these two were now almost family, I thought he'd hold back.

He waved at the waiter, and after a brief consultation with Elliot over which beers to order, he settled back down to smile at us.

"I've got a little announcement of my own. I'm stepping away from the business a bit more, giving myself more time to relax. I've worked too hard for too long, and it screwed up so much of my life. I want a life of my own."

All I could do was nod. He hadn't had a lot of time for me when I was younger, but maybe he'd have time to spend with his children, and even grandchildren when they did arrive.

"Dad, I ..."

"Nicola and I are going to make it official too. I wanted you to be the first to know. I know she's told you about the baby, and I do love her, Rebecca."

I placed my hand over his. "I know you do. It'll take a bit of getting used to."

"I always thought you'd make a good big sister. Just never thought there would be thirty years between you and a younger sibling."

I laughed. "Neither did I. I think you're good for Nicola. She needed someone to ground her, and looks like it's you."

"Becca?" Ruby's voice came from across the table.

"Yes, sweetie?"

"Can we have ice cream?"

I smirked, while Elliot cocked an eyebrow. "After dinner. Let's have a look at the menu and find something for you." I reached for her hand and squeezed it.

"They have a junior menu here, Rebecca. That's why I chose this place." Dad smiled kindly at Ruby, and she hid her face behind her hands.

I picked up the menu, half expecting to see chicken nuggets. That would be weird and out of place for this kinda restaurant.

"Oh. Chicken bites. Those are like nuggets, Ruby. They come with fries anyway."

Ruby nodded enthusiastically.

"You're sorted. Now for us." I glanced at Elliot. He was deep in conversation with my father and I grinned at the sight of them talking. It didn't even matter what it was about. Whatever it was, they seemed to be in agreement, all smiles and laughter.

The two men I loved more than anything else in the world.

RUBY FELL ASLEEP ABOUT thirty seconds after climbing into the bed in my spare room, Elliot tucking her in while I pottered around the kitchen, making a cup of tea. The chamomile was soothing, and I sat at the dining table with my eyes closed just sipping it

Warm, strong hands squeezed my shoulders, and I sighed as the tension rolled out of me.

"You could always be my personal masseuse if you can't find anything else," I said.

"I think I can manage this on top of a job. Are you okay?" Concern was evident in Elliot's voice.

"I'm fine. Just a little weirded out after seeing Dad the way he was."

"Your father is pretty cool, Rebecca."

"Cooler than I ever thought. I spent so many years trying to impress him. I never thought he was trying to do the same."

I placed the mug down on the table and stood, the tea having had the desired affect. I could stagger upstairs and flop on the bed and I'd be asleep before my head hit the pillow.

"He seemed to get pretty excited at the thought of you being pregnant," Elliot said, wrapping his arms around me and planting a kiss on the cleft between my breasts.

"That was only one thing about today that was weird. I didn't expect him to be so easy-going. He was just so relaxed and unlike himself."

"Maybe that's what he always wanted to be like, but thought you had expectations. Seems to me that he loves you so much he would do anything for you."

I flopped my arms over Elliot's shoulders, kissing him tenderly. "Let's go to bed."

"There's no reason why we couldn't have a baby. Once I've got a job, anyway. We've been together for a while; it's not like this is anything new."

I stared at him, dumbfounded. What the hell was it with the men in my life and babies?

"Besides," he continued, "it's not like you're getting any younger."

My jaw dropped as I narrowed my eyes at him. He just grinned and then kissed me again. "Come on, old girl. Bedtime."

"You'll pay for that."

"That's what I'm counting on."

27

A BIG SPIT bubble popped in my face, and Chloe's eyes widened as I laughed, wiping her slobber from my cheek.

"She's trying so hard to laugh. Logan's been hanging out for just a little giggle. That's as far as she gets," Olivia said. We sat out on the deck with a glass of wine each, absorbing the sun while I caught up on her post-wedding gossip.

"I still love her, even if she spits at me," I said, wrinkling my nose at the little girl who sat on my lap. She was such a sweetheart.

"So ..." Olivia looked down at the table.

"What? Is there something wrong?"

She looked up at me, lips clamped together.

"Olivia, what are you up to?"

"Nothing. I just wanted to make sure you were okay. We spoke so briefly after the night Logan picked you up, and he said you got a hard time from Elliot."

"I'm fine."

I grinned at Olivia, little Chloe almost head-butting me as she leaned closer.

"That's what I came to tell you. We're in a relationship."

She had a look on her face that almost resembled my father's when he'd found out about Elliot being in a band. That orbiting eyebrow thing.

"So you kissed and made up?"

"You're *so* nosy, Olivia," I said, letting out a little smile.

"And you know pretty much everything about my sex life, so spill the beans."

I hugged Chloe tighter. She smelled so good, I could hear my body pleading with me to make one of my own.

"He's been through a lot. His ex had cancer, and he found out he had a daughter. He was still trying to process that when he came back that night."

Her jaw dropped as she just stared at me.

"That would do it," she finally said.

"You know, we had a kind of friends-with-benefits thing. Frequent booty calls. I tried not to let it get too serious."

"But it is now."

The grin spread before I could help it as my feelings for Elliot rose to the surface just thinking about him.

"It is now."

Olivia leaned back in her chair and nodded. "Good. I'm glad. You always seemed at a loose end, and I've felt so many times I've been dealing with my own dramas and not being as good a friend as I could have been."

"You don't have anything to feel guilty about. I had other friends. One of them would hammer me into the mattress on a semi-regular basis. Didn't he, Chloe?" I rubbed my nose against hers and she let out a delighted gurgle.

"Oh, you are close to laughing. Are you going to laugh for me and annoy your father?"

The unmistakable sound of Logan's heavy boots behind me brought my laughter to the surface as I snuggled with Chloe.

"If you tell me she laughed for you first ..." His deep voice came from behind. Chloe's head shot up as she recognised it, and I had a squirmy, wiggly little girl in my arms who was no longer interested in me.

"She didn't. I got lots of spit bubbles, though," I said, gazing up as I handed his daughter to him.

She squealed as she went into his arms, and I grinned at Olivia, who sat there shaking her head. "Real Daddy's girl, aren't you?"

"Always," Logan said, cradling Chloe in one arm, a beer in the other hand.

Chloe let out a squeal again, and Logan laughed, shaking his head at her. "I know when I come home at least one person is really happy to see me."

Olivia laughed. "Not just her."

I stuck my tongue out, my finger in my mouth as I pretended to gag at what I knew would end up being their foreplay. Those two were so sexed up it wasn't funny. And I loved them both so much, I couldn't have been happier for them. Olivia for being my friend, and Logan for loving her. Though, that bit was easy.

"You're just jealous, Rebecca." Logan grinned at me.

"Oh no she's not. Rebecca and Elliot are serious." Olivia sang the words as if we were all teenagers talking about first loves, and to be honest it kinda felt like that after the emptiness I'd felt at times. To have Elliot as a friend had been awesome enough; to have him as so much more? Well, that was amazing.

"Is that right? Even after the way he acted?" Logan growled.

"It sounds like he had a lot to deal with." Olivia rubbed his arm.

"He did. He brought his daughter home to live with him after her mother died. She's four. So he's coping with all of that and then comes home to find me in another man's arms."

Olivia screwed up her face, that eyebrow inching up again. "Another man's arms?"

"It was that or let me fall on my face in a drunken stupor." I laughed.

"Just you make sure he's good to you. Like I said, he'll have me to answer to if he's not. Although, I have to admit I'm impressed you found someone who can keep up with you." Logan winked at me. He was like that big brother I'd never had.

"Well, he is younger than me. More Olivia's age."

"So he found a cougar too. Lucky man."

Olivia reached across the table and gave him a gentle slap on the arm. Logan grinned at her, winking as Chloe blew one of her spit bubbles and it broke, splashing across his face. He laughed, wiping his face with his hand. In response, she chortled, and the look on his face was priceless, his jaw dropping at the sound.

"Was that you giggling, Chloe? Did you giggle for Daddy?"

The sight of this tall, well-built, tough guy reduced to baby talk made my heart flutter. Not for Logan, but for the thought that one day that could be Elliot with our baby. *Oh, holy crap.*

"I'll bring him over some time so Olivia can meet him and you can see that he's not a douchebag."

"We'd love that," Olivia said.

"Seriously, that would be great," Logan said. "We'll need to make sure he fits into the family. You are a part of it, after all you have done for Olivia."

"I love Olivia, probably nearly as much as you but in a completely non-sexual, don't-want-to-hump-her-silly kinda way."

Logan grinned, shaking his head and then turned to look at Olivia with that intense gaze that made my stomach flip. I'd always loved the way he looked at her, even before she realised he wanted her as much as she adored him. Now I got that look from Elliot, the warmth that feeling generated was even more real.

Chloe squealed again, breaking the gaze, blowing bubbles at her father.

Daddy's girl.

28

THE HOUSE WAS STILL when I got home, the fading light casting long shadows in the living room. The aroma coming from the kitchen was divine. Elliot had left dinner in the slow cooker for me.

I was well looked after these days. Elliot worked when he could, Ruby was in day-care three days a week and I helped out where I could. At least now he was there all the time for his grandmother, none of this coming and going stuff. Between the two houses, we were making things work.

I drew the curtains and turned the on the lights, taking a deep breath and smiling at my stomach grumbling in response. I patted my belly. "Gonna go get you sorted."

Passing through the kitchen, I walked out to the deck, wondering if they were going to join me for dinner. There was more than enough food, but Elliot was so good at taking care of me, there was equal chance he'd show up afterward and split what was remaining into lunches to be frozen.

The house next door was dark, which was unusual since the sun was going down.

Lost in thought, I jumped as something pressed against my leg. I looked down, smiling at the big, grey, fluffy cat purring around me.

"Hey, fur ball. Whatcha doing?"

I bent, picking up the cat and stroking it while looking at the house for any sign of life. Weird. This time of day the lights would be on and Elliot's grandmother would be fussing around the kitchen, either cooking or watching over Elliot's shoulder.

Placing the cat back on the deck, I cocked my head.

"Have you had any food? I'm going to get something to eat. That smell is driving me crazy."

I walked back inside the kitchen, standing with the door open until the cat followed me in.

I ladled out a plate of the casserole and took a deep breath. The meat and potatoes were about to melt in my mouth, I was so very sure of that. Blowing on it, I laughed as the cat rubbed around my ankles, as mad about the smell as I was.

"Okay. I probably shouldn't, but I'll put some meat on a plate for you. Don't you dare tell anyone."

I spooned a few pieces out on a plate, waving my hand over it to cool it down and looked out the back window again. There were still no lights on next door and the sky was growing darker.

I hope everything's alright?

Fishing my phone out of my pocket, I dialled Elliot. The tinny sound of *The Lion King* theme filled the air. His phone sat on the table vibrating away.

I hung up. My first thought was how sweet it was that he had used that ringtone, a reminder of our first 'date'. My second thought was that his grandmother wasn't home, and Elliot had left without taking his phone. That set the alarm bells ringing in my head. He was always scrolling through Facebook or some other app, and wouldn't go anywhere without it. When he'd been away with no phone coverage, it'd driven him crazy.

For a few moments I just stood there, unsure of my next move. The cat kept rubbing against me, a constant reminder of my commitment to give him food, but I couldn't move. What should I do?

My stomach grumbled, and I shook off the worry, deciding to eat my meal and feed the cat. I bent, placing the plate on the floor. Wisps of steam still drifted off the meat and gravy, but the cat would know what to do.

I took my plate into the living room and sat on the couch. Flicking on the television, I tried my best to keep occupied. It was hard. Maybe there was nothing wrong and my big ol' brain was worrying over nothing. But it was odd.

We'd settled into our taking-it-slowly routine. I felt uneasy about it being broken. That thought made me smile. I'd lived such a haphazard life, but now had domesticity without sharing my house. Not yet anyway.

After eating seconds, I flicked the slow cooker to 'keep warm' and settled back on the couch, my eyes growing heavy as the background sound of the TV went on.

The cat padded across the floor, licking his lips, and jumped up on the couch beside me. He was Elliot's grandmother's cat and had been inside a few times since Elliot had been going back and forward, but never been allowed to sit on the furniture. Tonight, I'd make an exception.

My eyes sprung open as the phone rang. The number wasn't one I recognised, but I pressed the accept key.

"Hello?"

He was barely coherent on the phone, whispering between deep breaths that sounded almost like hiccups.

"Becs, can you come to the hospital? Nan had a stroke."

The words barely got out. This was bad, really bad.

"Of course I can. Which hospital are you at?"

"In the city. Come quick. I need you."

"I'm on my way."

Picking up my keys, I headed toward the door. The cat looked up from the couch with sleepy eyes, and I shook my head. "Sorry, fur ball. You gotta get outside. I'll let you back in when I come home. Whenever that is."

The cat buried his face back in his paws, and I rolled my eyes, walking to the couch to pick him up.

"I promise I'll make it up to you. You can have some more of that steak later. Right now I gotta go and look after Elliot."

He snuggled into me as I made it back to the door, placing him gently on the step.

The alarm on the car beeped as I pressed the button and climbed in, taking a deep breath. I had to focus on getting to this hospital in one piece. And Ruby. *Shit.* After everything that had happened with her mother, this was the last thing she needed to go through. Even if it was just to grab her and get out, I needed to get there. All I wanted was to wrap my arms around both of them and tell them it would be okay.

It would be, wouldn't it?

I gripped the steering wheel, backing down the driveway and onto the street. It wasn't a long drive to the hospital and finding parking would be the most difficult part of the journey, but I had to keep my mind on what I was doing and not be distracted.

As I approached the car park, I lucked out as someone else pulled out of their spot, getting a place nice and close. I looked up at the big building in front of me and realised I had no idea where to go. Elliot hadn't told me, and I hadn't thought to ask. My throat tightened in panic.

You're not an idiot, Rebecca, you just need to ask.

I pulled open the door and walked toward the massive reception desk.

"Hi, I'm looking for ..." My mind went blank at the thought of Elliot's grandmother's name. He had told me once, but I couldn't for the life of me remember.

Oh, for pity's sake.

"Becca, Becca." Ruby's voice came loud and clear from my right, and I turned in time to see her running toward me, her arms extended to hug me. I bent, opening my arms and grabbing hold of her, picking her up as I held her tight.

She frowned. "Nan is sick."

"I know, sweetheart. I'm here to make sure you and your dad are okay."

Elliot arrived seconds later, hugging us both. He shook, and I dropped Ruby to the ground so I could rub his back to reassure him.

"Hey," I whispered.

"I'm glad you're here."

"I'm so sorry," I whispered. "How is she?"

I let go, and he looked at his feet, sighing. "She's alive, but lost all sensation down one side. Mum and Dad are on their way; they'll be here any minute."

"You sounded terrible on the phone."

He gripped my hands in his. "I'm sorry. I'd just gotten to your place and put dinner on. She'd pressed her medical alarm so the ambulance was already on the way. It just all happened so fast."

"Oh, sweetie." I touched my palm to his cheek and he closed his eyes. The thought of him going through this by himself gave my heart an ache. It ached even more to think of what Ruby must have seen, even if she might not have understood it.

"I went to call you but I realised I left my phone at your place. They called Mum and Dad, but I had to get to a phone to call you. I'm sorry it wasn't earlier."

He leaned into my arms again.

"It's okay, Elliot. I'm here now. I fed the cat if it helps. He was hanging around my place."

His shoulders shook as he laughed. "That'll be my fault. He's followed the smell of food."

"Maybe. Everything is okay at home anyway. It was so thoughtful of you to sort out dinner. So, where's your nan now?"

"They're running some tests. I needed a break and to hear your voice."

"Want some fresh air? Maybe a coffee?"

Elliot nodded, and I kissed his cheek, letting him go so we could walk down toward the coffee shop.

"Hey, Ruby. Want to go get a drink and something to eat?"

She nodded, grabbing hold of my hand. We were getting so close, and I loved that she just did that instinctively. My heart warmed at her acceptance.

I linked arms with Elliot, and led them back the way I'd come through the hospital. As we entered the elevator, Elliot slid his arm around my waist. "Thank you for coming when I needed you."

"Isn't that what I'm here for?"

"I know. I just ... after all the time we weren't serious, it's kinda weird to have an actual partner."

"Well, get used to it."

He squeezed me tight, nuzzling my neck. "I love you," he said.

"I love you too."

"At least now you get to meet my parents. And they'll get to meet Ruby too."

My throat tightened as he said it. They had been planning to visit in a couple of weeks and I had looked forward to a relaxing meeting with his folks, not a stress-filled hospital meeting. But it was what it was, and all I could do was be there to support and love him.

"Sure do. Wish it was under better circumstances."

"Me too. But at least it gets it over and done with. They'll love you, Becs. I promise."

We made our way across the foyer to the coffee shop, and I found a table in the corner to sit. "Stay here. I'll get the coffee," I said, rubbing his back as he sat.

"Thanks." He ran his fingers through his hair, clearly frustrated about his situation. This would mean the loss of his grandmother's independence at the very least, and Elliot looked lost.

"Two lattes please," I said to the server. "Can I also get a lemonade and a cheese and bacon muffin?"

She nodded as she put the transaction through the till and I handed over my cash card. As I glanced toward Elliot, I spotted an older man and woman coming toward our table. He stood and embraced the woman.

That must be his mother.

His head drooped as he let go, misery pouring off him and my heart just ached to watch it.

I was so busy watching him I didn't notice the man walking toward me and looked up to find myself looking into eyes identical to Elliot's.

"Oh. Hi. You must be Elliot's father," I said.

He nodded. "Call me Lucas. You must be the famous Rebecca."

My cheeks burned as I nodded. So Elliot had told his parents all about me.

"It's good to meet you. I'm so glad Elliot has you. He's so close to his grandmother; it's a tough time for him."

"Whatever he needs." His eyes were so kind. I could see where Elliot got it.

I looked back at the counter. Ruby's muffin and drink were ready, and I grabbed them, smiling at the server and nodding and Lucas.

He moved past me to order and I took a deep breath, heading toward the table. Elliot and his mother had sat down and were deep in conversation. Ruby sat further around the table, swinging her legs and looking bored. I looked around, not wanting to interrupt, but he looked up at me and smiled. "Hey babe, come and meet my mum."

I grinned, and sat down between Elliot and Ruby, holding my hand out for Elliot's mum to shake. "Hi. I'm Rebecca."

She had such a sweet smile.. "Hi. I'm Carmen. I'm sorry we couldn't meet under better circumstances. Elliot has told us so much about you."

I cocked an eyebrow at him as he grinned back at me.

"We kept telling him to bring you to meet us, but he was so shy about it. I was beginning to think you were a figment of his imagination."

Laughing I shook my head. "Well, I'm very glad to meet you now. I hope Elliot's grandmother will be okay." I said.

Elliot leaned back and put his arm around my shoulder, kissing me on the cheek. "Hey, can Ruby stay with you tonight? I don't know how late everyone is going to be here and I need to know she's okay."

"Of course she can. I'll stay home as long as you need me to."

"YAY!" yelled Ruby.

I ruffled her hair. "Oh, you like that idea, do you?"

She nodded enthusiastically. *Wonder if she wants to stay with me, or just wants to get out of here. She must be so bored.*

"Hello, Ruby," Carmen said, waving from across the table.

"Oh, Mum, sorry. This is Ruby. Ruby, this is my mum and dad. So that would be your grandma and grandpa."

Ruby's eyes widened, and she snuggled into my side.

"She's a bit shy at first, but we're getting there," Elliot said.

"I can see that." Carmen smiled, that same gentle smile that Elliot had, and Ruby lessened her grip on my waist just a little.

"So, Rebecca, I understand you're in finance," Lucas said.

I nodded. "Mostly small business loans and investments."

"Find it interesting?"

I think he was the first person to ever ask me that. "It's not that exciting, but I work for my dad. He's the big numbers guru."

He grinned. "Maybe we'll get to meet him. We're going to be here for at least a few days."

"Sounds good. Maybe we can all have dinner one night." *Awesome. Yeah dinner with my dad and his girlfriend who is one of my best friends.*

"That'd be great. Elliot has raved about you, and I think you've handled the whole situation with Ruby so well. Elliot says she adores you."

"The feeling's mutual." I looked down at Ruby, now snuggled in tighter. She smiled up at me, her fingers digging into my side.

"You okay?" I whispered, bending down so no one could see her.

"I want to go home," she whispered back.

I nodded. "Not much longer, okay?"

She smiled, taking another bite of her muffin. We could hang out for the night; there was plenty of room at my place. Maybe tomorrow I could call someone to fill the pool. I'd drained it when it became just me in the house; I got all my exercise at the gym. But Ruby might get some use out of it and we could all use it for cooling off in the upcoming summer.

Before I knew it, Ruby's muffin had disappeared and she'd drained her drink.

"Let's go through and see what the doctors say," Lucas said.

Ruby and I trailed along behind the group. I didn't want to disappear too soon, and I really wanted to know what was happening with Elliot's grandmother. We'd lived next to one another for a few years before Elliot had appeared on the scene. Besides, I had to get the car seat out of Elliot's car and into my own. Maybe I should look into getting a second one.

As we drew close, I grabbed Elliot's hand. "I'll stay out here with Ruby. She doesn't need to be in there."

He nodded. "I agree."

"I'm going to need to get the seat out of your car too."

Elliot pecked me on the lips. "I won't be long."

I took a seat in the waiting room, patting the chair beside me. "Come on. Elliot won't be long and then we'll get out of here."

Ruby looked at me from under those long eyelashes of hers. "Can we get ice cream?"

"I'm teaching you my bad habits, aren't I?" I sighed. "Tell you what, there's yummy casserole at home, but we can stop on the way and get a tub of ice cream for afterward. You can choose the flavour. Deal?"

She grinned, nodding enthusiastically.

As the minutes ticked by, I handed her my phone to play with. She was smart; she'd have Angry Birds sorted in a short amount of time.

"What's this?" she asked.

I looked over her shoulder and laughed. The Facebook app was open and she'd carefully typed her name. It was the only word she knew the letters for, and following that was a whole bunch of gibberish letters she'd just posted.

"Now you've said hello to all my friends." It was okay; they'd all think I was drunk. And possibly that I'd gone home with a girl named Ruby. Stranger things had happened to me.

I tapped my foot without thinking about it, impatient to get Ruby home, frustrated not to know what was going on. What Elliot must be going through, I didn't know. Maybe Ruby being with me meant he could spend the whole night at mine and that I could keep an eye on him.

"Can we go?" Ruby asked, tugging at my hand.

"Just a little bit longer, sweetie. We'll wait until Elliot comes back out and lets us know what's going on, and then we'll get out of here. Are you hungry?"

She nodded. That muffin had barely touched the edges as she'd wolfed it down. It was time to get out of here and get her some real food and sleep.

"Okay, I'll stick my head in the door and grab Elliot."

I stood, moving toward the door. It opened, and Elliot appeared, looking shaken, his face speaking volumes. His eyes were sad, as if he was about to cry, his lips in a straight line, as if he didn't want to let whatever was going on out.

"Hey." I wrapped my arms around him, giving him a hug.

"She's going into a home, Becs. All movement down one side is gone. She needs rehab, and someone to look after her. I won't be enough."

"Oh, babe. I'm so sorry."

He shook his head. "I came here to look after her and I haven't done that great a job. I disappear for weeks on end, and come back with someone else to look after."

I glanced back at Ruby. She sat looking up and down the corridor, swinging her feet back and forward. "Elliot, nothing you did made things worse for your nan. It would have happened regardless."

He shrugged.

I sighed. "I've got to get Ruby home. She's hungry."

He nodded. "I really need to grow up, Becs. I can't just say the words; I have to do it."

I squeezed his hand in mine. "Do what you need to do. You know whatever happens I'll support you."

He looked at me, his brows knitted together in concern. "I don't want you to support me. I want to find a real job, earn decent money. Be able to support my family."

I laughed, and wrapped my arms around his neck. "I wasn't necessarily talking about financial support. I mean I'm behind you. Whatever you decide to do. You're smarter than you give yourself credit for. I'm pretty sure you can do anything."

He hugged me tight. "Love you."

"I love you too," I said.

"Hey, Ruby," Elliot said.

She looked up, beaming a brilliant smile at him. He let go of me, kneeling in front of her.

"Rebecca's going to take you to her place now and get you some dinner. I'm coming too, but later. I'll see you in the morning if I don't see you before you go to sleep."

Ruby nodded, wrapping her arms around his neck.

"I'm sorry you had to sit and wait for so long. Nan's really sick, but she's okay. Love you."

"I love you too, Daddy," she said.

Tears welled up in his eyes. This was something new; she hadn't called him that before, and as far as I knew she hadn't told him she loved him either.

He kissed her, rubbing his stubble against her cheek and she giggled, pushing him away.

"Have a good sleep. I'll come and give you a kiss before I go to sleep."

He stood, grabbing her by the hand and pulling her onto her feet. "Come on, let's go get your seat out of the car and then you can go home."

"We're having ice cream," she announced proudly.

He smiled, and it was like the clouds breaking apart. It wasn't forced; she had done that for him.

"Sounds awesome. Save some for me?"

Ruby shook her head. "I don't think there will be any left."

"We're buying a two-litre tub. There had better be," I muttered between my teeth.

Elliot grabbed my hand too, kissing it with a grin. He led us out to the car park, where his car wasn't too far from my own, and pulled the seat out from the back. "Here, I'll help you put it in. It's a bit tricky."

"I was thinking I might go and get another one tomorrow. You know, it'd be handy instead of moving it back and forward."

"That is the best idea I've heard all day." He sounded so tired. This whole thing must be so mentally exhausting. "Mum and Dad are going to stay at Nan's place. I'll come to yours when we come home. I just want to curl up in bed with you."

"I'll be waiting," I said.

He leaned in the back door of my car, buckling the seat in and helping Ruby into her harness. "Be good for Rebecca."

She nodded, looking at him solemnly, as if he'd entrusted her with the most important job on the planet.

"You're a good girl, Ruby." Elliot stood up, facing me. "So are you."

"Not all the time." I smiled innocently.

"That's what I love about you," he replied.

WE INDULGED in cartoons and ice cream after a big dinner for Ruby and a third helping for me. We sat in front of the television and found a cartoon channel where a cat was chasing a mouse. Ruby lasted about five minutes before crashing.

I tucked her into the spare bed, kissing her good night and

brought in the lamp from my bedside cabinet. The last thing I wanted was a frightened little girl waking up and not knowing where she was. As the soft lamp light filled the room, I sat for a moment and watched her sleep. So calm and peaceful.

When I got to my room I stripped off and fell into bed, wondering how long Elliot was going to be. He arrived a short time later, quietly undressing and slipping into bed beside me, wrapping those big, strong arms around me and holding me tight.

"Love you," he whispered.

"I love you too. How is everything?"

"Mum and Dad are next door. They'll stay a few days, or however long it takes to arrange for them to move her into a home. They're taking her back with them rather than having her up here by herself. I mean, she has me, but Dad wants her near him. I'll stay in the house while they work out what to do, but they'll be putting it on the market at some point."

I sighed. "It all just seems so final."

"They've had this all planned out since Poppa died." He kissed me tenderly, lifting his hand to my face to stroke my cheek with his thumb. "So while we're taking things slowly, Ruby and I can stay next door and come over to visit. If that's what you want."

"I guess you have to look after the house."

He nodded. "I mean, we'll spend more nights over here obviously, because I don't have anyone to stay with Ruby, but ..."

I shrugged. "We'll make it work."

29

IN THE MORNING, I was the one cooking bacon. I made eggs too. Elliot and Ruby needed taking care of now more than ever, and anything I could do for them I would.

Ruby woke first, climbing up onto a chair at the dining table and grinning up at me. She wore the same clothes she had the day before, and her hair hung in scruffy plaits.

"Have a good sleep?" I asked.

She nodded. "I'm hungry. I want something to eat."

I grinned. "Can you smell what I'm cooking?"

"Bacon?" she asked.

"Yes, and eggs. Do you like eggs?"

She kept nodding, and I caught her gaze, sharing a loving look with her. I'd do anything for this kid.

"Becca, where's Daddy?"

I picked up a fork, lifting a slice of bacon onto a plate with a fried egg already waiting. Grabbing a knife, I made my way over to the table and sliced up the bacon before giving her the fork.

"He's asleep, honey."

"Can we wake him up?"

I laughed, shaking my head. "I wanted both of you to get lots of sleep. You need it after yesterday. I'm going to stay home with you instead of going to work today."

A grin lit up her face, and she clapped her hands excitedly.

"I've got a man coming to fill the pool, too. When the weather is warmer, we can go swimming."

"You're filling the pool?" Elliot stood in the doorway, wearing just his T-shirt and underpants, scratching his head.

"Morning, Sleeping Beauty," I said. "And yes, I was trying to decide whether to get rid of it and develop the garden, but with you two around I thought it'd be nice for the summer."

"Can't you just put the hose in it and turn it on?"

I laughed. "Maybe, if I want it to take till the end of summer to fill."

I turned back to the benchtop, plating more bacon and eggs for Elliot and I, and returned to the table where he now sat.

Ruby had egg yolk all around her mouth and down her chin, and I shook my head as she grinned up at me. I guess it was a little too runny.

"I'll get you a paper towel, and next time I'll cook your eggs longer."

I placed the food in front of Elliot and he shovelled the eggs in, barely stopping for breath. Grabbing the paper towels from the edge of the bench, I pulled one off and wiped Ruby's mouth with it. "There you go. All clean again."

"Are you hungry, Daddy?" Ruby asked, giggling at Elliot's obvious appetite.

"Starving," he mumbled, his mouth full of food.

"There's plenty of food," I said.

"I remember a time when you had no food in this place."

I grinned. "Now I have you two to look after. Some of the time, anyway."

While they ate, I picked up the phone, dialling Dad's mobile.

"Rebecca," he said warmly.

"Hey Dad. I was wondering if you wanted to come over for dinner tonight. Elliot's parents are here for a little while, and I thought you could meet them."

Dad had never been one to organise anything at the last minute; his life was so organised because of his work, but he had said he was letting go a little.

"That sounds wonderful, Rebecca. I'll call Nicola to let her know and we'll come over. What time?"

"Around five-thirty? Dinner around six. Nothing too fancy, just a good family meal." My heart warmed to say the words.

"The first of many I hope. We'll see you then. Love you, sweetheart."

"Love you too." As I put the phone down, I looked up to see Elliot smiling at me. "Your dad coming over?"

"I thought that your parents might like to have dinner here tonight after a day at the hospital and now seems as good a time as any to get everyone together."

Elliot put down his knife and fork and stood, pushing his chair out and walking over to me. He nuzzled my cheek, planting a big, sloppy kiss on me, to Ruby's delight. She giggled and clapped.

"That's a fantastic idea. I'm sure Mum and Dad will really appreciate it. They've got a lot to sort out and this'll be a great way for them to relax."

I leaned against him. "I hope so. I'm going to call my mum next and see if she can make it."

He reached for my hand, squeezing it tight. His lips drew into a line, as he grew serious. "I hope she can. It'll be good to meet her too. Now, I'm in the shower and off next door. Ruby, we'll go and get you a change of clothes, okay?"

There were odd things he'd left behind. Enough to form a small collection of clothing. All Ruby's things were next door. We'd have to change that.

I watched him leave the room. A faint sniff came from the table, and I looked over to see Ruby, her lips downturned in a frown.

"What's wrong?" I asked.

"I want to stay with you."

Taking the handful of steps to the table, I squatted beside her. "You can stay with me today. Elliot's going to the hospital, and you'll be here with me. You just have to go and get changed into some fresh clothes. These ones are getting stinky."

Her lips quivered as the frown disappeared.

"You can draw and maybe when you come back over Elliot can bring some of your toys."

She liked that, as the small smile on her face grew bigger and bigger and she nodded.

"Do you want do that?"

"Yes."

I reached for her, wrapping my arms tight around this amazing child who had been through so much. I was good for her. More than ever I could see that. She was pretty good for me too.

MUM HAD AGREED to come over at four-thirty. I made her time earlier than Dad's to give her a chance to be late. She usually was. Besides, she had Elliot and Ruby to meet for the first time, and a little time together before everyone else arrived would be nice.

I looked up at the clock. 5.02 pm. Mum was a little more than half an hour late. Maybe I shouldn't read so much into that, but I couldn't help it. She was good at not being where she was supposed to be at the right time.

Taking a deep breath, I dialled her number, closing my eyes as no one answered. What if she was on her way and I was worried over nothing? That could happen, right?

"She's not there," I muttered, my finger hovering over the button to disconnect the call.

"Hello?" she answered, muffled, subdued, the familiar tone that told me she'd just woken up.

"Mum, it's Rebecca."

"Sweetheart. It's nice to hear your voice."

"Are you coming?" I asked.

The silence spoke volumes. She wasn't going anywhere. "I'm sorry, Rebecca. I really want to, but I'm so tired." Now she slurred the words and I closed my eyes, tears building. Mum had let me down again.

"Okay." That was all I could manage. There was no point in arguing and the last thing I wanted was for her to get in the car and drive in the state she was in. She was more likely to fall asleep.

"I'll see you soon, love."

I'd bet anything she'd be back in her chair in front of the television, snoring soon enough.

"Okay."

As I hung up the phone, warm, strong arms enveloped me. Elliot nuzzled my neck. "So, are you really okay?"

"Mum's not coming."

"I'm sorry, babe," he whispered, taking a deep breath into my hair. If anything, this whole thing had shown me just how supportive we were of each other. He'd get me through this, as I'd get him through his grandmother's illness.

"I'll be fine. I should be used to it by now." I sighed, and he let go, turning me around to face him.

"Love you." His smile was so warm, so loving. And all for me.

"I love you too."

Little hands gripped my thigh, and I looked down to see Ruby grinning up at me. I ruffled her hair. "Hey, Ruby monster. Want to make a cake for dessert?"

She nodded.

"I'll tell you what. You can help me crack the eggs."

Her eyes widened, and she let go of my leg, jumping up and down, clapping excitedly. Seeing her like that almost made up for the disappointment of my mother letting me down again.

"Did you double check if your dad is coming?" Elliot asked.

"I don't even need to. If he says he'll be here, he'll be here. Nicola too. She wouldn't stand me up."

He rubbed my back, kissing me on the nose.

I held my hand out to Ruby, and she gripped my fingers, with that big smile on her face. My heart warmed as we shared a loving look. How quickly I'd fallen for her, just as hard as I'd fallen for her father.

"Come on, Becca," she said, and I nodded, Elliot squeezing my other hand.

"Let's get this cake done," I said.

LUCAS AND CARMEN arrived a few minutes later. Both of them looked exhausted, Carmen with purple smudges under her eyes, and the light that had been in Lucas's eyes the night before had faded. It had been a long day for them.

Carmen hugged me as she came in the door. I think she needed the contact; she slouched as I put my arms around her.

"Thank you for inviting us for dinner, Rebecca." She sounded as tired as she looked. At least she didn't have to worry about making food. It was almost all done.

"You're welcome. Dinner's nearly done. My father and his girl-friend will be joining us too."

Lucas smiled. "Good. It'll be nice to meet him."

I led them into the living room, showing them to the couch. "Can I get you anything to drink?"

"I'd kill for a coffee." Carmen smiled.

"That sounds great," Lucas said.

"I'll sort that out. How do you take it?"

"We both have black, one sugar." Carmen leaned back and closed her eyes for a moment. They'd both sleep well tonight.

I looked up at the tap on the door. "I'll just get that. It'll be Dad."

I skipped to the door, turning and pulling at the handle.

Dad stood on the doorstep, Nicola beside him. She pushed past to hug me, and he just stood there, smiling as she squeezed me tight.

"It's good to see you, love," he said.

Nicola released me enough that I could breathe, and spoke. "I'm really glad you're here."

I smiled at Nicola. "Glad you're both here."

"Is your mother coming?" I should have known he'd ask that.

"She ... umm ... she couldn't make it."

Dad's face said it all—the slight flare of the nostrils, the warmth in his eyes disappearing. This was par for the course with Mum and he knew it, but it didn't make him any less irritated over it.

"Come in," I said, and he moved closer, kissing my cheek. "At least you two are here. My father and stepmother."

Out of the corner of my eye, I saw the colour drain from Nicola's face, as if she hadn't thought of that.

"Trouble," Dad said, grinning at me, and taking my hand in his to squeeze."

"Always. Now come in and meet Elliot's parents."

Dad made his way past Nicola and I, and she squeezed me again before we went back into the living room, arm in arm.

"Dad, this is Lucas and Carmen, Elliot's mum and dad."

He was used to dealing with people and he smiled with all the warmth he had. Not only were they my boyfriend's parents, they were hurting with all that they had endured in the past twenty-four hours. Dad would help put them at ease.

"Hi, I'm Neil. This is Nicola."

Carmen waved at Nicola as Lucas stood and shook Dad's hand. Nicola squeezed my fingers before making her way to the couch.

"Do you two want a drink?" I asked.

"Sounds great," Dad said. "A beer if you have one, and Nicola?"

"Just a juice if you've got some." She smiled brightly, and I couldn't help but grin back. I'd never seen her glow so much, appear so healthy. She was loved.

"Sure thing. Elliot is in the kitchen with his little helper. I'll get them out to say hello."

Elliot and Ruby stood by the bench, Ruby on a chair to see what he was doing. Elliot stirred gravy in a glass jug, and I smiled at the concentration on their faces as the gravy thickened.

"Your parents are here," I said. I flicked the kettle on and plucked cups and glasses from the crockery cupboard.

"I'll go and say hello. Gravy's done, the chicken is ready to take out the oven, and the potatoes are cooked. Vegetables are all steamed."

"Brilliant. Ruby, want to set the table with me? I'll just get some drinks ready and then you can help."

She nodded, jumping off the chair, her feet slapping the lino with a loud smack. Instantly, her hand went up over her mouth as she giggled.

I grinned, rolling my eyes at her, which made her giggle even more. That sound was music to my ears. The more time we spent together, the livelier she was.

Grabbing a beer from the fridge, I poured it into a glass. Normally Elliot would just drink out of the bottle, but this was a special occasion. As I poured the juice, I realised this was the first time I'd seen Dad and Nicola out together as a couple. What was going on with them? Were they moving in together? I'd kept my distance to let them settle into whatever it was they had developing. But now I wanted to know.

The water had boiled and I put together the coffees, placing everything on a tray and smiling as I entered the living room. Ruby trailed behind me, and I steadied myself as she clung to my leg. There were a lot of people out there for her to take in.

Dad and Lucas were deep in conversation, and I could hear sporting references popping up. Nicola was talking with Carmen and Elliot, laughing and happy, shining brighter than I think I'd ever seen her. Dad had been good for her, that much was obvious.

This is my family.

30

LOGAN COULDN'T MAKE himself look bigger and more menacing if he tried. It was like watching a father stalk the potential boyfriend of his teenage daughter. He wasn't about to give Elliot an inch. In fact, he was acting more father-like than my actual father had.

All I could do was giggle. It did my heart good to see him act like this. It was well meaning, even if it wasn't necessary. All I was waiting for now was for him to ask Elliot what his intentions were toward me. Not even my Dad had done that.

Logan held out a hand for Elliot to shake, as the two men sized each other up. Two peacocks strutting if ever I saw.

Behind Logan, Olivia had a smirk on her face, shaking her head and no doubt thinking the same thing I was. As I caught her eye, I bit down on my bottom lip, laughing and looking at the floor.

There was a slap as their hands met and finally a grin from Logan as he took in the strength of Elliot's handshake, or something. I could ask him what the hell he was being like that for, I liked being protected and cared for. I guess being his wife's best friend, he was just looking out for me.

"Elliot, it's so good to meet you properly."

Elliot nodded. "Last time we met I was a real dick."

"A jealous man can get a bit crazy. I'm glad you're here now; I was curious about meeting the man who tamed this wild one." Logan nodded toward me.

"I don't know about taming her. I doubt there's anyone who can do that." Elliot looked my way and winked. All I could do was grin like an idiot.

"And this is Ruby," Elliot said. She popped her head around from behind him and Logan waved at her.

"Hi, Ruby," Olivia said. "There are other kids here to play with and lots of toys."

Ruby's eyes lit up and she looked up at me, excitedly. "Can I play?"

"Of course you can, sweetheart," I said, as she slid her hand into mine. "Come on, let's go find those kids."

"Maddy and Andrew are here with Carly, so there's another little girl for her to play with. She's younger, but the three of them already have plenty of fun—one more is just going to make it better." Logan grinned at me as I led Ruby away, and out to the backyard where the other kids were playing.

Maddy and Andrew sat at the table on the deck, smiling at Ruby and I as we made our way out.

Ruby walked slightly behind me, almost disappearing behind my leg before we got outside. Jack, Thomas and Carly all took turns on the slide that had appeared since my last visit. There was squealing, yelling and so much laughter. Slowly, Ruby moved out to stand beside me.

I took a deep breath as Ruby let go of my hand and ran, not even looking back as she joined the others. I shook my head with a smile as she jumped right on in there, introducing herself and lining up to take a turn.

Pulling my phone out, I focused and snapped a photo. She might not be mine, but I was so proud of her.

So much like her father. So friendly and warm.

Something in the back of my head nagged at me. Maybe one day I could have one of my own with Elliot. Give Ruby a little brother or sister to play with. I'd gladly act in a motherly role for her if she needed me, but what about some half-siblings?

"She fits right in." Maddy drew level with me, nodding toward the slide.

"I'm kinda surprised she just jumped in there. She can be quite shy."

Maddy laughed. "Kids seem to just latch onto other kids. I think she'll be fine. It'll be nice for Carly to have another girl around. Chloe's a bit too little to play with yet." She turned and went back to the table where Andrew waited for her with a bottle of beer.

"Becca, look at me!" I looked back at Ruby, at the top of the slide and waving at me with her free hand.

"You be careful," I called.

She laughed, and pushed herself off. It wasn't a big slide, but she had enough time to yell a resounding 'wheeeee' as she slid.

Elliot wrapped his arms around my waist from behind, planting a kiss on my neck. "It's like she's always been here," he said, laughing.

I wriggled free, turning to face him.

"Move in with me," I said.

He smiled. "I thought we were taking it all slowly with Ruby and everything."

"I don't want to. I want you and Ruby to move in. I want us to be a family." All these emotions overwhelmed me and my heart swelled as I looked at him. I was so in love and proud of the pair of them.

"That sounds amazing, but I need to know you're ready for this. I don't know if this is the right place to make this kind of decision."

"I don't care where we are. Wherever I am with you two is home."

Elliot raised his palm to my left cheek, and I closed my eyes as he ran his thumb across my lips. "I've always felt at home with you. Does this mean you're not scared anymore?"

I nodded, opening my eyes to see his face, full of love for me. "I've never been so sure of anything in my whole life."

We stood, arms around each other's waists, watching Ruby. She queued with the other children, sliding over and over again. I leaned my head on Elliot's shoulder.

Everything was perfect.

***

"DID you know Maddy's a musician too? She can play the guitar, but apparently she's insanely good at the violin."

"Is that right?" I was miles away, folding laundry that I'd tried in vain to catch up on since we'd gotten home. I wanted Sunday to spend with Elliot and Ruby, and I didn't want to be distracted.

"Yeah. I thought sometime we could organise a play date for the kids. We can make beautiful music together."

I stopped, turning my head toward him. "You'd better be talking *music* music."

Elliot laughed. "Would I be talking about any other kind? Aside from the fact that I'm crazy in love with you, have you seen Andrew? He's not exactly small. Logan and him would be a pretty formidable team."

I grinned, shaking my head at him.

He leaned over, kissing me softly. "Thank you for today. It was so good for Ruby, and good for me."

"I loved going there with you two."

"Did you mean what you said about us moving in with you?"

I caught my breath. Ruby slept in the spare room tonight; Elliot would be in my bed with me. I didn't want them to be anywhere else.

"There is nothing I want more in this world right now," I said.

This time he kissed me harder, and I dropped whatever I was folding back in the basket to embrace him.

"It's what I want too. I can still keep an eye on the house from here until it's sold, and there'll be no more moving Ruby back and forward."

I nodded, hugging him tight. He planted a kiss on my neck. "Have I told you just how amazing you are?" he asked.

"I don't mind hearing it again," I whispered the words, overcome by him. I don't think I'd been so happy, so fulfilled in my entire life.

"You love me, and you've taken on Ruby without any doubts. At least, that's what it seems like to me. If you've ever had any second thoughts, you've never voiced them," he said.

I let go, holding onto his arms and smiling. His eyes were so full of love, and it would have been so easy to drown in them, and forget to answer.

"I never had any second thoughts. I tried to keep us casual at first because I was so scared of being hurt. But you became everything to me. Ruby was the easiest part of the whole deal. She needed me."

He wiped tears away that had gathered on my cheeks. "We both need you."

"I needed both of you. More than I ever realised. I feel whole now, like it was you and Ruby that were missing. Even when I thought I was happy before, it pales to how amazing this feels."

Elliot wrapped his arms around me again, holding me tight and stroking my hair. He kissed my temple, and I closed my eyes, leaning against him.

"We love you so much, Rebecca. Don't ever forget that. Let's go to bed. I think my lady could do with some loving."

I laughed, nodding and wiping my eyes on his shirt. After all, it was his beautiful words that had made me cry.

31

ELLIOT SAT ON THE COUCH, strumming his guitar and singing softly as I came in the door. The aroma of lamb filled the air, my mouth watering at the scent. Maybe he didn't have to get a job. Maybe he could just look after me for the rest of our lives.

"Dinner smells amazing," I said.

He looked up at me, the biggest grin on his face that just made me smile.

"We're celebrating."

"Celebrating what?"

He leaned the guitar against the couch and stood, moving toward me and wrapping his arms around my waist. "I got a job, babe. It's not the most money in the world, but once I've finished training I'll get a pay increase."

"That's fantastic. I hope it's doing something you enjoy."

"I'll be working with Logan."

My eyebrows inched up. This was an interesting development.

"I went past the garage and saw a sign wanting help. Didn't realise that it was his place from the street."

Shaking my head, I nestled my forehead into his chest. "That's so cool."

"He'll take me on as an apprentice, Becs. Train me up and I can learn the trade. Once I'm qualified I'll get paid more, but for now it's enough. And for the moment, I can work school hours so I can take Ruby to school and pick her up, when she starts."

My heart was swollen with pride, and with love for Logan for taking a chance on Elliot. My man was so determined to do well I just knew he'd be good at anything he set his mind to.

"Just do me a favour?" I asked.

"Anything."

"Don't you dare come home with any tattoos. Logan has enough for both of you."

His laughter echoed in his chest. "Are you anti-tattoo?"

I rubbed his arm. "No. I just like your skin the way it is. So creamy and smooth and unblemished." I lowered my voice. "Pure."

Elliot kissed the top of my head, chuckling into my hair. "You know you're creeping me out right now."

"That was my intention."

He squeezed me tight. "Okay. No tattoos. For a while at least. Anyway, I made your favourite for dinner, and then I picked up a chocolate cheesecake to celebrate."

I looked up at him, grinning. He appeared so content and happier than he had done during the past few days. "I'm glad you're happy," I said.

"Beats sitting around feeling sorry for myself. Nan is being taken care of, Mum and Dad loved you, Ruby and I are settled. Why be miserable? And I get to learn something new and something that interests me."

"Does it really interest you?" I hadn't heard of any great ambition to become a mechanic, and the last thing I wanted was him taking on something he hated.

"I'm good with my hands. I like finding out how things work. I got to the bottom of you after a year or so."

I shook my head with a laugh. "Didn't take long then, did it?"

He kissed me, making my toes tingle and my heart race, as it always did.

"I would have waited forever if I'd had to," he said.

I reached behind me, pulling his hands apart, lowering one to my butt, lifting the other to my breast. "So, umm, how long until dinner? Do you think we have time for—"

"Daddy!" Ruby called out.

Crap. They hadn't been living with me long, and sometimes I'd forget there were three of us.

"No. But after someone's bedtime we might be able to find some time." He waggled his eyebrows, and I laughed as he bent his head and kissed me.

"Love you, Becs," he whispered.

"Love you too. You better go and find out what your daughter wants." I squeezed his butt and gave my own eyebrows a little waggle.

He paused in the doorway, wiggled his hips and looked back over his shoulder, winking.

That man.

———

THE BEDROOM DOOR flew open with a crash, and I sat up, rubbing my eyes. Ruby stood by the bed.

"Becca." Her voice cracked as she spoke. Something had upset her.

"What is it? What's wrong?" I flicked on the bedside lamp.

Her bottom lip wobbled. "I had a bad dream."

"Oh, sweetie."

Relieved I'd thrown on a T-shirt to sleep in, I pulled back the blanket so she could snuggle in beside me. I hugged her close. "You okay?"

She nodded, closing her eyes. Guess she was spending the rest of the night in our bed.

Elliot slung his arm over me in the morning. "Huh?" He sat up, looking past me, and smiled with a nod.

"She had a bad dream."

"I should have told you. She had a few when we were living with Nan. I just let her jump into bed with me for the rest of the night. She went straight back to sleep without any more issues."

Ruby snorted, wriggling beside me. I kissed the top of her head, stroking her hair.

"What do you think the bad dreams are about?" I asked.

"She didn't really tell me. When I stayed with her and her mum she didn't wake up that I know of. Maybe it has something to do with her missing Toni."

Just the mention of Ruby's mother's name brought tears to my eyes, and I clung to Ruby even tighter. I'd had my fair share of nights when I'd climbed in with Dad for the comfort of having him there. I understood the loneliness even when there was someone around to be there for you.

"I'm glad she feels comfortable enough with you to hop in beside you," Elliot whispered.

Closing my eyes, I took a deep breath, smelling the sweet scent of blueberry shampoo from Ruby's hair. I'd spent months working out that I wanted to be serious with Elliot, months deciding to be a grown-up again.

Maybe I needed this little girl as much as she needed me.

I'd move heaven and earth to protect her now. Do whatever it took to take the bad dreams away.

32

LIFE WITH ELLIOT and Ruby took some getting used to. I had always been up and out of bed, off to the office as early as I could get there. I'd worked to get ahead and impress Dad, worked to take my mind off my own issues.

Now things were better than ever with Dad, and the issues I'd had were a thing of the past. I relaxed, taking my time in the mornings and making sure my family was taken care of before going to work.

I wasn't alone.

My family.

They'd been living with me for a few weeks. We all had to adjust, Ruby most of all. What an upside-down world she must have been in. Losing her mother, moving in with Elliot and his nan, and now me. At least now, her home wouldn't change and she would always have us. Of that much I was sure.

I knew what it was like to feel lost. I just wished I could end those bad dreams of hers.

We'd had a week of no bad dreams, though. It was a start, but I was nervous every night when I tucked her in. Every night she slept right through, I felt more settled and hoped she did too. There was nothing I wouldn't do for her.

I woke to Elliot nuzzling my right breast, planting gentle kisses on the skin, rolling his tongue over my ... *Holy crap that hurt.*

"As much as I love you doing that, I need you to stop." I sighed as I ran my fingers through his hair.

He looked up, his eyes sad with confusion and hurt. "Why?"

"They're really sore and tender. I'm sorry, babe, must be coming up to that time of the month."

"Or you're pregnant."

The words hung in the air as we locked gazes. Hell it was always a possibility, but not that likely.

I shook my head. "No. I'll just be pre-menstrual."

"In the time we've been together, you've never pushed me away like that. Have they been that sore before?"

"No, but there's always a first time for everything."

His brows lifted, and he pursed his lips in frustration. "You're ignoring the obvious. We haven't exactly been strict about contraception since I moved in. It only takes one early morning half-asleep quickie."

I shrugged. "I don't feel pregnant."

"Would it be so bad?"

I smiled, stroking his cheek with my palm, pulling him up for a kiss.

"Probably not. It wasn't what I had planned."

His eyebrow snaked up. "What did you have planned?"

"I don't know. A while with just us before we started a family. I know you joke about it, but I do want children. I'm just not in a hurry yet."

Elliot sighed. "You really do my head in sometimes. Not in a hurry, but not worried about occasionally skipping the condom."

"You should know by now I'm that kind of girl. Can't make up my mind about *anything*."

He kissed me softly, stroking my breast but avoiding the nipple. "We have been having a *lot* of sex."

I chuckled. "I don't think it's the quantity that matters."

"Just the quality." Elliot waggled his eyebrows.

"If you need any quality control, I'm your girl," I whispered.

"Oh, I have lots of quality. But practice is the key to maintaining perfection."

I laughed, slapping his arm, but deep down, I wondered if he was right.

"WHAT ARE YOU DOING?" Olivia called as I ran past her and into the bathroom. "Oh."

I opened the box and pulled out the test, staring at the ceiling as I pulled the cap off and stuck it under me. At least in a couple of minutes I would be put out of my misery one way or another.

When the deed was done, I slid the cap on the end and placed it on the vanity. I wiped it clean with some toilet tissue and washed my hands, taking back out to where Olivia stood with two cups of coffee in her hands.

"I'd just made one. Thought you might need it."

She staggered as I hugged her, her arms held out to stop the coffee spilling.

"Rebecca? Are you okay?"

"I don't know."

She examined my face as I let go, as if looking for some sign of what was going on.

"Coffee is a great idea," I said. "I have something I need you to do for me."

She handed me a cup, and I placed the stick in her hand. Her eyes widened at the sight, and she cocked an eyebrow at me as she sat down on the couch. I sat along with her.

"I wiped it off with tissue, it's not got wee all over it."

Olivia laughed, and tilted her head. "I didn't think you'd give it to me dirty. I'm just curious about you giving it to me at all. Isn't this something you want to share with Elliot?"

I lifted my hands, lowering them again palm up. "Yes. He's so insistent that I must be pregnant based on a few things that have happened." I locked gazes with Olivia. "I'm just so scared of giving him false hope. If I turn up with this and it's negative, he'll be gutted. I just didn't want to do this alone."

She reached over and squeezed my hand. "Fine. Want me to look at it? It must be enough time now."

I nodded, my stomach clenching at the thought of finding out the results.

Olivia held up her other hand, and I stared at her, trying to read her expression. She was never very good at hiding the way she felt about things; she had such an honest face.

This time, the look never changed. It was calm, not surprised, shocked, happy, or sad.

"So?"

"There are two little lines."

"What the hell does that mean?" I knew what it meant, I just didn't know if I wanted to believe it.

"You're pregnant."

I exhaled, and burst into tears as Olivia looked at me, open-mouthed in horror. "Oh my God, I'm so sorry. I'm guessing that isn't what you wanted to hear?" she asked. She dropped the plastic stick on the couch, wrapping her arms around my neck as I sobbed into her shoulder.

"We got carried away a couple of times and didn't use a condom. But we both decided not to worry about it. Whatever happened, happened. Having Ruby with us made me want a baby of my own, but I didn't think it'd happen this fast. Elliot was teasing me, and seemed so sure. I was convinced that I knew my own body better than that," I said between sniffs.

"What matters is that you're okay with it. And that you're ready to talk to him if you're not."

She let go and I leaned back to look at her. Her eyes were so sad, and I just knew that big heart of hers would be aching, seeing me like this.

"I'll be fine. It's just a shock. I was so sure. Elliot is never, ever going to let me hear the end of this."

The corners of Olivia's mouth cracked as they slowly curled into a smile. "He loves you, Rebecca. I'm sure he'll be over the moon. And I'm sure he'll support you whatever you want to do."

Tears flowed down my cheeks as I smiled at my amazing friend.

ELLIOT WAS COOKING dinner when I got home, Ruby standing on a dining chair beside him as he chopped vegetables on the kitchen counter to go into the boiling pot on the stove.

"Hey," I said.

"Becca!" Ruby climbed down from the chair and jumped up and down in front of me.

"Hey, baby," I said, bending to hug her. She wrapped her little arms around my neck and I groaned as I picked her up.

"You are so big," I said. "I need to drop you down on the chair."

She giggled, and I moved to the side of the chair, placing her back.

"How was day-care?" I asked.

"Good."

"What did you learn today?"

She leaned on the bench. "We read a story, and I got to go on the slide."

"Did you?"

Ruby nodded.

I moved around the chair, rubbing Elliot's back. "And what did you do today?"

"I spent some hours in the workshop. Helped Logan pull an engine out of a car. I think he's glad to have the extra help."

Kissing his shoulder, I breathed in his smell. I loved this man so much, but I'd have to wait for Ruby to go to bed to tell him the news. Then we could decide when the right time was to tell her. Waiting would be agony.

Elliot picked up the chopping block, sliding the vegetables into the pot. "There, once those are done, we should be good for dinner." He turned, wiping his hands on the towel, before sliding them around my neck.

He kissed me tenderly. "So, how was your day?"

"Oh, bit up and down. I'll tell you all about it later."

Elliot slid his hands down my back, hugging me tighter. "Things not for little ears?" he whispered.

"Something like that."

He kissed me again, squeezing my butt. "Well, dinner's nearly ready and then the munchkin can have a bath and go to bed. There's a bottle of wine in the fridge we can open later."

"Sounds good." I smiled. No point telling him I wasn't going to drink wine just yet; it would only pique his curiosity.

"Hey, can you stay home with her tomorrow? I tried to get her into day-care, but they didn't have a space. My fault for trying to do it at the last minute."

My diary was clear as far as I could remember, and if it wasn't Grace could sort that out. "Of course I can. I know it'll take us a while to get into a new routine."

"Have I told you lately just how amazing you are?" Elliot grazed his lips against my neck and I sighed with the promise of things to come.

"You can tell me like that any time you like."

"Oh, I intend to."

WE'D SKIPPED the wine anyway, and headed to bed. Living together was still a novelty, and part of me wanted to have wild, crazy sex with him—the other part was so tired, I just wanted to curl up and go to sleep.

I yawned as I climbed into bed.

"Am I boring you?"

I laughed, shaking my head. "No, just really tired. I think I need a good night's sleep." I lifted my hand to my neck, rubbing my tired muscles. "Today was a bit crazy. I had to make a huge decision about a client, and things have been so good. It was pretty stressful." That much was true. After my emotional visit to Olivia, I had another company I'd had to decline finance for. It still sucked.

His lips met mine as he kissed me softly, lovingly. I could kiss this man forever, it was so good.

"Then it's my job to relax you. Roll over."

I screwed up my nose. "Why? What do *you* have planned?"

"A back rub. What did you think?"

I shrugged. "I don't know. I've been in all kinds of positions with you. Just wondering what you were up to."

"I'll be up in you if I have my way. But first, a massage for my lady."

Pulling my T-shirt over my head, Elliot unhooked my bra from behind and I flopped on the bed. His warm, strong hands landed on my shoulders, gripping and squeezing while I moaned because it felt so good. It was funny how much tension could build in your body without you even knowing it.

I closed my eyes, Elliot's hands continuing to rub my bare skin. Maybe I could convince him to make this a regular thing. Yet another reason to love him.

I need to tell him about the baby.

My eyelids were so heavy and I began to drift off, fighting it all the way, but I was so comfortable and relaxed and groaned as Elliot rolled me onto my back.

"What are you doing?" I asked, with another yawn.

"That was part one."

I laughed, so tired but still needing his hands on me. I'd never loved so much, never wanted so much to be so close to someone as him.

He reached for the waistband of my skirt, pulling it down along with my panties.

And then for a most glorious part two, he went down on me, making me gasp as I struggled to catch a breath. I was still so warm and relaxed, my eyelids grew heavy again. He was so good at what he was doing, his hands gripping my thighs as I closed my eyes, breathing deeply, feeling myself drifting off.

So tired.

Going.

Going.

Gone.

33

"BECCA."

I rolled over, opening my eyes to see Ruby in the spot where her father slept. The bed was still warm from him; he couldn't have been out of it long.

"Hey," I croaked, still half-asleep.

"Daddy's gone to work."

I reached over, pulling the sheet tight to me and stroking her hair. "I guessed that. Is his side of the bed snuggly?"

She nodded, grinning.

Somewhere in the distance, I could smell bacon. It made me smile how Elliot still maintained that tradition. Only the smell wasn't as nice as it used to be. In fact ...

Oh crap.

I grabbed the mink blanket that sat on a chair beside the bed and rolled out from under the sheet, stumbling to the bathroom. Ruby watched as I lost the limited contents of my stomach in the toilet.

I guess this is what morning sickness is all about.

"Becca. Are you sick?" She patted me on the back, which was

irritating, I hated being touched when I felt ill. But at the same time, it was soothing that she cared about me.

"Just a little upset tummy. Are you hungry? Want some breakfast?"

She nodded, her eyebrows dipping as she frowned.

"I'll be fine. Let's see what's in the kitchen to eat." I stood, twisting the tap in the vanity basin, and splashed water on my face. Grabbing a towel from the rail, I dried it and looked at myself. My skin was pale, with barely any colour in my cheeks at all. Probably caused by my still aching stomach. And yet I was ravenous.

"Why don't you go and turn some cartoons on while I get dressed."

Ruby nodded, skipping away. Returning to the bedroom, I couldn't help but smile at the memory of the night before and how I'd have to make it up to Elliot for falling asleep.

The tiredness had been overwhelming. *Yay for pregnancy hormones.*

Making my way out to the kitchen, Ruby joined me. In the fridge, encased in plastic wrap were two bacon sandwiches. I grinned, taking one out for Ruby. "Want this?"

She nodded and I unwrapped it, threw it in the microwave for a few seconds to take the chill off, and placed it on a plate, putting it on the table in front of her.

"I'll get you a juice. I might just have some toast."

Dry toast—the breakfast of champions, or something like that. It lined my stomach, but the ache still sat there. I'd just have to fight my way through it.

My mobile sat on the kitchen counter, and I picked it up, smiling at the text message that was waiting for me.

> Can't believe you fell asleep like that. Must have been relaxing.

There was a huge smiley face emoticon after the words.

It was. I didn't know I was so tired. I'm
sorry. Promise I'll make it up to you.

I sent the message back and dialled work.

"You're not coming in?" Grace didn't even say hello. Next time I'd have to work out how to suppress my number so it didn't pop up on her caller ID.

"No, I'm with Ruby. I think I'll just take the day off. Call me if anything urgent pops up, but I'm going to spend the day with her."

The end of the conversation was as abrupt as the start, and I rolled my eyes. At least she was nice to customers.

My phone buzzed.

I'm counting on it. Love you. Have a good
day with Ruby.

There were boxes in Ruby's room that we needed to unpack. Today would be a good day for that.

TOYS WERE SCATTERED ALL over the living room. I think Ruby had brought out every single thing she had to show me and I hadn't made her put it all back.

I'll sort it out later. She's having fun now. It was too hot for me to care, all the doors and windows were open and it was still stupidly hot. I just sat watching her.

Now she sat on the floor, playing with two dolls. They were having an animated conversation about the new house they were living in, and I couldn't help but smile at her imagination running wild.

"Hey, Ruby. Want to go for a swim?"

She frowned. "I don't have any togs."

"It's just us girls. You don't need togs."

Her little lips quivered as she frowned. Clearly this was something that bothered her.

"Tell you what. How about we go and buy some togs and then we'll come back and go for a swim before lunch?"

She lit up, beaming as she threw herself at my leg. "Really?"

I laughed. "Sure. We'll need to get you some for school anyway, so let's go find something now."

All the way to the mall, she sang the alphabet, bouncing in her seat. I sang along with her, loving how close we were growing. She still had her moments from time to time when she cried for her mother, but I'd hold her tight and rock her until she stopped crying or fell asleep.

I loved her, just as I loved her dad. My heart was finally fulfilled, as if the two of them were what I'd been waiting for.

The drive was short, and as soon as we walked in the door of the store, she headed straight for what she wanted. I sighed, shaking my head as I looked on.

"Fine. If those are the ones we want, we'll get them. Just don't blame me when your father doesn't like them."

Ruby giggled, grinning up at me with that big Elliot-like smile. She was so much like him. "I want these ones."

"Okay. Is there anything else we need while we're here? Let's take a look."

She held my hand all the way around the store as we picked her up a new school bag and lunch box. It wasn't long until she would start, and even I was excited to buy them. Ruby was growing up.

We had to stop at the Thomas ride so she could play for a few minutes before heading home and I stood, my hand on Thomas's stack as she laughed and pressed the buttons, her bag and clothing in my hand.

Smiling at her excitement and waiting for the ride to stop, I looked around the food court. Nearby, Alexander sat, having lunch with another lawyer I recognised from his firm. He looked at me with one eyebrow raised, and for the first time since our break up, he had no effect on me whatsoever. In the past, no matter how much I'd thought I was over him, seeing him stirred something in me, even if it was just a residual bit of resentment. This time, nothing.

That realisation made me smile even more, and I cocked my head as I looked back at Ruby. She pouted as her ride finished.

"Want to go home for that swim?"

She nodded and I took my hand off Thomas and held it out to her. Ruby grinned, grabbing hold of my hand and leaping from the ride, landing beside me.

"That was a big jump."

"I went wheeeeee." She giggled again, clapping her hand across her mouth, thinking she'd made the funniest joke.

"Yes you did." I grinned, squeezing her hand tight.

She tightened her grip in response, and I led her back out of the mall and to the car without looking back over my shoulder. My life was better than perfect right now. Nothing was going to get me down.

WE'D PLAYED in the pool for an hour before having sandwiches for lunch, and Ruby lay on the floor, still wearing the togs which she refused to remove, drawing pictures for me.

"Becca, look."

Ruby held up her latest work of art. This time there were four people in the picture.

"Who's that?" I asked.

"Me, Mummy, Daddy and you."

My head swum as tears threatened to overwhelm me. My heart belonged to both Elliot and Ruby now, and this showed me just how much Ruby loved us all.

"It's beautiful, sweetheart."

"Can we put it on the fridge?" She had a grin so big and cheesy on her face, showing off all her tiny white teeth, and I laughed.

"Of course we can. We can show your dad when he gets home."

She nodded slowly, crossing her eyes as she did it.

"I love you, Ruby."

"Love you too, Becca."

I scooped her up and into my arms, hugging her tight. "I'm so glad you came to live with me."

"Ahem."

Elliot stood in the doorway, one eyebrow raised at the sight of us.

"Daddy!" Ruby wriggled to be free, running and flinging herself into his arms. He lifted her up, swinging her around.

"Look at you, fancy pants. Have you been swimming?"

She nodded. "Becca got me some togs."

"I can see that. *Frozen* togs?" He shifted his gaze to me, his eyebrow still raised.

I shrugged. "I let her pick what she wanted. The sun was so nice this morning; it was a good day for a swim."

"But *Frozen*? You know what kids are like, Becs. It starts with one thing and next thing it'll be *Frozen* lunch boxes and school bags and—"

"Daddy! Becca got me a new bag. For when I go to school."

I bit down on my bottom lip to suppress the laughter just begging to come out. Elliot smiled at his daughter. "Did she, sweetie?"

"It's got a snowman on it."

"Don't tell me ..."

"It's Olaf," she said, giggling and pressing her nose to his.

"Rebecca," Elliot growled. Ruby laughed louder and reached out for me, pulling me into a kind of awkward three-way hug.

Elliot sighed. "I guess I can forgive you. Whatever monster you create will be your problem."

"It's a deal." I winked at Ruby. "Right, Ruby monster?"

She nodded, with the biggest grin I'd ever seen on her face. This was what made my heart sing—the loving family we'd created for her. She still talked about her mother, and drew pictures of her. I'd encouraged her to do it. My mother was very much alive, but there was that distance that I just couldn't close.

Ruby still felt that closeness to her mum through her drawings.

Maybe I'd try that too.

———

ELLIOT and I stood in the doorway to Ruby's room, watching her sleep. Snowflakes danced around the walls and a soft blue light covered the entire room.

"I can't believe you bought her the duvet and the nightlight too," he said, wrapping his arms around my waist from behind, nuzzling my neck.

"They made her happy."

"Rebecca, you can't do everything to make her happy. The last thing I want is for her to think she can get everything she wants."

I unclasped his hands, turning around. "Are you telling me off?"

"How can I when she's so happy?"

Wrapping my arms around his neck, I snuggled into his chest.

"I love her, Elliot. Just as much as I love you."

"She loves you too. Very much."

"I think she'll make a great big sister."

I raised my face to see his reaction. His eyebrows were arched as he gazed at me. "I'm sure she will." He broke the silence, and my heart beat faster as he just kept on looking at me, as if he was waiting for something more.

"We'll find out soon." I pursed my lips, cocking my head.

His lips spread into a grin, his dimples twitching.

"So I was right?" he asked.

I nodded, squeezing him tight. "You were right."

Anything else I might have wanted to say was lost as his mouth met mine.

A celebratory kiss.

34

ONE PREGNANCY LATER ...

"WHAT DO you think of the name Nala?" Elliot asked, stroking the baby's face.

"What?"

"From *The Lion King*. You know, that's what Simba's mate was called."

My heart was touched by him remembering that fact, but I wasn't so sure about the name. "I feel like I should be telling you not to be so stupid, but that is so sweet. And no."

Elliot grinned, and I pressed my finger to the dimple on his right cheek. "I hope she gets those."

"Gets what?"

"Those damn dimples."

He waggled his eyebrows. "Do they do something for you, Ms Wallace?"

"Ordinarily yes. Right after I've given birth? No. Apart from wanting our child to inherit them."

Elliot leaned over and kissed me. He'd been at hospital with me for the night, sleeping in the chair beside the bed after I'd given birth just before midnight. Once I got the all clear from the doctor, I was out of this place. I couldn't get home fast enough with my family.

"I'll go and get Ruby while you're waiting. She'll be excited about meeting her little sister and driving Olivia's boys crazy right about now."

I laughed. That'd be right.

He kissed me again. "I just want to get you both home with us."

"I want that too. I want to sleep in my own bed. One night in this place is enough to drive me bonkers."

"Can't have that."

He handed me the baby, grinning as he left. This was the most amazing feeling in the world. In my arms was the bond we'd always share.

I clucked at her as she looked at me with big, blue eyes, taking in as much as she could.

"Hello, little baby. Your big sister will be so excited to see you. Yes she will."

Thoughts of being home gave me pangs, although that could have also been twinges of afterbirth pain. This little one would be happy in the home Elliot, Ruby and I had made together, full of love and laughter. At one time I'd thought that would never be a thing for me.

I picked up my phone and flicked through Facebook. Elliot had made a birth announcement for us and right at the top of his wall was a picture of the baby and I. I hadn't even realised he'd taken a photo, I'd been so engrossed in our daughter. There were so many messages of support, of love.

Dialling my father, I held back the tears when he answered. We'd sent him a text and a picture at stupid o'clock, and it felt so good to hear his voice.

"Hey, baby girl."

"I just wanted to make sure you'd seen the picture."

"I did. She's beautiful, Rebecca. So much like you were."

Tears welled in my eyes, and I rocked my daughter in my arms, wishing like anything my father was with me. Wishing like anything my mother could be here. I was almost afraid to call her too—she'd probably be hungover and missed the messages I'd sent. At least I'd be home soon and Dad would visit us there.

"I can't wait to see her. My granddaughter. Has Ruby seen her yet?"

I sniffed. "Elliot has just gone to get her. She stayed with a friend overnight."

"Give both my girls a big hug. We'll let you get settled in at home before we visit. Nicola is champing at the bit to catch up with you."

"Congrats, Rebecca." I heard her in the background. They'd been living together for months, but I was still adjusting to it. Their happiness came first, and they were blissfully in love. Her parents were even okay about it after the initial shock. I think baby Noah had taken care of that.

"I will, and please say hello to Nicola. I'll tell her all about it when you come over."

"Have you spoken to your mother?"

I gulped. The baby wriggled in my arms as if reminding me she was there. Her eyes were closed, and she distracted me for a moment. I wondered if she was dreaming and if so, what she was dreaming about.

"I ... umm ... not yet. She's next."

"She's trying. Really hard."

Tears rolled down my cheeks. I wanted to be closer to Mum, feel the same way I did about Dad, but it had always been so difficult to get near her before she pushed me away.

"Okay."

"Don't cry, sweet pea. I love you so very much and I'm so happy for you and Elliot. We'll see you soon."

"Okay. Bye, Dad," I whispered.

Hanging up the phone, I hugged my baby tight, planting kisses all over her face. "You will never have to worry about anything like that, I swear. I love you."

I sniffed again, wiping the tears from my face. Dumb hormones.

I couldn't face calling Mum yet—maybe when I got home. Dad said she was trying, but I wasn't sure I could handle it if she was hungover and not really listening, or still drunk from the night before.

The baby capsule sat in the corner on a chair. We'd brought it in with us the night before, and I climbed off the bed now, and picked it up with my free hand. Placing it on the bed, I put the baby in her little crib beside me and fussed with the harness, getting it ready to put her in it and take her home for the first time.

At home, we had her nursery ready. She would sleep in our room alongside our bed for the first few weeks at least, but Ruby and I had decorated the baby's room together. Sure, it had its share of Disney princesses, but it was a project we had loved doing together. I couldn't wait for Ruby to see her little sister.

I turned at the sound of a tap on the door, and the doctor entered.

Last night, I'd felt as if I'd been on display to half the hospital. This morning, I had no problems answering questions that might have otherwise made me blush. But we got the all clear to go and that was all that mattered.

My phone buzzed, and I smiled as I picked it up.

> I've just parked. If you're good to go, get our daughter ready. I want to take you two home.

Sweet, sentimental Elliot. What a big softy. I rolled my eyes, but smiled to myself. I couldn't wait to get home either.

I scooped the baby up and into my arms, lifting her gently into the capsule. She snuffled and looked around, as far as her eyes could see, anyway. My beautiful girl.

The door opened, and Ruby came running in with her father right behind her. She hugged me around the leg, and smiled up at me, jumping up and down.

"We're going home?" Elliot asked, nodding at the capsule.

"We sure are. I can't wait to get out of here." I ruffled Ruby's hair. She held up her arms for a cuddle. "Sorry, sweetie. Not for a couple of days. I'm still a bit sore and tired from the baby being born."

Ruby bounced up and down. "I want to see the baby."

"Come on." I nodded. "Get Dad to help you up on the bed and you can see her."

Elliot lifted her up to sit on the bed and she gasped as she looked into the capsule. "She's so little."

I looked up at Elliot in time to catch the wistful look in his eyes. He'd never had that time with Ruby when she was so new.

"I bet you that your mum snuggled you up like this when you were a baby, too. I think she looks a lot like you, don't you?" I ran my fingers through Ruby's hair, playing with the crooked plait Elliot had put in it.

"She has no hair." Ruby sounded flat, disappointed.

"She will soon. Wonder if it'll be dark like mine, or light like you and Daddy."

Pouting, she turned back toward me. "I hope she's like me."

I opened my arms and she leaned over for a hug. I loved this little girl with all my heart, and in my crazy, emotional state, the tears rolled down my cheeks.

Ruby looked up at me. "Becca? Why are you crying?"

I wiped the tears with my free hand. "I'm just so happy. I have you and Daddy and the baby. We need to work out what to call the baby, Ruby. What do you think?"

She smiled at me. "That's easy. Olaf." Her hand covered her mouth as she giggled, and I shook my head with a smile.

"That's from *Frozen*, right? God damn it, Rebecca. This is your fault." Elliot sounded bemused rather than annoyed.

"Ruby?" I leaned my head on my shoulder, looking at her.

"Anna. She's Anna."

Elliot sighed. "Let me guess. That's from that movie too."

"It is, but it's not a bad suggestion." I turned my head to smile at him, only to see a huge grin on his face.

He ran his fingers through his hair, sighing again. "No, it's not. Damn it."

"That's a naughty word, Daddy," Ruby said, wagging a finger at him. "You said it twice."

He smirked, pulling her off the bed and swinging her around. "Yes it is. I'm naughty."

She giggled again. That still sounded so good, especially when I thought of the shy little girl who had come to see me that first day. I was settled and content, knowing I would be spending the next few months at home with the baby and spending more time with Ruby.

My two little girls.

DAD TURNED up at home in the afternoon with Nicola and Mum. I didn't want to ask how that had happened, but Mum seemed okay, rushing to hug me before even looking at the baby.

"Congratulations, darling. I'm so proud of you," she said.

Nicola grinned. "Hurt like hell, didn't it?"

It was still weird to see my father with a baby in his arms. My little brother, Noah. But Dad seemed content.

I nodded. "Sure did. After she came out, I swore I'd never have another one, but not even twenty-four hours later here I am thinking about round two."

Elliot looked up in surprise. He'd been sitting on the floor with Ruby, holding Anna's hand and smiling at her.

"Not now. One day." We shared that loving look I'd always envied between Olivia and Logan. This one was all mine.

Nicola took Noah from Dad's arms and sat on the couch beside me. The little boy smiled at me, and I tickled him under the chin. This wasn't weird at all, my mother on one side, Nicola on the other.

Dad leaned over to give me a hug and a kiss, producing a small wrapped parcel from their nappy bag.

"Ruby, I got you something," he said.

Ruby looked up with big eyes, her face glowing as she stood and jumped to Dad. He squatted beside her. "I know it's hard when the baby gets so much attention, and I know you love her very much. But here's a little something for you because we love you, too."

He gave her the parcel, stroking her hair and she hugged him tight. "Thanks, Poppa."

Dad grinned. I think he loved this just as much as he loved being a father again.

"Come and see Anna," Ruby said, grabbing his hand. She sat beside him, tearing open the gift as he clucked over the baby with Elliot.

"Becca. It's a necklace." Ruby ran over to me, holding the precious jewellery in her hands. It was a little heart pendant with her name engraved on it.

"We got that because we wanted you to have something special just for you," Nicola said.

I unclipped it, hanging it around Ruby's neck, and she patted it before running back to Dad.

"She's going to make such a good big sister," Mum said.

In that moment, the sorrow I felt for Mum was overwhelming. Here Elliot and I were, over the moon with our new baby. Dad had finally moved on and was settled with Nicola and Noah. Mum was all alone.

"She will do," I said.

"Rebecca, I'm going to meetings."

That handful of words held so much meaning, although it wasn't the first time she'd promised me she would go.

"I've been sober for three months. It's hard, but I just have to keep going."

I watched her face as she spoke. She meant it; I could see that. Maybe having the new arrival could help focus her; she could help me more.

"You know you're welcome any time, Mum. While I'm home it'd

be nice to spend some time with you and good for you to spend time with Anna and Ruby."

She took hold of my hand, and we were closer than we had been in years in that moment. I squeezed her fingers, and she smiled. "Your father called me to see if I was coming to visit, and he and Nicola were kind enough to pick me up. But they needn't worry, and neither should you. I'll come over whenever you need me. I want your trust back."

All this time she knew I'd struggled with believing anything she'd said. It had nearly killed our relationship, but maybe this little added incentive might help keep her on track.

I wasn't sure about trusting her to look after my children yet, but we were one step closer to becoming friends again. Something we hadn't been in years.

Nicola nudged my arm. "Look down there."

Dad and Elliot were deep in conversation, completely absorbed by Anna and Ruby.

All I could do was smile.

LUNCHES AT LE Grande were a thing of the past now. We'd all moved on.

I unlatched and pushed the wooden gate open, walking into Katya's backyard. The lady herself was in a lounger, soaking up the rays beside the pool, her pregnant belly sticking up to greet the sun. She looked beautiful, but I wouldn't have expected anything less.

"That food smells amazing." Elliot came in the gate behind me, the capsule in his hand. Anna had fallen asleep in the car and he carried it gingerly, even though a herd of elephants couldn't disturb that girl from her slumber.

"Can we go in the pool?" Ruby tugged at my hand. We might have a pool at home, but this was somewhere new, exciting, and her swimming costume was on under her clothing.

"I just want to say hello to the girls and then we can go for a swim."

"Katya," I said, making my way through the inner pool gate. She took off her sunglasses and smiled.

"Rebecca, it's so good to see you. And the family." Ruby tucked herself half behind my leg.

"Look who's here. My girls." Dad's voice came from the right. Of course he'd be here with Nicola.

Ruby let go of me, running straight into Dad's arms as he scooped her up, kissing me on the cheek as he came close. "Hi, Dad."

"We're going swimming," Ruby said.

"Are you, sweetheart?"

She nodded. "I've got my togs on under my clothes."

"You're all prepared, then." He smiled as she hugged him tight. I loved seeing him so relaxed, so happy.

"Tim and Alexander are making some lunch on the barbecue. There's a lot of food," Katya said.

"Oh, joy," I muttered between my teeth. It had never crossed my mind that Alexander might be there, even though he was good friends with Tim.

Katya reached up, grabbing hold of my hand. "Show me that baby of yours."

I grinned, turning back to Elliot and taking the capsule from his hand. Katya sat up, grinning at the sight of Anna, fast asleep and snuggled under her blanket.

"She is so beautiful," Katya said.

Anna yawned, stretching and opening her eyes with that cross-eyed baby look as she tried to focus on me.

"Come and meet Auntie Katya," I said, unclipping her harness and lifting her out of the seat.

I handed her over to the waiting Katya, who started to rock her, stroking Anna's hands with her fingers.

"She's so precious," she whispered. "I can't wait to have my own."

"Poppa, can I go swimming?" Ruby asked Dad.

"Sure you can. If it's okay with your dad and Rebecca."

Elliot grinned. "Go for it. She's getting more confident, but she just needs to stay in the shallow end. Don't you, Ruby?"

Ruby nodded.

"I'll just paddle my feet while she goes for a dip," Dad said.

I watched as he made the short walk to the pool, sitting on the edge as Ruby stripped off her dress and showed him the big picture on her swimming costume. He beamed as they spoke, and I wondered if this was helping him make up for my disjointed childhood. He hadn't been there as much as I'd wanted when I was little, but he was there for Ruby and would be there for Anna.

"Oh, crap," I said, turning my face toward Elliot, leaning against his shoulder.

"What?" he whispered, kissing my temple.

"Here comes my ex."

"She looks so much like you, Rebecca." Alexander came up behind Katya, looking over her shoulder and nodding at Anna.

"I don't know about that. She's got her father's eyes, and I think she looks quite a bit like her big sister," I said.

"I think she looks like both of us." Elliot's arm landed on my shoulder, and I leaned in tighter against him.

"She's got your eyes, Elliot," Katya said.

"I'm just hoping she ends up with his dimples." I gazed at Elliot, lovingly. This man was everything I'd ever wanted, even when I didn't know it. I slid my arm around his waist as he kissed my temple.

"You might be lucky. She does have those little dimpled hands." Katya gathered Anna's hands in hers and brought them up to her lips to kiss them. "Oh, you are such a pretty girl."

"Oh. Elliot, this is Alexander. Alexander, Elliot."

Elliot extended his hand and Alexander took it. They studied one another for a moment as they shook hands. Elliot had blanked his expression, and I'd have given anything to know what he was thinking.

"Congratulations, Rebecca." Alexander leaned over and kissed my cheek.

"Alex, Alex. Come here." Clarissa's shrill voice broke the peaceful moment, and I couldn't stop my smirk.

"Excuse me." Alexander smiled at both of us.

I nodded slowly as he left, squeezing Elliot's waist tight.

"That was your ex?"

I kept on nodding.

"I'm glad you don't yell at me like that."

I snickered, turning around to face Elliot, hugging him tight. "I don't have any need to yell at you. You're always where you're supposed to be when you're supposed to be."

"I swear I'll never give you any cause to throw icy Fanta at me," he murmured.

He lowered his head, kissing me softly.

Nothing could darken this day.

CHAPTER 35

We were back at the zoo, our little family. Ruby wanted to see the giraffes. She'd been reading a book all about them, and the opportunity to get her up close and personal, feeding one, was just too good to say no to.

Right on feeding time, I took her hand and the two of us went onto the platform with the keeper.

He bent, handing her a piece of celery. "Here. They like celery because it's sweet. His tongue is going to come out and grab it like a hand, so don't freak out, just let it go."

She looked up at me, apprehension in her eyes.

"I'm right here. We'll do it together if you want."

Ruby was heavy, but I could still pick her up, and I did so, much to Elliot's irritation. "I'll come and do it," he called.

"We're fine." I kissed Ruby on the nose. "Here we go."

The giant spotty head appeared from below and Ruby gasped. "There he is," she whispered.

The keeper patted the giraffe's head and gave it a stick of celery. Ruby tensed in my arms and I hugged her tighter. "It's okay, Ruby. See how much he loves the celery?"

I took a step closer, and she frowned. "I'm scared."

"I'm not surprised. His head is almost as big as you are. But I'm right here. Do you trust me?"

She nodded.

"Then let's do it together."

Her hand in mine, we offered up the celery. The long, brown tongue of the giraffe came out, wrapping around the stick, gently tugging at it as we released our grip.

Ruby stared, watching as the giraffe sucked in the succulent food.

"That was AWESOME." She lost all fear as she yelled in my ear, and I laughed as she wriggled around.

I placed her down on the platform beside me. "Thank you," I said to the keeper.

Ruby squeezed my hand as we walked back toward her father. He stood, the pram in front of him, with his phone in his hand, snapping photos of the two of us.

"Did you see the giraffe, Daddy?"

He grinned. "I did, honey. You were so brave. It looked so big."

Her eyes widened. "Its tongue was HUGE."

People around us watched her with smiles on their faces. Happiness shone from her in a way that warmed my heart. Every day that we got through without her getting upset or having a nightmare was a good day. And there were plenty of those now.

The night light I'd bought her had helped. The love we all shared helped more.

We continued our walk until we got around to the lion enclosure. Ruby skipped alongside me as Elliot pushed Anna. One day I'd bring her back when she was old enough to love the animals as much as Ruby did.

"These are your favourites, Daddy?" Ruby knew. She'd watched *The Lion King* so many times with her father. It was one of those things they'd bonded over.

"They sure are. I heard they have a baby here too."

Ruby's jaw dropped as she saw the cub. "It's so cute."

"Just like our baby."

She rolled her eyes. "Daddy, Anna is a baby, not a lion."

Elliot grinned at me, shaking his head. I looked back at the lions, the cub rolling around while the others sat, looking bored. At least the little one seemed to be having fun, the only other movement being the lioness occasionally reaching for her cub to pat the baby with a paw and settle her down.

"Becca." Ruby tugged on my shirt.

"Hang on, sweetie. Look at the cub rolling over. Just like that fur ball at home wanting a tummy scratch."

"Becca," she said again, this time sounding more irritable.

"What is it?"

I looked down at her. She had that Elliot grin on her face and in her hand was a small velvet box. I squatted beside her. "What's this, Ruby?"

She handed it to me and I switched my attention to Elliot. "What are you up to?"

"Open it," he said.

"Becca, open it," his little parrot repeated.

The box's hinge snapped open as I lifted the lid. Inside was a ring with a diamond solitaire stone. "This was Nan's engagement ring. She wanted us to have it."

Tears pricked my eyes as I looked at it, unable meet Elliot or Ruby's gazes.

"It's lovely."

"You have to put it on," Ruby whispered.

"Oh, do I?" I reached for her with my free hand, hugging her tight. "Love you, Ruby monster."

She giggled. "Love you too."

I stood, and Elliot grabbed my hand. "What do you say, Ms Wallace? Are you going to put it on?"

I wanted to kiss those damn dimples of his. "I don't know."

His face dropped. "What do you mean you don't know?"

"I mean, why would I be wearing it?"

Elliot pulled me to him, taking the box from my hand. "Rebecca Wallace, will you accept this ring and marry the hell outta me?"

I grinned as he took the ring from the box and slid it onto my left ring finger. It was a little loose, but nothing we couldn't take care of. "Of course I will. I love you."

He kissed me long enough for Ruby to pull at my shirt again. "Hey, you guys."

Elliot and I laughed, looking down at her and pulling her into a hug with the two of us.

Maybe we'd all come together in not so conventional circumstances, but the important thing was that we were together.

And we'd be a family forever.

***

He used to play in a band sometimes, and will do again someday. I'd never stand in the way of the things he loves. But now he spends his evenings singing lullabies to our little girl as her eyelids flutter, fighting the urge to sleep.

Watching them together is the most beautiful thing I think I've ever seen. Emotion overwhelms me at times, and I tear up at the smallest of things. Because of them.

It's amazing how organised we've become, two of the least likely people to end up this way. While I had my work routine, the rest of my life was so haphazard. Now I know where I'm going to be at any given time, and I wouldn't want to be anywhere else.

I have a meaningful relationship with my father now too, more so than I have at any other time in my life. He dotes on Anna and Ruby, and I've never seen so much of him. During weekends, he can often be found sitting on our couch watching sport and drinking beer with Elliot. The pair of them are so close.

Dad and Nicola are still as in love as ever. Their little boy will grow up with my daughter. Maybe it's not traditional, but no one could ever have accused me of being that anyway. We make it work.

We see Mum from time to time. She's working hard at going to her meetings and doing her best to stay sober for her grandchildren. I will regret all those years she didn't try for me, but they're in the past.

Ruby grows bigger every day, and I couldn't be more proud of her if she were my own. She's top of her school class and thriving in the loving environment Elliot and I have created. It brings me to tears thinking how her transition to being with us was eased by the love we all share. That little girl has been through so much for her young years, and now I'll do everything in my power to protect her.

We balance childcare, and I work from home, or when Elliot isn't working for Logan, he's at home with Anna. It's working for us for now, and if something changes, we'll adapt. That's what families do.

I never knew just how much the human heart could love, but now I know it's a lot, judging from the state of mine.

And sometimes, if I'm lucky, in the morning the house smells of bacon.

ALSO BY WENDY SMITH

Coming Home

Doctor's Orders

Baker's Dozen

Hunter's Mark

Teacher's Pet

A Very Campbell Christmas

Fall and Rise Duet

Falling

Rising

Fall and Rise - The Complete Duet

The Aeon Series

Game On

Build a Nerd

Bar None

Hollywood Kiwis Series

Common Ground

Even Ground

Under Ground

Rocky Ground

Coming soon Solid Ground

Stand alones

For the Love of Chloe

Only Ever You

The Friends Duet
Loving Rowan
Three Days

The Forever Series
Something Real
The Right One
Unexpected

Chances Series
Another Chance
Taking Chances

Lifetime Series
In a Lifetime
In an Instant
In a Heartbeat
In the End
At the Start

ABOUT THE AUTHOR

Wendy Smith is a multi-platform bestselling author, whose book In the End, written as Ariadne Wayne, was named one of Apple's best books of 2017. She lives with her two children and two cats in New Zealand where she bases her books because she loves living there. All her stories come with a quirky sense of humour, and she cries over everything.

Find me online
www.wendysmith.co.nz
wendy@wendysmith.co.nz